Desires

OF A

Baron

ROSE GORDON

DESIRES OF A BARON
Copyright © 2014 C. Rose Gordon
Cover image copyright Aileen Fish
All rights reserved.

Parchment & Plume, LLC
www.parchmentandplume.com

If Giles Goddard, Lord Norcourt, were anyone else he might think he'd had a miserable life. Sent away from Dolsey, his parents' country estate, at eight years old to be raised by nuns at a convent in Ireland when the baroness had announced she was breeding once again.

At the time, Giles was too young to understand why he needed to leave. Twenty years later, Giles knew why: he'd been unwanted.

Though the firstborn and heir to the barony, Giles had little else to recommend himself to his parents, most notably his father. Born with his life's cord wrapped around his neck and his skin a pale blue that would match the creek that ran behind his father's estate, he was slow to cry or scream to announce his presence and later he was slow to walk, slow to talk, and undeniably slow to comprehend. Giles' aging father couldn't abide Giles' presence any more than he could fathom the idea that a simpleton would one day take over his title.

So when Lady Norcourt announced she'd missed her monthly flux three times, the old baron made arrangements that he hoped would be sufficient to allow his second son to become his heir.

During Lady Norcourt's second gestation period, the baron forbade her to leave her room. The servants were ordered to bring all of her meals and entertainment to her before she had a chance to ask. She was not to be allowed on her feet more than an hour each day and was to be carried from her bed to her chaise if she wished to change locations. And most importantly, she was to have absolutely *no* association with the child that was robbed of his mind by the devil!

Her body was a vessel. One meant to deliver a smart and healthy heir. She'd failed once, and the baron had seen to it she understood that she was not to fail him again.

However, on the slim possibility that Lady Norcourt proved to be incompetent in her ability to give him a suitable heir once more, the old man with more than seventy years of wisdom between his ears made arrangements to protect his barony if his simple son should inherit.

Unfortunately for the old baron, between his raging excitement to ensure nothing happened to his wife, his vessel, during her confinement and his joy that his simple son wouldn't inherit, the old man's heart gave out on him while out celebrating his new plan. His wife, though blackmailed into being unable to communicate with Giles, thwarted the old baron all the same and married another within a month of his passing. Thus, her second son, both healthy and smart, was not eligible to inherit the title through any schemes of the late baron. Which meant that despite his father's hatred and obvious disdain for his firstborn son, Giles had inherited a barony. The very last thing he ever wanted.

Well, perhaps being a baron wasn't the *last* thing he'd wanted. Having a title fell a short second to the situation he'd recently found himself in: face-to-face with his mother. At a house party. In Telford.

Seeing her wasn't quite so bad.

Listening to her prattle on about nothing of any import, however, was enough to make him, a grown man of eight-and-twenty contemplate pulling out all of his hair. He was *this* close to doing just that. In fact, the only reason he didn't was because it might hurt. No, it wouldn't "might" hurt, it *would* hurt. Hair pulling hurt. No matter who pulled. And to pull it hard enough for the hair to come out, it'd hurt something fierce. He was certain of it.

Instead, he balled his hands into fists. That didn't hurt. Much. His nails were a little sharper than they should be and dug into his palms, but the pain in his palms was less than it'd be if he ripped his hair out. It had to be.

"Giles, I'd love to hear more about the time you spent in Spain," the dowager Lady Norcourt, now Mrs. Appleton, also known to be his mother, said from where she sat perched on a settee not five feet away from him.

Giles squeezed his fingers into a tighter fist, if such a thing were possible. He didn't wish to talk about his time in Spain. He'd already told her everything she deserved to know: it was good.

"Giles?"

He swallowed. "Yes?"

"Tell me about the bulls, Giles. Did you see them chase the men?" the woman who'd once been so dear to him asked. Her sweet smile only served to make his stomach clench as waves of memories of her running after him as a young lad in leading strings came to mind.

He thrust away the thought. Just like his father, she hadn't wanted him. If she had, she'd have never sent him away. "They chased me," he said softly around the lump of emotion—part hurt, part anger—that had formed in his throat and was on the verge of choking the life right out of him.

Lady Norcourt, as he'd taken to referring to her in his mind since the word "mother" not only didn't fit her, but made his gut ache whenever he heard it, stared at him, her blue eyes wide and her mouth slightly agape.

She snapped her mouth closed and forced a smile. "I suppose I could see that. You always were a fast runner. Why I remember when you were a boy..."

Giles stared at her, but didn't hear her words. Since arriving at this inane and tedious house party, the last word of which he used very loosely, he'd been driven nearly to tears of frustration by the countless young ladies paraded in front of him. They'd talked of silly things like hair ribbons and reticules. And that was it. The only statement any of them had said that had caught his attention was when one of the young ladies told another to "stuff it". A slow smile pulled at Giles' lips. Having grown up in an orphanage run by nuns, he'd never heard such a term before and only assumed it was a less-than-polite way to ask the young lady who was chattering like a bird to stop talking.

But what if she'd really stuffed it? What would she stuff it with? What if Lady Norcourt stuffed it? He started. The dratted woman had been so interested in him these past few days it bordered on annoying. He most definitely would like to see her mouth be stuffed with *something*. Cotton. Leaves. A ball of yarn. The list was limitless if it'd get her to stop talking to him for any amount of time.

"Are you all right, dear?" Lady Norcourt asked, startling him from his drifting thoughts.

He was spared from having to tell her what he was thinking about, because he could not tell a lie, when the doorknob twisted, drawing both of their attention.

Relieved and glad for any distraction, Giles stared at the door waiting for the intruder to let himself—hopefully it'd be a "him", he didn't think he could tolerate much more useless chatting about ribbons and bows—into the room.

His relief didn't hold, however, when the man revealed himself: Simon Appleton, his younger brother.

"Simon," Lady Norcourt greeted. "Do come in and join us."

Mr. Appleton came into the room and quietly closed the door behind him. "Mother." He turned to look at Giles. "Lord Norcourt."

"What brings you about?" Lady Norcourt asked.

Simon's face took on an expression that Giles couldn't determine. "I've come to speak to Lord Norcourt." When a broad smile took his mother's lips, Simon added, "Alone."

Lady Norcourt's smile faded and she shot a glance to Giles that he couldn't interpret. "I don't know if that's a good idea."

Irritation bubbled inside of Giles. As much as everyone liked to pretend he was, he wasn't a child and incapable of having thoughts for himself. They might not always come to him quickly or make sense to others, but he was capable of some things. He scowled at them. "I do."

"You do what?" Lady Norcourt asked, her eyebrows drawn together.

"We'll talk alone."

Lady Norcourt's lips thinned. "I don't think—"

"We'll be fine, Mother. I don't plan to eat him," Simon said, opening the door to the library for his mother.

She cast one last glance toward Giles, then gathered her green skirts and made her exit. Giles was a hint jealous that it was her and not him who was escaping.

After she'd crossed the threshold, Simon closed the door. "Have you and my mother become bosom friends yet?"

"She's my mother, too," Giles said quietly.

"Indeed." Simon walked to a high backed chair and gripped the wooden frame of the back until his knuckles turned white.

Giles stared at his half-brother. From where he sat, it was easy to tell that Simon was as tall as Giles, though not as broad. Their hair and eyes were exactly the same shades: chestnut brown and emerald green respectively. That's where their similarities ended. They'd had breakfast together the other morning and Simon had seen fit to talk endlessly about every subject he knew anything about. Giles preferred to listen. He'd learned, not the easiest way, either, that he was less likely to make a fool of himself if he didn't speak, or just said very little when necessary.

He swallowed. He hoped he wouldn't make a fool out of himself in front of Simon right now.

Mindlessly, Giles tapped his foot. What was taking the man so long to speak? "Come to talk?"

"You do know why you were invited here, do you not?"

"Yes." He didn't like it, but he understood very well why he'd been coerced into attending Lady Cosgrove's house party.

"Because Mother thinks to right her wrong by finding you a bride?"

Giles clenched his fists as tightly as he could and commanded his face to stay impassive. He couldn't let on to the hurt soaring inside him at Simon's cold, but truthful reminder that he'd been unwanted. "You're a fortunate man, then."

"Me?" Simon jabbed a finger at his chest. "She didn't invite those young ladies here for me to peruse, they're here for you."

"Not interested. Have your pick."

"My pick?" He shook his head. "I don't need a swarm of ladies to choose from. I've already found my bride."

Giles' mind raced. Was Simon speaking of Isabelle Knight? He had to be, she was the only female Giles had seen him with at this party. "She's taken," he said evenly.

Simon frowned. "Yes, by me."

"No. She's Sebastian's wife," Giles said quietly. His friend Sebastian, Lord Belgrave had told him that himself. He'd never signed the annulment papers. That meant they were still married, didn't it?

"*Was*, Lord Belgrave's wife," Simon corrected. His voice an odd mixture of annoyance and frustration, likely at Giles' arguing.

"Still is," Giles said flatly.

"No, they had their marriage annulled. That means they were married, but they're not any longer."

"No, they're still married," Giles said adamantly. Sebastian had told him so. Sebastian was the only friend he'd ever had. He wouldn't lie to Giles. He never had. If Sebastian said they were still married, Giles had no reason to believe otherwise.

Simon's green eyes narrowed. "Did Lord Belgrave tell you this?"

Giles nodded slowly and watched silently as a myriad of emotions crossed the younger man's face. Giles hadn't any idea what most of them meant, nor did he care to ask.

A moment later, Simon's face was dark red and his lips were in a thin, tight line that made the edges of his mouth turn white. He looked furious.

Giles just stared at the man as he breathed so hard his nostrils flared. He'd told the truth. He'd done nothing wrong, and yet, he felt as if he'd once again pushed away a potential friend. Not something foreign to Giles.

Then, without so much as a fare-thee-well, Simon spun on his heel and quit the room.

Chapter One

Shrewsbury

Lucy Whitaker frowned as she climbed the rickety stairs to the apartments above the smithy's shop on the ever-hustling Flynt Street. She crested the top of the stairs and a chill ran down her spine. Something wasn't right about this. Her son, Seth, had met her when she'd returned from working at the bakery with a pot of soup that was already made and poured into a carafe for traveling. He'd then told her that there was an ailing man in the village, gave her his direction and begged her to hurry and deliver him the soup.

Only because she loved her son and didn't want to see him hurting over yet another of his friends dying, just another disappointment he'd face in his short life, she'd reluctantly agreed to go.

Lucy tightened her hold around the handle of the carafe. She'd promised Seth she'd come and deliver the man a bowl of soup and medicine. But that was as far as her Christian charity went. Once she gave him what she'd brought, she'd be on her way.

She found his apartment, 2B, and knocked twice on the door before letting herself inside. She stepped inside and froze. Before her stood a man, virile and young. Decidedly not sick in the least. "Pardon me, I must have the wrong direction," she rushed to say, taking a step back.

The young man with light blond hair and blue eyes reached for her. His touch made her skin grow cold and turn nearly frigid when he gave her what he might think was an affectionate squeeze. "I don't think so."

Panic welled up inside Lucy and she wrenched her arm away from him, taking another step toward the door.

His rich chuckle filled the room. "The boy said you might be upset." He gestured to the faded blue divan in front of the window.

"Come, we'll talk first."

Boy? Talk? *First?* So many partial questions formed in her mind, the least of which was what exactly did Seth have to do with this? "Sir, I think you have the wrong idea. I'm not here for—for —" she waved her hand in a circular motion in the air— *"that."*

He frowned and crossed his arms, the sun glinting off his signet ring, filling Lucy with a sense of dread. Not only was he handsome, but he was titled. "But I thought—"

"Yes," she cut in crisply, doing her best to tamp down her true feelings for men of his ilk. "I'm sure you did and I was led to believe I was coming here to deliver soup and herbs to a man nearing his deathbed." A bubble of irritation swelled up inside Lucy as the memory of her son's words that he was so sick came back to her: *He's nearly delirious with fever,* Seth said, thrusting the soup in her direction. *He could die at any moment, so please go now.*

"I see," the handsome stranger said slowly, pulling her back to present. "I suppose then you're not interested in..." He trailed off with a lopsided shrug and a wolfish smile.

"No," she snapped. "I need to get back home to my son."

"Son?" he echoed, a myriad of emotions passing over his face.

"Yes, the young fellow who suggested this—this—this *assignation,* is my son," she confirmed, her face heating.

He had the decency to flush, but only a little. "I see." He cleared his throat. "You must understand, I don't usually take recommendations of this sort from young boys, it's just—"

She waved him off before he could say another word and further mortify them both. "He didn't know what he was doing."

The strange man stared at her, then blinked slowly.

"He's just trying to find himself a father," Lucy burst out before she could think better of it. Another burning wave of embarrassment came over her.

"Uh—uh—uh," the young lord stammered, his face turning as violently red as she imagined hers was. "I'm not interested in that. I was just—"

"Yes, I know what you wanted," she cut in, pursing her lips

8

and narrowing her eyes on him. "Nonetheless, Seth did not know that was your intention." She sighed as a defeating sadness threatened to overcome her. "He's just a boy and doesn't understand the way of the world," she whispered aloud, more for her own benefit than for the man who was standing before her looking decidedly uncomfortable. Pushing away the feelings of failure and anger that were swiftly overcoming her, she inclined her chin and forced herself to meet the still wide eyes of the man in front of her. "I do hope you have learned a lesson today."

"Indeed. I shall never again accept the help of a village imp."

"Perhaps the word *never* is a bit strong. Surely, you could accept his assistance to hold your lead while you visit a shop or give you directions to the smithy's without the expectation of soon becoming his father." At the man's choked laughter, more choking than laughter, of course, Lucy allowed herself a small smile then excused herself from the room.

Once outside, the emotions came with the force of a team of the king's finest horses charging at her as if she were the enemy and he must capture her and behead her at once. Anger. Humiliation. Confusion. Sadness. And finally, helplessness. Through the tears that now burned her eyes and blurred her vision, she made her way to the lane that would lead her back to the crumbling stone cottage she rented on the fringes of the village.

She took a deep breath to calm her fraying nerves and steady her uneasy gait. Twelve years ago she'd made a mistake. A mistake that not only would taint her name for the rest of her life, but had ruined the life of an innocent child. Biting back the vile curse that resounded over and over in her head for the man who'd put her into this position, she walked on and directed that curse at herself. She'd been the one who'd believed his lies and given herself to him. She'd also been the one who'd tried her best to protect her son from what he really was: a bastard. A cold sweat came over her and she was only vaguely aware that she was violently shaking when the carafe of soup that was dangling from the crook of her arm hit her in the rib.

"*Ooof,*" she muttered, not slowing her steps. A million

thoughts flew through her mind, but the one that stood out the most was she had no choice but to explain Seth's parentage to him. The truth. All of it. He was almost twelve now, he deserved to know; and for as painful as it might be for both of them, he might understand why his efforts weren't appreciated. Her chest constricted, crushing her heart and lungs and making it nearly impossible for her to drag in another breath. He didn't deserve that. He didn't deserve any of it. But that didn't make it go away. She'd made a horrible mistake and he'd been made to suffer just as much, if not more than, she. She'd always known it, but after her recent conversation with Lord Virile and Primal, it seemed so real and definite. Crushing.

"Mama! Mama! Come quick. I found you a man!" came the excited voice of her son, jarring her to present. He skidded to a halt in front of her, blinking his moss-green eyes at her. "Have you been crying?"

His innocent question made her eyes flood with tears once more. "We'll talk at home."

His eyes grew wide and his cheeks pinkened, presumably at realizing his earlier actions were about to lead him into trouble. "Yes, ma'am," he said solemnly. "But first—"

"No. We're going home, now." She reached for his arm to keep him close by, but he pulled away and wildly shook his head, sending his sandy blond hair all over the place.

"Mama, there's a man who needs help—"

"I'm sure there is," she retorted, pursing her lips. "But he can get whatever help he needs from someone else."

"There isn't anyone else," he argued.

"Seth," she said on a sigh. "I cannot—no, *will not*—help that man with whatever it is that's ailing him."

His eyes grew wider if that were possible. "But isn't it your Christian duty?"

She would have laughed at the absurdity of the situation if that wouldn't have meant laughing at the innocence of her son in the ways of the world. "Seth, let's go home. It's time we talk."

"All right, Mama. I'll talk about anything you want to—pastry dough, sewing, flowers, anything—but please help this man first. He's hurt."

"Genuinely hurt?"

Seth nodded.

"Physically?"

Seth's brows knit together and Lucy sighed again.

"What can you tell me about this man, Seth?" Why was she even asking? After her recent experience in the village at the hands of her meddling son, the last thing she wanted to do was to go see another "ailing" man. But something within was stirred. It might have been the panic in her son's eyes or the way he spoke with such conviction. She didn't know, but something inside of her she couldn't make sense of wanted to know more.

"He's rich," Seth said simply.

That did it. Lucy steeled her spine and reached for her son's arm above the elbow. "While I thank you for your efforts, my boy, they are for naught. We are going home. Now."

He pulled away from her and began running.

"Seth, wait!" she called, dropping her carafe of soup and running off after her son. The sun was already so low in the sky that in an hour or so it'd be completely dark. While she was confident he could find his way home if necessary, she didn't want him to be out wandering around while a strange man lurked in the woods. Her heart jumped to her throat. What if this man grew angry when Seth didn't bring Lucy back with him? She ran as fast as she could to keep up. It was hopeless to believe she, a woman of nine-and-twenty, could keep up with a boy of eleven, but as long as she could still see him, she wouldn't panic. Yet.

He led her through the woods and in the direction of his favorite place: the Old Elm. She should have known. It was his favorite place to go during the day. While most boys his age would have stripped off all the tree's branches and fashioned swords out of them, Seth preferred to sit under the shade the Old Elm provided and read. She swallowed another round of emotion. Just another way her son was different.

Seth came to an abrupt stop and Lucy almost ran into the back of him, then dropped her eyes to the ground and a strangled sob erupted from her throat at what lay on the ground in front of her.

"I told you he needed help," Seth said, his voice full of raw emotion.

Lucy fell to her knees at the side of the lifeless, dark haired stranger. Discarding all reservations and decorum, she reached a hand toward his blood-covered face. His skin was still warm. Whether that was a sign of life within or the blood that covered so much of him, she couldn't know until she examined him better. She moved closer and rolled him over onto his back.

"I thought you said he was rich," she said, trying to keep herself calm as her eyes scanned over this man's beaten and bloodied body.

"I presume he was—before he was robbed," Seth said simply, dropping to his knees next to her.

Lucy couldn't stop the slim smile that spread her lips. Her boy was clever, he was. He might be a bastard and seemingly unable to fully comprehend what that would mean to him and the things he'd never have because of his bastardy, but he was clever and the only ray of joy in her life these past eleven and a half years.

Not sure if the man who was lying before her was still alive or not, but not wanting to hurt him more if he was, she gingerly touched his wrist and felt for a pulse. She felt one. Barely. Releasing a breath she didn't know she was holding, she looked up to her son and met his tear-filled eyes.

"He'll be all right," she lied. "But I need you to help me."

He nodded wordlessly.

"We need to carry him back to the house so I can clean him up and examine him better." She moved to stand at the man's shoulders. "I'll lift him under his arms and carry him as best I can. I need you to hold his ankles and make sure we don't drag him."

Seth looked at her for a moment in disbelief, then shrugged and grabbed the man's ankles while Lucy slid her hands under his shoulders and closed her fingers in his armpits. Then, together, they lifted. And grunted. The man was heavy. No, not just heavy. There had to be another word that was more accurate. She just didn't know what it was.

Fortunately their house was only a quarter mile away.

Even more fortunate, for Lucy, Seth *and* the man they carried, they only dropped him twice and neither time was on his head!

Of course it did take them thirty minutes to get back to their house, but without those breaks every two to three minutes they might have all been dead.

"Let's put him on my bed," Lucy said on a gasp. It'd be a wonder if she didn't collapse any moment.

Seth grunted as he helped heft the chunk of lead shaped like a human up onto her bed.

When the man was secure on top of her mattress, mother and son exchanged a quick look before Lucy gave her son orders to go fetch a basin of water and an unused sheet from the hall.

"You'd better not die on me," she whispered to the dark-haired man lying motionless on her bed. "I'm about to rip up my last sheet for you. The least you owe me is to live."

A moment later Seth entered the room with a white sheet draped over his shoulder and dragging on the ground behind him and a basin of water in his hands so full that with each step he took some splashed over the side.

Normally she'd chastise him for making such a mess, but not today. There was more than enough to chastise him for later. Right now, she needed his help if this man was to have half a chance at life.

Seth set the basin down on the crude table beside her bed and without being told started shredding the sheets. Lucy checked for a pulse again. It was as weak as before, which she took as a good sign. They hadn't killed him on their way to the house.

Lucy picked up a strip of linen that Seth had pulled from the sheet and soaked it in water. She wrung out the excess and brought it to the man's face. Exerting a hint of pressure so she could actually clean off his face, but not hurt him, she gently wiped away the blood that surrounded his mouth. The cloth absorbed so much blood she rinsed it out, then made another swath. Then another. Slowly, she cleaned the majority of his face, leaving the water a dirty reddish-brown color. She dropped the rag into the water and took a moment to look him over. Despite the bruises forming on his chin and around his eyes and the cuts that covered his face, he was undoubtedly very handsome. High cheekbones, a strong angular jaw and chestnut brown hair. He looked young, too.

Her eyes traveled down to the rest of him. His clothes, though once undoubtedly among some of the most expensive to be found in London, were tattered and dirty, indicating that his injuries were likely greater than just those on his face. Tentatively, she unfastened the buttons of his light brown waistcoat.

"Are you undressing him?" Seth asked.

"I don't have a choice," she murmured, not daring to look up at him.

A moment passed, then his hands joined hers in undressing the good-looking stranger.

Wordlessly, the pair removed his clothing, gasping and shuddering as more painful bruises and abrasions were revealed. It was a miracle the man was still alive.

Seth dropped the man's torn silk stocking to the floor and looked back to where his mother was unfastening the man's black trousers.

"You plan to undress him *all the way?*" The terror in his voice was unmistakable.

Lucy nodded, but couldn't force herself to meet her son's eyes. He was reaching an age, if he hadn't already reached it, where changes would happen. Changes she couldn't bring herself to talk about with him. A lump formed in her throat. He really did need a father. She blinked back those traitorous tears and said, "I don't have a choice. He might have been hurt—"

Seth made a sound that would suggest *he'd* been the one hit or kicked there. "I'll do that," he said a moment later, the conviction in his voice stole Lucy's attention momentarily.

She stilled her hands and looked at her son as he seemed to straighten to his full height of four feet and eight inches.

"I'm a man, like him," he continued, his face turning crimson. "There's no need to embarrass you—or him."

Or him.

The words stole her breath away. Seth did have some concerns. Ones he'd likely never bring to her. She licked her lips, but couldn't speak and just moved out of the way when he took over unfastening the man's trousers.

Wordlessly, she made her way out of the room and to the hall where she leaned against the wall, closed her eyes and covered her face with her hands. If the idea of Lucy seeing a man's naked form caused her son to panic so much, the very idea of just how he came into existence might kill him. Especially since it'd be her who'd have to inform him.

Chapter Two

When she awoke, the sun was already shining in her window, letting her know she was late for her post at the bakery. She scrambled off the settee she'd dragged into Seth's room to sleep on and after giving the beaten man a very quick once-over, she rushed to work. Mr. Swenson, her employer, wouldn't be pleased she was late, but she prayed he'd be understanding when she explained the events of the previous evening.

He wasn't.

Worse yet, she was sacked.

"But I need this post," she said before she could stop herself. There was nothing worse than begging; but though she detested begging, she did need this position. Without it she and Seth couldn't afford to stay in their house past the end of the month.

"Then ye shouldn't be late."

"But it was only the first time. Surely—"

"No," he snapped, his lips thinning. "If yer too tired after a night of entertainin' a strange man in yer bed, then ye don't need the post that bad."

Understanding filled her then. Two months after she'd begun working for Mr. Swenson, he'd offered her a proposition that would allow her the freedom of staying home to tend her house and make friends about the village while spending her nights with him. She'd declined. She might be a fallen woman, but she would be no man's mistress. Ever.

Biting her tongue to keep in a stinging retort that would likely only make her look bad, she bobbed a quick understanding and with a chest filled with dread exited the bakery.

They'd likely have to move.

Once news got out that she'd been sacked from Swenson's Bakery, and *why*, she might not be able to get another decent post.

No. She shouldn't think like that. She'd worked at the bakery for three years. Surely she'd be able to find another position.

Mulling over her other employment options, she took the longer way home. The dark-haired stranger who was still sleeping (and breathing) when she'd left hadn't been wearing a coat. She wondered if perhaps she'd find it somewhere along the lane or among the sticks and trees.

She saw nothing.

Not even her carafe.

Of course.

"Mama, he's awake!" Seth hollered just as she'd come into view of the house.

Finally some welcome news, she thought as Seth ran over to her. "That's wonderful, Seth." And she meant that. "Has he said anything?"

He nodded and fell in step beside Lucy. "Lots."

"Oh?"

"Well, he's from London. He works with his father who does something with a bank so he has pots of money."

"I see you asked him the important questions," Lucy said only a fraction sarcastically.

"Indeed," he chirped, not daunted one jot by her tone. "He's unattached. Not even a betrothed or anything."

Lucy wanted to groan, but before she could, her son continued.

"Just think, Mama, you could marry—"

Lucy halted her steps and pulled him to a stop. "Seth," she began, turning to face him. "I know you'd like a—" she swallowed so she wouldn't choke on her words— "father, but Mr.—" she waved her hand through the air then frowned. "We don't even know his name."

"We could ask him," he said with a carefree shrug.

Lucy didn't even want to know why that wasn't the first thing Seth had thought to ask the man, but neither did she want to. "And we will ask him," she said matter-of-factly. Then she'd ask who his family was so she could post a letter to have them come collect him so she could stop worrying about him and start looking for another position.

Seth tugged on her hand. "Why are we just standing here?"

Indeed. Why just stand there when there was a naked man in her bed to go interrogate?

***

Simon Appleton was damned uncomfortable lying in a strange bed with nothing more than a thin sheet covering his naked body from the world. But that was hardly anything compared to the scrapes and bruises that covered his body or the steady tattoo of painful drumming that sounded in his head. Not to mention the never-ending string of questions from a boy who Simon still couldn't determine if he was real or a figment of his imagination. Perhaps taking the indirect way back to London from Telford wasn't the best idea he'd ever had. He wanted a chance to wander and think. Instead, he was in pain and had been interrogated.

He closed his eyes and took a deep breath. *The boy was real.* He might not be present right now, but why on earth would Simon's mind have made up a story about a young boy and his mother having carried him into their house and disrobing him? He wanted to groan, but didn't have the energy to. Perhaps that was a figment of his imagination, too.

Oh, hell, he didn't know what was real and what wasn't. But if the boy was real, then he'd been robbed, beaten, and then carried here to be cared for by said boy and his mother. This time he did groan. The identity of the boy—and even his existence—was still very foggy to Simon, but the aching of his body declared that he had indeed been beaten quite severely.

A door creaked in the distance and Simon snapped his eyes open. Were those voices?

The voices grew closer. One he recognized right away as that of the boy who'd plagued him with inane questions, presumably to keep him conscious, if he were indeed conscious to begin with, then regaled him with his own heroic tale. The other was new. Perhaps it was the boy's mother? He closed his eyes to regain his bearings, banishing the voice along with his view of the room.

Suddenly, the boy's excited voice floated to his ears, and just as suddenly, it was gone.

"Perhaps he went back to sleep," a decidedly female voice soothed.

Simon's eyes snapped open as quickly as they could under the circumstances. That voice sounded like that of an angel, and he *must* see her form to verify. Of a medium height, with raven hair and blue eyes, she stood gracefully near the side of his, no *her,* bed. She looked younger than he'd expected the boy's mother to be so she must be a sister or cousin. Or just someone from the village. Not that he cared just what her relation to the boy was she was welcome to his bedside anytime.

Simon cleared his throat and his thoughts simultaneously. "Good afternoon, Miss…"

"Whitaker," she supplied, tucking a tendril of her long, dark hair behind her ear. "My name is Lucy Whitaker, and you are?"

"Simon Appleton," he said without hesitation.

"And I'm Seth," the boy standing near Lucy said.

Simon nodded his understanding of the boy but didn't take his eyes off Lucy. She was a very beautiful young woman. More beautiful than— He twisted his lips in disgust that his mind had even thought of *her*. He grimaced in pain.

"Is something wrong?" Lucy asked as she rushed to his side.

He forced a smile and shook his head. "No, not at all."

She slowly nodded once and gave him a wary, sidelong glance.

Simon nearly cursed himself for his sarcasm and cleared his throat. He looked to the boy to offer him some sort of distraction, and just as quickly jerked his eyes away. That inquisitive young fellow stood down by Simon's feet, grinning. Simon scowled, then grimaced once again.

"Have another momentary lapse?" Lucy asked, her tone light.

Despite himself, Simon laughed. "Indeed."

Lucy shook her head; what appeared to be a slight smile pulled on her lips, but didn't meet her eyes. It was hard to guess her age. She was older than him, but it couldn't be by much. Not that he could dare ask her. "Other than suffering at your own hands by stretching your lips and contorting your face, are you hurting anywhere else?" she asked, pulling him from his thoughts.

"No, ma'am," he lied. Truth was, there wasn't anywhere on his body that didn't hurt. But that mattered very little. He might be a commoner, but even he knew that any young lady, whether of breeding or not, wouldn't be inclined to nurse a gentleman beyond fetching him a glass of water or a cool rag.

"That's good," Lucy said.

From the corner of his eye, Simon saw Seth making an eating motion with his hands. "I'm ravenous," Simon burst out.

"Oh," she said, her face turning a fetching pink. She smoothed her skirts. "Of course, I'll go start a pot of soup."

Simon and Seth exchanged a look, but their victory came to an abrupt end when Lucy spoke again. "While it's cooking, I'll write a letter to your family to let them know you're all right."

A flash of hope sparked in Simon. She'd only said she'd write them to inform them he was all right, she hadn't said anything about making arrangements for him to return home. Catching sight of her lifted brow, he realized she was waiting for a name. He racked his brain. Who should he have her contact? He had no relations other than his parents. His mother would be on Lucy's doorstep in a trice, making a fuss that could be rivaled only by a wounded war hero returning home. He shuddered. Of course she'd love the chance to fawn over him and reassure him that the sudden emergence by his half-brother that he never knew he had hadn't changed the way she felt for Simon.

That was not what he needed. Nor did he wish for his father to come. Simon was injured, but not so severely that he was about to be visited by the Angel of Death. If his father, Walter Appleton, had any reason to believe Simon wasn't still at that blasted house party in Telford, he'd insist that Simon be the one to go visit Lord Drakely about his investments. Lord Drakely himself was pleasant enough, it was that bewitching, tart-tongued shrew he housed that Simon would rather avoid. Simon shuddered again. His last encounter with one Miss Henrietta Hughes had been more than enough for him to know spending any more time with her was at the bottom of the list of things he wished to do.

"So many relations," she teased.

"Do you have to contact any of them?"

"Yes," she said, the same time Seth said, "No."

Simon and Seth grinned at each other. He had no idea what the connection between Lucy and Seth was, but it would seem that Seth would be a wonderful ally in softening Lucy. "You've got a good number of bruises and cuts," Lucy began. "Though nothing looked too deadly—"

A coughing attack came over Simon. Lucy had seen Simon's injuries? That'd mean... *Lucy* was Seth's *mother?* No, she couldn't be. She was too young to be his mother. Through squinted eyes he looked from one to the other. Seth's eyes were green and his hair sandy blond. Lucy's eyes were blue and her hair was dark. Seth must favor his father.

"Indeed, he does," Lucy said in a cool tone, startling Simon. He hadn't realized he'd said that aloud. Lucy lifted her chin and cleared her throat. "Who is it that I shall be notifying of your whereabouts, Mr. Appleton?"

"My brother," Simon blurted, distracted. He hadn't meant to insult her; he was just trying to make sense of who she was. He didn't care that she was obviously more than just a few years his senior. Nor that she had an imp.

"And just who is your brother and how shall I reach him?"

"He's currently at Lady Cosgrove's house party in Telford," he muttered offhandedly as a slow smile pulled on his lips. Perhaps his connection to Giles might be to some benefit to him after all. Not that he expected Giles to actually come to claim him. The two barely knew each other. Giles wouldn't come; but Lucy didn't need to know that. He'd just pretend not to understand why Giles didn't come for him and enjoy his time with Lucy—mayhap even persuade her that he could be a good husband to her.

"And his name?" her crisp voice sent chills down his spine. Did she have a problem with those nobles who did nothing but attend house parties all season? He flashed her a reassuring smile. He detested those sorts, too. They'd get along nicely.

"Lord Norcourt," he answered through gritted teeth. She nodded stiffly and quit the room.

Chapter Three

Telford
Later that day

"A missive for you, my lord," Clarke, the butler said, holding out a silver salver toward Giles.

Giles snapped up the missive and flipped it over. He frowned. There was no wax seal. Odd. He shrugged and unfolded the note that gave him a reason to ignore his mother's prattle.

Dear Lord Norcourt,

Your brother has been recovered. He is at my home, but would likely prefer to return to his home to finish recovering. Please come to collect him at your earliest convenience.

Sincerely,
L. Whitaker

Giles frowned at the words written out on the parchment he held in his hand. If his "brother" had been recovered, then why did he need to be taken to his own home to recover? He blinked. No matter. He was intrigued, which was far more than he could say he was at the conversation between his mother and Lady Mary that swirled around him.

"I'm off to—" he looked down at the missive in his hand to the direction scribbled at the bottom— "Shrewsbury." He gave a quick nod to where his mother and Lady Mary sat staring at him with slack jaws then exited the room.

He went straight to his room and rang for Franks, the valet he'd hired when he'd arrived in London. He had never planned to have such a man. It was silly really to have a man help you dress and shave. He was capable of those things. Why did he need anyone to help him? He didn't, but it "wasn't done", to not have such a man. Or so he'd heard during his second visit to White's. He shook his head. It still didn't make any sense to him, but right now, it seemed like just another stroke of good fortune on his part.

When the man arrived, Giles informed him that he would be leaving as soon as Franks could get him packed.

"How long do you plan to be gone for, my lord?"

"Forever."

"You don't wish to stay for the duration? It's only—"

"No," Giles cut in, grabbing hold of all of his clothes that hung pristinely in his closet. He walked to the bed and carelessly dropped them in a heap. Franks' sharp gasp startled Giles. They were only clothes.

"I'll pack your room, my lord," he said. "Why don't you go say goodbye to your mother?"

Giles froze. Say another goodbye to his mother? No. That held less appeal than visiting an outdoor privy in the dead of winter. She'd developed this strange fascination with him at some point in the last year and other than manipulating things to force him to return and see her, she was dratted annoying with all of her inquiries and inane chatter. No, he thought as he scanned his bedchamber, saying goodbye to her wasn't a priority to him.

Now, packing his art supplies was a priority.

He walked over to the desk in the corner where he'd put his pencils and papers upon arrival. With the same care Franks was exercising in packing his clothes, Giles went about packing his drawing materials for his departure.

He placed the tall stack of parchment perfectly upright in the side of his satchel then reached for the smaller case of pencils. He mindlessly flipped open the top of the case and stared at the line of pencils within. They needed to be sharpened. He dropped his eyes to where his knife still lay on the side of the desk. *Giles use a knife? Never! He'll cut his finger off—and only a finger if he's fortunate.*

Giles blinked back the thought and continued packing his

supplies. He was a man now. A man. Men weren't careless with sharp tools. Nor did they care what others thought of them, he reminded himself once again. They just did whatever they wanted —no matter what anyone else thought. He hadn't spent much time in his father's presence, but he'd spent enough to know that.

"Where shall I tell McDougal you will be traveling, my lord?"

Giles withdrew the missive from his breast pocket and handed it to Franks.

If the man found his behavior odd, he didn't show it. Which was for the best. Giles might be a man of few words, but "You're sacked," were two he was fairly certain he could string together. He frowned. He'd never really understood the origin of that phrase, either. At least with telling someone to stuff it, there was a literal meaning. The one who said the phrase was implying the offending person stuff their mouth with something to make them unable to say anything more. When someone was sacked, what happened? Did someone pack all of their belongings—including the person being "sacked" into a large bag? He didn't think so. It would be quite a humorous sight if it did, but it didn't seem logical.

Then again, logical wasn't a word many people often used in connection with Giles anyway, so perhaps that is what happened to someone who was sacked. Giles shrugged. He didn't really care, but neither did he want to see such a fate befall Franks. He rather liked the man.

"Your carriage will be pulling up the drive shortly, my lord," Franks said, coming up behind Giles.

Giles nodded once to show his understanding. His brother had left early the morning before—presumably to escape having to spend any more time in Giles' company after the uncomfortable conversation about the state of Sebastian and Isabelle's marriage. He shrugged again. That was of no consequence to him. The two hadn't been getting along well before that. In fact, the two hadn't gotten along very well since the first time they met less than a fortnight earlier.

He scanned the room one last time to make sure he wasn't leaving anything in his haste then quickly glanced out the window through the break in the curtains. The sun was lower than he remembered it being when he'd come upstairs. It must have taken him longer than he realized to get ready to leave. No matter. It wouldn't take him long to collect his brother. They could make it back to London around midnight.

Downstairs, his carriage waited for him in the drive. He wasted no time getting inside and rapping on the roof. The last thing he wanted to do was linger and risk being accosted by his mother again. He closed his eyes and leaned his head back against the blue velvet squabs. She meant well. At least he thought she did. A sudden tightness gripped him. What if she didn't mean well and she'd manipulated his return to mock him? That's why most people were kind to him. Then as soon as he trusted them, they did something to hurt him.

His mind traveled back to when he was only twelve and a lad named Charlie Mercer who lived at the orphanage with him had convinced him that he should swim in the pond without any clothes. He'd claimed that was how everyone else swam. Then, after Giles had removed his clothes and started swimming, Charlie left and returned moments later with an angry nun in tow.

The intense cramping that had overcome his hands, arms, shoulders, and chest from clenching his hands so tightly at the memory jarred him back to present.

He forced himself to relax his muscles. His mother wasn't like that. Or was she? She'd once sent him away with nothing more than a few whispered lies about loving him and seeing him soon. Giles might not have ever received the education for a boy of his station, nor attended university, but even he knew that twenty years wasn't soon by anyone's definition. He sighed. He'd been hurt too often to put much stock in his mother's actions. Or his brother's for that matter. Which is what made this latest development so interesting. If he took Simon to his house to be cared for, they'd be forced to spend time in each other's company and maybe they could become friends. He lowered his lashes and swallowed hard. *Friends?* Not bloody likely. The man positively hated him. And for no good reason. Giles had tried to remember his manners when they shared company.

He sighed again and pressed his forehead against the glass window. He'd always loved to look out the window while in a carriage. It was amazing what was just outside the window: trees, lush fields, occasionally a house, and animals. His heart lifted. Just a few feet from the road was a field with one, two, three, four, no five horses grazing. Four were chestnut and the fifth was black and at least three hands taller than the others. What it might be like to ride him! He licked his lips and admired the animals. But soon they were gone and empty fields filled his view. Then a dense thicket of trees of various heights and outlines came into view.

Suddenly, the horses slowed and Giles leaned back against the squabs and took a deep breath to settle the sudden bout of nerves that had come on when the horses had changed their speed and he realized that they must almost be to their destination.

Chapter Four

Lucy cupped her hands in the basin of cool water then splashed it on her face. With a sigh, she idly ran her wet hands over her face. That boy—*her* boy—would be the death of her and he was not yet twelve.

All morning he'd pleaded with her not to send word of Mr. Appleton's condition to Lord Norcourt.

She ignored his pleas and hummed as she dashed out her missive to his lordship.

He just wants a father, a voice somewhere in the back of her mind reasoned as she stared aimlessly out of the little window in her kitchen.

She squeezed her eyes shut and clenched her fists. *This* was not the way to get one. Well, neither was sending her on "discreet" assignations. Lucy was a fallen woman. Everyone knew it and accepted it. Everyone except the child she conceived and bore out of wedlock, that is.

She clenched her fists. After Lord Norcourt reclaimed his brother, she'd just have to explain the facts to Seth and pray he wouldn't hate her.

Whether because he realized he couldn't dissuade her or because he thought to try a different tack, Seth had holed himself up in the room with Mr. Appleton and had refused to speak to her from the moment she'd returned from the village to use the majority of her savings to pay a messenger to take the note to Telford post haste. She needed the money of course, but she needed Mr. Appleton out of her home before Seth had more of a chance to grow a fondness.

The echoing sound of hoofs clopping up the drive stole Lucy's attention. *He's here.* Lord Norcourt, whoever that was, had arrived. She exhaled and steeled her spine. She'd grown up on the estate of a wealthy viscount and knew just how haughty some of those lords could be. She had little doubt this one, though only a baron as Seth had informed her some time ago, would be much different.

Trying not to appear too anxious by meeting him at his coach, she took measured steps and made her way to the parlor, but not without first glancing into her bedchamber and getting a quick peek at Seth and Mr. Appleton having a conversation. Well, perhaps conversation wasn't entirely accurate. It seemed to her that Seth was doing most of the talking. Explaining what it was like to live out here and asking the man random questions about his life in London.

Likely Mr. Appleton would be just as delighted to leave as she'd be after this was all over. She shook out and smoothed her skirts then went to the parlor.

Just as she entered, the baron's servant knocked on the door.

Suppressing her disdain for the nobility and forcing a smile, she walked to the door, pulled it open and caught her breath.

***

Giles instinctively tightened his fingers around the leather strap of his satchel and stared at the woman who stood just across the threshold, unsure what to say.

"Would you like to come in?" she invited.

He bobbed his head once and stepped into the dwelling. Once inside, he continued to stare at her as the scent of honeysuckle surrounded him, calming him. Odd.

She returned his gaze and it was all he could do to hold it. *You must look at their eyes, Giles,* Sister Catherine had scolded him almost daily. It was easy to do with this woman as she had the most beautiful blue eyes he'd ever seen. *Her husband won't be happy when he comes out and sees you staring at his wife.* His body jerked and every muscle in his body tightened painfully. "Mr. Whitaker," he croaked.

A wide smile came over her face. "I've been called many things, my lord, but never that."

Giles stood motionless. She'd just made a jest, he realized, otherwise she wouldn't be smiling so broadly. How unfortunate that he didn't understand it. "Where is he?" he practically barked, flushing.

"Forgive me, my lord," she murmured softly. "I was only jesting. I didn't mean to make sport of you."

He clenched his jaw. Wasn't jesting and making sport of the same thing? Of course they were. The other boys always "jested" about him and roared with laughter. She wasn't laughing, though. Not even smiling anymore. Perhaps, it was just a misunderstanding. Exhaling, he repeated, "Where is Mr. Whitaker?"

"Dead." She covered her mouth with her hand. Her face colored a violent red and she lowered her hand. "I'm Lucy Whitaker, the one who sent you the note. I signed it L. Whitaker because I didn't think you'd come if you knew I was a single woman. Actually that's not true," she amended; her cheeks coloring. She frowned, then cleared her throat, but didn't say anything further.

Something Giles didn't recognize twisted in his gut as the word *dead* echoed in his mind. What a shame that such a fine woman was left to be a widow. Moreover, how unfortunate that she'd been left to care for Simon alone. "I'm sorry."

She knit her brow. "Whatever for?"

"Your loss."

"My loss," she said slowly. A few seconds later the left corner of her lips turned up. "My father has been gone for a while now, but thank you."

Father? He'd meant her husband. Surely a young woman such as her had had a husband. Any man would be fortunate indeed to have a woman like her as his wife. An uncomfortable and inexplicable lump formed in his throat. He blinked to clear his thoughts and swallowed. He'd spent the majority of his life uncomfortable, but it wasn't the same feeling of discomfort as he had talking to her. He didn't feel like running and hiding or wanting the floor to open up beneath him. Rather, his pulse raced and a hot tendril coiled in his gut. It was quite unnerving.

"Would you like to see your brother?"

Giles started. "Of course." A different sort of tension came over him as he followed Miss Whitaker down the hall. He and Simon might be brothers, but there was absolutely no brotherly love between them. Which still seemed to beg the question of why Simon would have sent for him.

"He's just through there," Miss Whitaker said, gesturing to the room.

Giles forced his heavy legs to carry him across the threshold and came to an abrupt halt. Simon lay in the bed, bruises and cuts covering every part of skin exposed—and his eyebrows lifted nearly to his hairline. "Didn't expect me, did you?"

An unreadable expression came over Simon's face. "No, I didn't."

Giles could accept those words as the truth, though he couldn't place the softness in Simon's tone as he said them. He cocked his head to the side and studied his brother, not sure what he was looking for exactly. Perhaps the man felt just as awkward in Giles' presence as Giles felt in Simon's and like him, didn't know what to say.

"Seth, why don't you go with your mother," Simon said, bringing Giles to present.

Giles swung his gaze over in the direction of a boy who was sitting in a chair to the left of the bed. Their eyes locked and Giles offered him a smile.

The boy didn't move, but Giles couldn't understand why not. He might be two marks past six feet and as thick and solid as an oak tree, but he wasn't going to hurt the boy. "That's quite a nasty facer the boy planted you, Simon," Giles teased merely for the boy's benefit. Simon, he knew, would see no humor in it.

A wide grin split the boy's face accompanied by a slight laugh —and a stifled giggle.

Giles turned around and saw Lucy standing behind him. She once again had her delicate fingers covering her mouth, as if to keep from laughing while her eyes sparkled with what looked like tears. Hopefully they were the good kind. Surely his words hadn't upset her. He opened his mouth to clarify why he'd said that, but confound it all, he couldn't think of a single thing to say.

"Come, Seth," she said in a high-pitched tone. "Let's give Mr. Appleton his privacy while Lord Norcourt attends him."

A strangled sound erupted from Giles' throat. "Attend?"

He barely recognized the word, but thankfully Lucy had and said, "He's scuffed up a good bit, but not so much that he can't travel, I shouldn't think."

Giles nodded slowly and searched Simon's face, but the younger man gave nothing away. It still made no sense why Simon would have sent for him. Nonetheless, he'd do what he could to help him.

"I can help, if you'd like, my lord," Seth said quietly.

"Oh?" Giles said, not sure what else to say to that.

"I'm a good help. I helped Mama carry him here and care for his wounds."

A small measure of pride for the boy flowed through Giles. "You are a good help."

The boy pushed his chest out and Giles bit back a grin.

"Is there anything you need, Simon?"

The only thing on Simon that moved was his nostrils. They flared. Why was he so angry? It wasn't Giles who'd beaten him senseless—no matter how much he might like to.

"I'll go get his clothes off the line. They should be dry by now," Lucy murmured.

"What are we going to do?" Seth exclaimed as soon as his mother's footsteps couldn't be heard any longer.

Simon closed his eyes for an extended blink and groaned. "The plan," he said between gritted teeth.

"Right," the boy chirped excitedly.

"What plan?" Giles asked.

Seth said something that Giles couldn't hear over Simon's voice. "Nothing you need to worry about."

Giles pressed his lips together. He'd heard a tone similar to Simon's often enough to know he'd upset him. But damned if he knew what he'd done. Must be his mere presence. He balled his hands into fists and waited for Miss Whitaker to return. She had a way of diffusing the tension in a room and he preferred it that way.

His gaze traveled around the sparsely decorated room and landed on the boy who was biting his lip and shifting from one foot to the other. Mischief was on his brain, no doubt. Giles schooled his features to appear disinterested, though he was anything but, and continued to wait wordlessly for Miss Whitaker.

"This is all he was wearing," Miss Whitaker said, blushing. She handed Simon's clothes to Giles. "I'll just be—"

Simon cut off her words with a brutal sounding coughing attack that had him bent over. Followed by a series of deep groans.

Giles might have laughed at the absurdity of Simon's theatrics if he wasn't so distracted by trying to understand what his goal was.

Miss Whitaker's eyes widened and she rushed to Simon's side. "Are you all right?"

He coughed again then promptly moaned.

Seth picked up a metal cup from the bureau and extended it toward Simon who was patting his chest vigorously and groaning.

"Thank you," Simon gasped. He took the cup from Seth with his free hand and brought it to his lips. He spilled more down his chin than he managed to get into his mouth. When he was finished making a mess of himself, he handed the cup back to Seth, still clutching his chest as if he were having heart palpitations.

"Better?" Miss Whitaker asked tonelessly.

Simon shook his head. "No, ma'am. My chest—it hurts."

"I'm sure it does. You were slamming it with your palm for no apparent reason."

Simon's green eyes widened in response.

"Mr. Appleton, I think you forget that Seth is my son. I've borne witness to many of his schemes—" her gaze shifted to her son— "but, this was one of the worst yet."

Giles bit the inside of his cheek to keep from grinning. Not that he found it funny that Seth was being scolded. He'd been in his position more times than he could count. But there was something rather humorous about seeing Simon receiving a much-needed set down. Although he still didn't understand what the two had been trying to accomplish. He mentally shrugged. It didn't matter.

"Sorry, Mama," the boy said quietly. "I was just—"

"Yes, I know," she burst out quickly, then sighed. "Perhaps you can join me in the kitchen while Lord Norcourt helps Mr. Appleton get dressed."

"But I wanted to help."

"And you can help. Me." Her voice offered no room for the lad to refuse and with a loud sigh he followed his mother from the room, leaving Giles and Simon alone for only the second time in their entire lives.

"Do you need help?" Giles slightly shook the folded clothes in his hands for emphasis.

Simon groaned. "No. You can wait out in the hall. I'll dress and be out in a moment."

With a shrug of acceptance, Giles tossed Simon's clothes onto the bed and quit the room to wait in the parlor, but not without first peeking into the kitchen where a flush-faced Miss Whitaker was whispering something to her son.

His pulse raced at the sight of her and he forced himself to keep walking.

"My lord," McDougal, his coachman, said when he entered the room.

"Yes?"

"Can I see ye ou'side?"

Wordlessly, Giles followed.

Chapter Five

This was not when Lucy wanted to do this, but Seth and his schemes were leaving her little choice. She wasn't so naïve she didn't see through the charade he and Mr. Appleton had tried to fool her with. If she didn't just address it now, those two might never leave and that wouldn't do.

She gestured for him to sit down in one of the two dining chairs they had. "Seth," she started, curling her hands into her skirts. How did she say this in a way he'd understand? "I know you mean well, but I can't marry." There, that was simple enough.

Seth pressed his lips together. "Yes, you can, and Mr. Appleton seems the perfect sort."

Lucy tried not to snort. "We barely know him," she said evasively. That was true enough.

"No, *you* barely know him."

Lucy arched a brow.

"I spent the afternoon with him. I know lots of things about him."

Lucy didn't even want to know what her son had deemed important enough to ask Mr. Appleton. She released a deep breath. "Seth, I'm sure he's a nice gentleman, but he has no interest in becoming my husband."

"How do you know?" Seth retorted. "You have hardly spoken to him."

"No, I haven't," she agreed. "But I don't need to speak to him to know that he has no interest in marrying me."

"Perhaps he would if you spent a little time with him."

Lucy suppressed a groan. "That won't be happening."

"I don't understand why you don't want to give him a chance," Seth argued, the color heightening in his cheeks.

"I can't," she said more sharply than she'd meant to. "Gentlemen of rank don't usually have honorable intentions

35

toward unmarried mothers."

"He doesn't have a title. His brother does."

She frowned at Seth's flippant tone. "I know." Which was all the more reason not to get tangled up with either of them. She froze. *Either of them.* Where had that come from? Seth might have found Lord Norcourt's false compliment about Seth giving Mr. Appleton a nasty facer just as inappropriately humorous as she did, but Seth hadn't suggested anything about Lord Norcourt. He was still quite taken with Mr. Appleton. Catching sight of the curious expression on Seth's face, Lucy said, "It doesn't matter which one has a title. Neither is interested in making a fallen woman his wife," she said quietly.

Confusion marred her son's innocent face and Lucy steeled her spine for the questions he might ask. But she deserved them and she'd answer them. He deserved that. She'd shielded him too long.

"Have you met Mr. Appleton and Lord Norcourt before?"

Lucy was taken aback and a little confused by his question. "No."

"Then how do you know?"

She licked her lips and idly ran the tips of her fingernails into one of the deepest scratches that covered the top of their dining table. "When I was a girl your age, I had two playmates. One was the heir to a viscountcy and the other was his brother."

"But Lord Norcourt isn't a viscount," he interrupted. "He's just a baron."

"Indeed, but while he's *just* a baron as you put it, he's still titled and Mr. Appleton is still his brother."

"Were those boys cruel to you?" Seth asked.

"No, only one," Lucy said carefully.

"Was it the heir or the spare?"

Lucy sent him a sharp look. "That's unimportant." A wave half-filled of sadness and half-filled with bitterness swept over her. Paul Grimes, the younger brother treated her very well and had been genuine. Sam, the heir, however, had not. And foolish girl she was, had made the wrong choice. She pushed away the memories, then met her son's sad eyes and forced a wobbly smile. "Seth, you need to understand that I made a poor choice many years ago which I can't explain while they're still here; but what I can tell you now is that because of that I cannot marry either of those two gentlemen and we need them to leave immediately." Not that she'd have had a chance to marry either of them had she not had a bastard. She was born the daughter of a servant—not the kind of lady any man of their station would ever consider for a wife.

Seth looked like he wanted to argue but was halted when the tall, imposing form of Lord Norcourt entered the room. "May I borrow a horse?"

Lucy stared at him as if he were addled and bit her tongue to keep from saying something that might be considered disrespectful. "We don't have one, my lord."

He stood still, a blank expression on his face. "Can Simon stay?"

Lucy felt her eyes widen. "Wh-what?" She cast a quick glance to her son who was shaking his head. "Why?"

"One of my horses has thrown a shoe," he said as if that explained everything.

Which it did. It was too late now for Lord Norcourt's coachman to take the horse to the village to get it shod. "I suppose you'll want a place to sleep, too." She tried to hide the unease in her voice, but Seth's wince told her she'd failed. Lord Norcourt seemed unaffected, however.

"No, ma'am. I'll walk to the village."

Lucy blinked. Surely she hadn't heard him right. "You will?"

"Yes. But Simon won't make it."

"I know," Lucy whispered, still in shock. It had been a long time since she'd been in the company of Sam and Paul, but she remembered well enough that Sam had always believed he deserved special treatment over his brother solely because of his title, even if he hadn't yet inherited it. Oh, for heaven's sake, this was completely different. Irritated with where her wayward thoughts kept leading her, she stood and said, "All right. He can stay and so can you."

Chapter Six

Giles couldn't think of a more awkward arrangement. It was bad enough that Simon was spending the night here, but he was hurt and it couldn't be helped. That could be overlooked. But a healthy and virile gentleman staying overnight? It'd have her reputation in tatters within the week. He couldn't be responsible for that. "Thank you, but no."

A shadow crossed Miss Whitaker's face. "Just as well. The village is just a mile or so in the direction your coach was traveling before turning down my drive."

"I trust you can explain this change to my brother, lad?" Giles asked the boy.

Seth bobbed his head with vigor and instinctively, Giles reached out and tousled the boy's hair. "When will you return, my lord?"

"Sunup." And he meant it. He couldn't explain why, but just the thought of seeing one Miss Lucy Whitaker again tomorrow made his body surge with excitement and he didn't want to waste a single moment he might be afforded in her company. Preposterous, he thought with a simple shake of his head.

"Are you feeling unwell, my lord?" Lucy asked.

Giles started and instinctively brought his hand to his unsettled stomach. "I'm fine."

She furrowed her brows and took a step toward him "Are you sure? You look flushed." She reached up to touch his forehead and he jerked back. But not fast enough, for she skimmed her fingertips just above his eyebrow. "You're quite warm. Feverish, almost," she commented, retracting her hand.

Giles choked on his own tongue. Of course he was feverish, his pulse raced like a criminal on the run just by being in her presence. "I'm fine."

"I don't think you are." Lucy reached for him again.

He took an uneasy step back and nearly sighed with relief when she pulled her hand back. "I'm fine," he repeated, grunting.

"No, you're stubborn," she said, crossing her arms.

Giles blinked at her. Nobody had ever called him stubborn before. He'd been called aggravating, dimwitted, and a nuisance before, but never stubborn. "Was that a compliment?" he asked sincerely.

A slow smile spread across her lips and she shook her head. "I suppose it was."

Giles returned her grin. "Thank you."

She lowered her head a fraction and touched the fingertips of her right hand to her forehead. "You're welcome." A moment later, she looked up and cocked her head to the side, her vivid blue eyes staring right at Giles in a way that made those dratted tingles crawl up his skin anew. "Seth, why don't you go check on Mr. Appleton," she murmured.

Giles sidestepped to the left to allow the boy to pass, then turned his attention back to Lucy.

She was smoothing her skirts, a gesture he'd often noticed ladies do when they were uncomfortable. She was uncomfortable. With him. He swallowed and took a step back.

"Lord Norcourt," she said, licking her lips.

Giles stared unblinkingly at her.

"I have a favor to ask of you," she said with a swallow.

"A favor?" What the devil kind of favor could he possibly do for her?

"Yes, a favor." She smiled at him and gripped her hands in front of her. "As you already know, it's just Seth and me who live here and well, it wasn't too far away that we found your brother, and…" She made a harsh sound in her throat. "Well, as you saw, he was beaten badly, what if the men who did that come back to find him?"

Giles continued to stare at her. What the blazes did she mean? "If they come back?" he asked though he felt like a fool.

"Yes. What if they come back, looking for him?"

"They'll find him," he said automatically. *Why is her mouth hanging open?* he wondered.

"Lord Norcourt," she said in a tone he couldn't place.

"Yes?"

She sighed. "And what shall I do then?"

Let them take him. He pressed his lips together to keep from laughing at the inappropriate response that had come to his mind. Then froze. Since when had his responses—whether appropriate or not—come to his mind so quickly? Never. What had happened? Had he finally been cured of whatever curse had been put on his mind? If he'd known it would take merely the swipe of a beautiful lady's fingers to free his mind, he'd have been more encouraging of the ladies in Paris. From the recesses of his mind, he heard his name. "Yes?" he said, blinking.

"My lord, I don't think you understand."

"I usually don't," Giles admitted.

Lucy ran her hands over the front of her skirts again.

Taking pity on her, Giles said, "Ma'am, I am a simple man. If there is something you must say, just say it."

***

If ever there were a time to have the floor beneath her open up and swallow her whole, now would be perfect. Why did the dratted man have to play games? It was obvious he'd been quite pleased with her earlier unintentional compliment, but why did he have to make a dramatic production out of accepting her invitation to stay the night? It was obvious that he wasn't feverish, and even more obvious that he didn't like the idea of being thought weak, which is why she'd thought of the idea of playing on his male pride to convince him to stay.

Unfortunately, that wasn't working so well.

She offered Lord Norcourt her best attempt at a shy smile, but the truth was, she'd been smiling at him so much since he'd arrived that he had to either think she was a simpleton or besotted. Which she wasn't! Clutching her skirts, she steeled her spine and met his green eyes.

"Lord Norcourt," she tried again. "If those men return, I would be powerless to stop them from taking your brother."

Lord Norcourt seemed unaffected.

"I suppose he's not a favorite relation of yours," she ventured. Memories of the hatred and disdain Sam, the heir, held for his younger brother Paul, the spare, filled her mind and a bitter taste flooded her mouth. Apparently Lord Norcourt was exactly the same and now the idea of him staying in her home—sick or not— was less appealing than it had been before he'd first arrived. "Now that I think about it, I think we'll be fine. They—"

"Could hurt *you*," Lord Norcourt cut in, his eyes as big as saucers. Then, if it were possible, they got larger. *"And Seth."*

Now it was Lucy's turn for her eyes to widen. "I'm sure it'll be fine."

Lord Norcourt shook his head vigorously. "No. I'll stay."

"Truly, that's not necessary. I'm sure they won't be back," Lucy said, inwardly cursing herself for ever trying to convince him to stay. She should have just let him go. Damn her caring instinct.

"No," he said fiercely. "I'm staying."

Chapter Seven

"Do you think the house might collapse?" Seth grumbled as he pulled his pillow over his head and repositioned himself on the settee where he'd tried to sleep.

Lucy grinned. "If it hasn't happened yet, I think we might be safe." She rolled out of Seth's bed. "Why don't you lie in the bed for a while and see if you can sleep?"

Seth grunted and made his way to the bed where he flopped down in an undignified heap.

Lucy tucked the blankets around her son then slipped out of the room and into the hall where she leaned against the wall and said a silent prayer that Lord Norcourt's coachman would return soon. She was more than ready for her uninvited guests to leave so she could go to town in search of another post. That would be impossible as long as they were still in residence. Not to mention that she'd been unable to sleep last night and it had nothing to do with Simon's snoring.

"Everyone's safe," Lord Norcourt, the reason she'd been unable to sleep, declared.

Lucy opened her eyes to look at him. Standing in the hall and cloaked in shadows he cut a fine figure. She shivered. "Thank you."

He made a strangled noise, but didn't say anything. Either he was embarrassed for some unknown reason or perhaps he didn't know how to graciously accept a thank you. She nearly snorted. He was a lord, so naturally it was the latter reason.

"Would you like some breakfast?"

"Please."

Lucy made her way to the kitchen, aware he was directly behind her. If his heavy boot falls hadn't been enough of an indication, the heat his body radiated would have let her know just how close he was. Inside the kitchen, she moved to put some distance between them and went to the window above her worktable and opened the curtains. Taking longer than necessary to move the curtains just so, she racked her brain for what she'd be able to make for breakfast. Nothing she had was acceptable to feed a lord. Sighing, she turned around and gasped.

Quickly, she turned toward the door to her little room where she stored her food.

"Is something wrong?" Lord Norcourt asked.

Yes, you're carelessly burning the last of my tallow candles! She shook her head, but didn't look at him. "No, my lord." She took a deep breath. A gentleman of his station didn't know what it was like to do without or the struggle of having to make a few meager supplies last until the means could be scraped together to get more. She clenched her hands together to keep them from shaking and took another breath. *Just feed them and they'll go away.*

But she had nothing to feed them. Though she worked in a bakery and knew how to make breads and cakes, she couldn't afford the ingredients necessary to make anything of the like in her own home. "You don't happen to have a fondness for gruel, do you?" she muttered in a self-mocking tone.

"Don't mind it," Lord Norcourt said.

Lucy straightened and chanced a glance over her shoulder at him. He stood with his left shoulder leaning against the wall and his arms crossed, impaling her with his stare.

"I beg your pardon, my lord."

"What for?"

"My suggestion. I—I—" She swallowed. "Unfortunately, I haven't been to market recently and I fear I don't have anything your lordship might enjoy."

"Gruel."

She pursed her lips. Was he mocking her? "Perhaps you'd enjoy some kippers and coddled eggs from the inn in Shrewsbury."

"Gruel will be fine."

Lucy didn't know if it was his mocking words or his tone and superior stance, but something in her snapped. "You wish for gruel, and that is exactly what you shall get."

A blank expression came over his handsome face. "I like gruel."

"No, you don't," she said with a harsh laugh. "Nobody *likes* gruel. We just eat it when we're forced to."

Lord Norcourt's body went stiff as a fire poker. "Force?" he barked, a stricken look coming over his face.

She put her hand on her hip. What was it about him that made her react this way? "You know what I meant."

He shook his head. "No, I do not."

Frowning, she said, "Lord Norcourt, why do I feel that you're purposely being diffi—" His lowered lashes and slumped stance halted her words. Was it possible that he was being genuine? Shame washed over her. She didn't know how or why she suddenly understood, but she did. She still didn't understand completely, but his earlier statement about being a simple man resounded in her head. He was the sort who was very literal and said exactly what he meant. No games. She could see that now and appreciated him more for being that way, for there'd never be any pretenses with him. Noticing his eyes were still downcast and his cheeks still tinged pink, she snapped her fingers to catch his attention. "If gruel is what you like, then gruel is what I shall make for you," she said, favoring him with her best grin.

Trying to ignore the way she felt like a fool for such an idiotic statement, Lucy reached for the metal water pail that was on the shelf near where Lord Norcourt was standing.

"Allow me," he said, his hand reaching out and covering her hand that held the handle of the bucket with his.

Lucy started, but didn't release her grip on the pail. "The well is just behind the house," she said as easily as she could considering her heart was slamming against her ribcage and a warmth akin to a small fire blazed up her arm.

He nodded his understanding and gave her bucket a slight jerk.

Lucy's body pulled forward. "I can't let go," she whispered. *Nor did she want to.* Her face flushed at the thought and she jerked at her hand that was still trapped under his.

It all happened so fast, but a second later there was a loud clanging sound reverberating throughout the room as the pail hit the cold stone floor. Lucy brought her hand to her chest.

"Sorry," he grunted. "I—I—" He closed his mouth and snapped up the bucket then stomped outside.

Lucy buried her head in her hands. *No. Not again. Anything but this*, she thought as memories of the first time she'd had interest in a gentleman flooded her mind. A lord, no less.

She dropped her hands to her side and went to the pantry to busy herself until he returned with the water. Distance. That's all it would take to make her heart stop thumping and settle her blood. And she'd have distance soon enough. In fact, sooner than she'd originally thought. She didn't have to stay here until the coachman returned with their horse. As soon as breakfast was ready, she'd leave to look for another post. They should both be gone by the time she returned.

"Here." Lord Norcourt plunked the heavy bucket of water on the table so hard a little splashed over the side.

"Thank you."

He grunted his response.

Doing her best to ignore the imposing figure that watched her, she went about making gruel. When it was finished, she called her son to the room.

"Shall I go wake Mr. Appleton?" Seth asked.

"It's little wonder he hasn't woken himself already," Lucy muttered, nodding her affirmation. From the corner of her eye, she caught Lord Norcourt smiling a little at her jest. "I'm sorry."

He waved his hand in front of his face. "Don't."

A moment later a grinning Seth returned.

"Aren't you missing someone?" Lucy asked.

"He has to piss," Seth said offhandedly.

Lucy's jaw dropped in mortification and she barely registered that Lord Norcourt said something to her son.

"Excuse me," Seth said to her quietly. "I didn't mean to be—" he looked to Lord Norcourt who bent and whispered something in his ear— "indelicate."

Stunned at what had just happened, Lucy mumbled an acceptance and looked to Lord Norcourt who seemed oblivious to her state of surprise.

"I beg your forgiveness for being tardy," Mr. Appleton said as he entered the room just then. He ran a hand over the top of his combed hair then straightened his collar. "A gentleman must always remember to attend his *toilette* when in the presence of a fine lady."

His brother scowled. "You're missing half of your wardrobe," he remarked.

Simon shot him what Lucy took to be an annoyed look and ignoring Lord Norcourt, pulled a chair out. "Ma'am."

"Thank you, but I won't be eating."

All eyes swung to her.

"Why not, Mama?"

She gave Seth what she hoped would be a quelling stare.

No such luck.

"You don't have a post to get to since you were late to work yesterday and got sacked."

Mortification came over Lucy in overwhelming waves.

"You have new employment now," Lord Norcourt intoned.

"Pardon me?" Lucy asked, confused. Was he asking her or telling her?

Lord Norcourt clasped his hands behind his back. "I have a post for you."

Lucy's face burned with indignation and she pursed her lips. She could only imagine what kind of post he had in mind for her. It wasn't that she minded being boarded off into the country to do some menial post at his estate. It was the fact of whose estate it'd be. "No, thank you." She raised her chin. "I will find my own post."

"Nonsense, my mother will be happy to have help," Mr. Appleton said with a flick of his wrist.

Giles stiffened at the mention of their mother, but said nothing.

"Again, no, thank you," Lucy said. "I don't think I'd be a very good lady's companion." That was true enough, she wouldn't and it had nothing to do with the fact that if she worked for the dowager Lady Norcourt that she'd have to see Lord Norcourt again.

"She doesn't need one," Simon said with a somewhat mocking twist of his lips. "My mother remarried after the old Lord Norcourt cocked up his toes and now she runs the lending library in London."

"The lending library," Lucy echoed.

Simon nodded. "She's always saying she could use help."

The lending library would be a wonderful place to work, but she couldn't work for Lady Norcourt. That had trouble stamped all over it. "No, thank you. I don't need anyone's charity."

Chapter Eight

Giles' heart squeezed. He knew too well what it was like to be offered something solely out of Christian charity. "I apologize," he said earnestly. He never should have offered her a position. What a stupid, heartless thing for him to do! He tightened his clasped hands past the point of pain and straight to numbness.

"It's not charity…" Simon's voice floated to Giles' ears. "My mother could use the help." The irritating man continued on, but Giles didn't bother to listen.

Instead, he thought about how much he might like to flick his brother. She was Giles' mother, too. Or was she? Biologically, yes, but in every other sense of the word, she was more Simon's mother than his. He forced himself to release his clenched hands before he snapped the bones in his fingers. "No," he barked.

"I beg your pardon," Simon said, crossing his arms.

"She said no," Giles snapped at his brother.

"Perhaps to your proposal, but I'm offering her respectable employment…"

Respectable employment? Giles didn't hear the rest of what his brother said over the blood that was suddenly thundering in his ears and the words echoing in his head. His offer was respectable, too. His head snapped in Lucy's direction. "I—I—I wasn't—" he blustered not sure how to word what he wanted to convey. The blood in his ears roared louder and he couldn't make out the faces of anyone in the room as his eyes rapidly darted between the three. A strangled sound emerged from his throat and he tried again, "I didn't—" He abruptly broke off. It was useless. His broken mind wouldn't work quickly enough to tell his tongue what to say. Frustrated with his own simple stupidity, he quit the room and went to the ramshackle barn where McDougal had put his horses for the night.

He scowled. There were no saddles and he knew better than to ride a carriage horse bareback. No matter. He'd walk to the village and buy a horse there. Surely someone would be willing to sell his mount if the price was right.

Grunting, he reached into his breast pocket and removed the blank notebook he often carried with him. He flipped past the sketches he often drew when he was disinterested and ripped out a blank sheet from the back before reaching into his breast pocket again and pulling out a broken pencil he used to draw. He placed the sheet of paper on top of his notebook and scribbled, *Went home.* He set the note on the coachman's bench then left the barn to walk to the village and put distance between him and his brother. And her. He swallowed the lump in his throat. This was for the best. She'd never want to have anything to do with him. Nobody did. He picked up his pace. She was too fine, too smart for someone like him. It was best to forget about her.

He was to Shrewsbury before he knew it and as he'd predicted, he'd gotten a deal on a horse. Not a good one, mind you. He might be slow, but even he realized he'd overpaid for the horse. Unfortunately, the realization didn't happen until an hour after he'd left. He shrugged and rode on. He hadn't really been taken advantage of. He'd have paid just about anything for a mount. The other fellow knew it and just took the opportunity to help himself. Giles couldn't blame him for that.

Shrewsbury was less than a day's ride from London and just as it was time to take his evening meal, he was on the steps of his townhouse, perfectly safe from the demeaning attitude of his brother and the spell of the woman who'd so easily captured him completely. He closed his eyes. No. He wouldn't think of her again. He couldn't. Not if he wanted to keep what little sanity he possessed, that is.

***

Lucy was dumbfounded by the exchange between the two brothers. To be honest, though, she had to admit that she didn't understand about half of it. There certainly had to be more to their disagreement than what she'd just witnessed.

Unsure what to say to break the suffocating silence that had come over them, Lucy eased down into the chair Mr. Appleton had earlier pulled out for her. She should go to town, she reasoned in her mind. She needed to find a new post. But for a reason she couldn't place, she felt pulled to stay and wait for Lord Norcourt to come back.

But he didn't come back.

"He must have walked to the village," Mr. Appleton, or Simon as he'd asked her to call him, deduced with a shrug that made him grimace in pain.

Lucy nodded slowly. "For the best," she said under her breath.

Simon raked his hand through his hair and cast a quick glance over his shoulder to where the coachman stood by the open door to the Norcourt coach. "Have you reconsidered my earlier offer?"

"No. I'll find work here."

"And if you don't?"

She didn't want to contemplate that. "I will."

He pressed his lips together and gave a terse nod. "Well, if you don't, my mother would be happy for the help." He patted his chest and frowned. "I wish I had one of my calling cards to give you, but they were in my coat."

"That's not necessary," she said honestly at the same time that Seth said, "No need for a calling card, sir. I gots a good memory. What's the name and direction?"

Grinning at Seth, Simon spouted off the name and address to the lending library.

Lucy didn't bother to take note of his words.

A short time later their uninvited guest climbed up into his brother's coach. As the coach made its way down the lane, Seth surprised her by running after it.

Her heart squeezed at the gesture. She couldn't really say if Simon had been just as taken with Seth as Seth was with him, but she doubted it. A man might tolerate a lady's family if it was beneficial to him in some way. Frowning, she went inside her house and readied herself to go to town to find a new post.

Unfortunately, it was futile.

Though nobody would give her a full answer, nor look her in the eye, it was quite obvious she wouldn't find employment. At least not the respectable kind. She shivered and returned home deflated. They'd have to move—which would devastate Seth since he'd become so comfortable since they'd moved there three years prior.

Or perhaps it wouldn't devastate him as much as she'd thought.

"That settles it, then," Seth said with a wide grin. "We'll have to move to London where you can work for Mrs. Appleton until Simon is ready to marry you."

Lucy would have laughed at the absurdity of his statement if she weren't so distraught about the whispers she'd heard about herself in town. Which was preposterous. She'd been the object of whispers for many years. She should be used to it by now. But she wasn't. Well, she was used to it, but it still bothered her. Which she hated.

Gritting her teeth, she said, "We will not be moving to London for me to work at the lending library."

"So we *are* moving to London, then?"

Though she knew he was only teasing, Lucy had the strangest urge to rap her son's knuckles with a wooden spoon. Instead, she settled for a playful tap on his backside and told him to go outside until it was time to come in for dinner.

Chapter Nine

Two days later

Giles had just about worn a hole in the large plush rug in his sparsely decorated study. Ever since he'd returned from Shrewsbury, he'd taken to pacing like he did when he was a young lad who couldn't make sense of everything. He pulled to a stop and gripped the hearth. Why did it matter so much what *she* thought of him? *Because he hadn't meant to shame her!* He tightened his grip on the edge of the hearth until his knuckles went white and he let out a savage growl. It doesn't matter. *Yes, it does.*

With a grunt of vexation, he pushed himself away from the hearth then let out a heavy sigh. Why did he have to say such a stupid thing and then not even be able to say the right thing to clarify? He hated it. Hated himself at times for this…this…idiocy of his.

"Is something troubling you?"

Giles jerked and slowly turned around to face the brown eyes of his longtime friend Sebastian, Lord Belgrave, from where he stood just inside the door. "You startled me."

"Sorry," Sebastian murmured. He walked over to one of the wing-backed chairs near Giles' spotless desk and made himself comfortable. "When did you come back to Town?"

"I left the day after you." He folded his arms over his chest and leaned his hip against his desk. "Simon was injured."

"Injured? How?"

"Beaten. Robbers, I suppose." He shrugged. Simon hadn't exactly been interested in speaking to him that night in Shrewsbury any more than he had before or since.

"I take it that it's Simon who's put that troubled expression on your face."

Giles instinctively ran his hand over his face. Was it possible for Sebastian to tell he was concerned about something? Could one tell that by looking at someone's face? He couldn't. "What do you mean?"

"Most of the time you wear a blank expression, Giles. One that would suggest you're disinterested. Today you don't seem quite so tranquil. Your brows are furrowed and your jaw is clenched. If I didn't know any better I'd think you were worried about something." He paused. "Are you?"

Giles dropped his gaze to study the floor. He could trust Sebastian. He was one of the only people he'd ever met who hadn't judged him or treated him harshly. But how did he explain what had happened?

"Giles?"

"Sebastian?"

Sebastian chuckled. "If it makes it any easier for you to know, you're not the only one who has been affected by these recent events."

Giles' head snapped up. What did Sebastian know? Before he could find a way to ask without giving himself and his vulnerability away, Sebastian continued.

"When Simon was trying to court Belle at the house party, he kept getting distracted. By you."

An odd mixture of relief and irritation coursed through Giles. "I don't see why."

"I think you do," Sebastian said quietly.

Giles shrugged and made his way to a chair on the other side of his desk. "Where is your wife?"

Sebastian bared his teeth in a look Giles had once heard described as a grimace, then lowered his lashes. "I'm not sure. We didn't part on good terms."

"And you say I'm troubled."

Sebastian twisted his lips and nodded. "Indeed. But I do have a plan." His face went back to normal. "I just hope it works."

"It will."

"I appreciate your vote of confidence," Sebastian said in a low tone. "Now, about you."

Giles shook his head. Sebastian wouldn't mock him, but he couldn't help him, either.

"Is Lord Cosgrove still pushing for you to find a bride?"

Giles stiffened. He'd forgotten all about that. "No."

"What changed his mind?"

"Don't know." He shrugged. "He hasn't spoken to me about it again."

A moment of silence engulfed them. "Do you think—" Sebastian cleared his throat and shifted in his seat. "We never discussed your past while we were touring the continent." He scoffed. "Hell, I didn't even know that you were a lord, let alone that you had a brother. You keep your secrets well, Giles, and this might not be my place to ask, but is it possible that Lord Cosgrove isn't quite as interested in seeing you married as someone else might be?"

Giles stared at his friend. Who else would care? Nobody. There wasn't anyone else who'd care. They'd probably rather he not secure an heir so his title could pass to someone else. Which was fine with Giles. He didn't want to be baron. The only reason he'd even come to London at Lord Cosgrove's demands was because of his threat to begin selling off anything Giles owned that wasn't entailed. He didn't care about losing the assets, but he knew better than to believe he'd be the one who'd receive the funds from the sale of those assets.

"Giles?"

Sebastian's voice pulled Giles to present. "Yes?"

"I know you like to keep things private, but if you tell me what's going on, I can help you."

"With Lord Cosgrove or Lucy?" The words were out before he realized it. At Sebastian's slow grin, Giles' face heated.

"Who's Lucy?"

"No one." Giles jumped at the sharpness in his own voice. "Just a lady I met."

"One who seems to have had quite a serious effect on you, I'd wager."

Giles flushed. "I said something foolish."

Sebastian didn't respond right away. "Are you sure it's irreparable?"

"Doesn't matter."

"I think it might."

"She can have Simon." Just saying the words made his throat constrict as if he might suffocate at any moment. But it didn't make it any less true. Simon was smarter. He wouldn't say thoughtless things to shame her. He could say exactly what he wanted to the first time. The sharp pain in his palms drew his attention and he released his fists.

"If she can make someone as calm as you react this way, I believe she's worth seeking out to make amends."

"It's no use."

"So you say, and yet, it's turned you into a bundle of nerves."

Giles frowned. "I'm not a bundle of nerves. I'm made up of cells."

Sebastian shook his head. "Indeed. What I meant was that you've never cared what anyone's thought about you before and now you do."

"I shamed her," Giles burst out, fighting the remorse that was threatening to wash over him.

"You should go to her and try to explain," Sebastian said in his usual calm voice.

"I can't."

"Why not?"

"It won't matter. She'll marry Simon."

"That didn't take long," Sebastian muttered. He waved a hand through the air. "Giles, I don't have all the details and I won't press you for them, but it's only been three days since I last saw you and Simon and at that time Simon was still very much trying to court my wife. I cannot imagine that he's already become engaged to another."

"I didn't say he was."

Sebastian drummed his fingers on the chair and now it was Giles' turn to shift uncomfortably in his chair. Were he still living with the nuns, either Mother Superior or Father Thomas would have yelled at him by now, or would with their next statement. Sebastian never had, but surely one day his patience would wear thin. Unfortunately, Giles had never been very good at articulating.

"I still think you should clarify what you meant," Sebastian said a moment later. "Even if you think she might marry your brother, it wouldn't do for you to have an uncomfortable relationship with your new sister-in-law."

"Why does it matter?"

"You mean because you don't even have a relationship with Simon?" At Giles' nod, Sebastian continued. "That goes back to what I was talking about before. I probably shouldn't tell you this, but since you're my friend, I want you to know. Belle mentioned that Simon told her that your mother means to make amends by helping you find a bride."

"I know."

"But I don't just mean by asking Lady Cosgrove to host the house party, Giles." He ran his hand through his dark hair. "Do you think it might be possible that your mother might have asked Lord Cosgrove to help bring you here?"

Giles sat stock-still. His mother had seemed extremely interested in him since his return. She'd agreed to host a dinner party when he'd asked her to a month ago. She'd even gone so far as resuming her title Lady Norcourt for the evening to act as hostess when she'd been content to be styled as Mrs. Appleton for twenty years. Then, at the house party, she'd sought him out whenever she could and had introduced him to some of who she'd considered to be the "finest" unattached young ladies. He'd found them annoying, but apparently she didn't. She'd even told him that she'd like to help him find a match. But did her desire to find him a match go so far as to issue threats to get him to return? His heart pounded and sweat beaded along his brow. He looked to Sebastian. Sebastian didn't lie. Not to Giles. He wouldn't suggest this if he didn't think it was a real possibility.

Hurt and anger swelled up inside of him, then just as quickly vanished. Just as it had when she'd admitted to having had the house party planned to help Giles find a match. Did it really matter that she'd used deceitful tactics to get him to return to England? He sighed. No. Almost everyone he'd ever met manipulated him. Why should his own mother be any different? "Thank you, Sebastian."

"For what?"

"The truth," Giles said simply, standing.

Sebastian leapt to his feet. "Are you going to confront her?"

"No."

"Then where are you going?"

"You were right."

"About?"

"Everything."

Sebastian arched an eyebrow. "I doubt my wife would agree with that statement."

Giles didn't know what to say to that. "My mother is quite desperate to have a relationship so I'd better go apologize for what I said to Lucy."

An expression Giles didn't understand came over Sebastian's face, then he stepped to the side and used both of his hands to gesture toward the door while giving a slight bow. Sebastian was a strange friend, to be sure, but many probably thought the same about Giles. Which was likely why they'd gotten along as well as they had in the past six years.

Less than five minutes later Giles found himself standing in front of the tall, light grey stone building that housed the Norcourt Lending Library. Though he was told he owned it, he'd never actually been inside before.

Clenching his hands into fists, he commanded his heavier-than-lead legs to carry him inside. The overwhelming smell of paper and glue filled his nose as soon as he opened the door. A second later he was assailed by a cloud of dust.

"Do forgive me," chirped a red-haired urchin holding a limp feather duster. "Mrs. Appleton hates it when any dust is visible on the books." She lowered her voice. "She thinks people will assume the dusty ones are the ones not worth readin'."

His mother was smart. Very smart. Of course he already knew she was clever and deceitful, but she was also smart. How ironic, those three adjectives often went together. "Is L—er—Miss Whitaker here?"

The girl turned her head to the side. "Who?"

"Miss Whitaker. She's about this tall—" he lifted his hand to the middle of his chest— "she has black hair and blue eyes."

"I don't know if I've seen her come in," the girl said as she spun the feather stick between her hands, making the dust swirl around them.

"She works here," Giles clarified with a cough.

"Works here?" The girl stopped spinning her duster. "The only person who works here other than me is Mrs. Appleton."

"I'll find her."

He didn't take three steps away from the girl before his mother appeared in his line of vision.

"Giles?" she called out to him. Her lips stretched into a wide smile. "I'm so glad you came to see me. Come, let's sit and talk."

Giles ground his teeth and forced himself to go over to her. "Is Miss Whitaker here?" he asked without ceremony.

"Who?"

Giles frowned. "When Simon returned. Was there—" He broke off. The girl at the front of the store had mentioned a Mrs. Appleton who worked here and now his mother seemed oblivious to who Miss Whitaker was. Was it possible that Simon had already married her? Could he have so quickly? Giles had never paid much attention when people got married except to know there was a short ceremony where they each pledged their lives to each other.

"Giles?"

He tried to swallow the unease in his throat, but couldn't. "The woman."

A vertical line formed between his mother's eyes. "What woman?"

"With Simon."

"You mean Isabelle Knight?"

Giles shook his head vigorously. "No. Lucy Whitaker."

"Who?"

A sound of vexation ripped from his throat. Why couldn't she understand him?

"Calm down, Giles," his mother said, placing her hand on his forearm.

He shook it off as if her touch burned. "Don't. I don't like it."

She backed away as if he'd stuck her. "I'm sorry. I didn't realize..." She smoothed her skirts. "I won't touch you again."

It wasn't being touched he didn't like. It was— It was— He shook his head to dispel the thought he knew wouldn't form completely until it didn't matter anymore.

"Tell me what you need, Giles?"

"I need to talk to her."

"All right. Who?"

"The woman with Simon," he practically bellowed in frustration.

"Simon didn't have anyone with him when he returned," she said calmly as if suddenly she understood everything.

"He didn't?"

She shook her head. "When I returned from Telford yesterday he told me a little of what happened, but he never mentioned a woman, Giles, and I mean that." She blinked her eyes rapidly as if she were trying to keep from crying. "Thank you for your kindness. I know the two of you don't get along, but I was hoping —"

"No," Giles cut in. "He doesn't like me."

"That's not true," his mother said immediately. "He just needs time."

Giles doubted that and just shrugged in response. It didn't bother him that Simon didn't care for him.

"Would you like to join us for dinner on Friday night?"

No, he wouldn't. "No, thank you."

She dropped her hands to her sides and let out a deep breath. "I'm trying, Giles. I know you haven't had an easy time of it and that's partly my fault, but would you please give me a chance?"

"A chance?" A chance for what? To hurt him again? To manipulate him some more? To use his position for her gain? He took another step back. "No."

She swiped at the tears that had slipped from her blue eyes. "I'm sorry that I couldn't be more help in your search for Miss Whitaker," she said, her voice uneven. "Simon never spoke of her, but if you'd like to ask him if he knows of her whereabouts he's recovering over at my house."

Giles frowned. "That won't be necessary." Surely, if Simon had indeed brought her back, his mother would have known of her existence since Simon was staying with her.

Then, without another word, because there was nothing more to say to her, Giles spun on his heel and left the lending library.

Chapter Ten

Lucy wrung her hands together and looked around the almost empty parlor. There wasn't much left of their meager belongings. Just the dining table and chairs and a faded, threadbare settee she'd found behind the bakery a year ago. It couldn't possibly be worth more than a half penny, but that'd be a half penny they could use.

"Why do we have to move to York?" Seth demanded of her, his face red and angry.

Lucy's heart clenched and anger, mostly directed at herself, bubbled up inside of her. "We're going to start over somewhere we've never been," she said. "It'll be fun like one of those adventures you like to read about."

Seth stared at her, unmoved. "I don't understand it. Can't you find another post in town or go to London and work for Lady Norcourt?"

"No," she said a little more sharply than she'd meant to. But the truth was, every business owner she'd gone to seek employment from was only interested in offering her one type of employment. And she wasn't interested in becoming *that* kind of woman. Nor did she want to go to London and work for Lady Norcourt.

"I don't understand why you won't marry Mr. Appleton."

"Other than the fact he hasn't asked?" Lucy said sarcastically.

Seth plopped down on the threadbare settee. "So if he asked —"

"No," she snapped. She rubbed her hands over her face. "Seth, I've already told you, gentlemen like Mr. Appleton do not marry women like me."

"I think he might. He said he thought you were fetching."

She was sure he did. "While that is the finest compliment a lady could ask for, that does not mean he wishes to marry me."

"It could," Seth said, oblivious to her previous sarcasm.

Lucy sighed. "I know you like him, but it'd be better if you stopped thinking about him." She swallowed and screwed up her courage. "Gentlemen like him, young, handsome, wealthy, they see women like me as amusements. Not as wives."

"Amusements?"

Lucy groaned. As much as she didn't want to prevail upon Paul, Sam's brother, for support, she might have to bring herself to ask him to explain the things to Seth that she couldn't. Heat crept up her neck. No. Too much had passed between the three of them that she could never ask that of him. "Seth, I won't discuss this with you any further. You are not to ever mention Mr. Appleton to me again, do you understand?"

Seth jumped up from the settee. "No, I don't understand," he said as he fought back the tears. "I don't understand you at all and I never will." Then, without allowing her a chance to explain, he ran from the house, slamming the door as he went.

Lucy started after him as he ran. But she couldn't keep up and fell to her knees on the ground, silent sobs wracking her body. "I'm trying, Seth," she cried out quietly into the setting sun. Tears stung the backs of her eyes. Which was ridiculous. She was the one who'd created this mess. Well, not just her, there was a *he* involved, too. But she should have known better. That familiar bitter taste that always accompanied thoughts of *him* filled her mouth, making her want to act most unladylike and spit. Which was probably fine since she wasn't a lady in any sense of the word. Instead, she rose to her feet and went back to her house. Seth would come back soon enough. This wasn't the first time he'd gotten angry with her and run off. He'd come back.

Twenty minutes later there was a swift, *bang, bang, bang* at her front door. Lucy stood from where she was packing their remaining clothes into the one trunk they'd have to share with all the personal belongings they'd be able to keep.

"Hello," she said, opening the door a couple of inches.

Two men were standing outside, both leering at her. She shuddered. The shorter one, Mr. Bronson, she recognized right away. He worked in the livery down the street from the bakery where she'd worked.

"I hear ye have a table," Mr. Bronson said.

"Yes, most people do." Her grip on the interior doorknob tightened. She had no desire to let them inside her home.

"I hear it's for sale," he continued.

"Not anymore," she said; then quickly shut the door and slid the lock.

Loud, raucous laughter filled the air. "Come now, Miss Whitaker, we just want to have a quick look-see at it."

She grimaced. "No. It's not for sale."

"We'll pay a more than fair price," the other man said. His voice sent a shiver down her spine. "We just want to test the sturdiness of it first."

More drunken laughter ensued.

Panic built in Lucy's chest. Perhaps selling her things had been a mistake. Just one more to a long list of many she'd made, she reckoned.

When their laughter died, their shouts began.

"We intend to pay," one slurred. "We have enough coins."

Coins jingled. Then more earnest banging began. After a minute, one of them called out to her again.

"Either you can let us in or we'll come in on our own. But if we have to come in on our own, we might not see to pay you as well."

Less than a second later, the unmistakable sound of glass shattering rent the air. Glass fell to the wooden floor next to her foot in a cascade of *clinks*. Lucy dashed to the back of the house. She had to get away and her best chance was to climb out the bedroom window.

Just then, there was a loud crashing sound and the cottage shook. Lucy closed the bedroom door and slid the lock. It wouldn't keep them out entirely, but it might slow them down just enough to afford her a few extra seconds to get away from here and find Seth.

She froze. Find Seth. She had an idea of where he was: the Old Elm tree. But she wasn't positive. Had these men already found him? Had they hurt him? She'd never forgive herself if anything had happened to her son. Trying to push thoughts of him in pain out of her mind, she unlatched the window and tried to lift it up. It wouldn't budge. She tightened her grip and used all the muscles she possessed. It didn't move and the wooden door behind her splintered and came crashing open.

"There ye are," said the man she didn't recognize. Even cloaked in shadows he looked fierce. He reached for her and grabbed onto the top of her pale blue dress, then yanked her toward him. "Yer a feisty one." He clucked his tongue. "I like that."

All fight left her body instantly. It was enough that he had her where he wanted her and he would have no resistance in getting his way. The last thing she wanted to give him was any further satisfaction about it. If he enjoyed it when those who he attacked fought and screamed and tried to break loose, she wouldn't.

"Hmm, docile as a church mousie, are ye now?" he mused, spraying her with his spittle on every word.

She didn't answer, which seemed to upset him.

"I think I know wot would put that spark back in yer eye." Then, a second later, he grabbed onto her hair and dragged her to the parlor.

Her heart nearly burst out of her chest. *Seth.* Mr. Bronson was holding onto him in such a way that Seth stood motionless with his arm pinned behind his back.

"Don't move, boy," Mr. Bronson sneered, a self-satisfied smile on his lips. "We're gwine shew you wot women like yer ma are good fer."

Mr. Bronson must have tightened his grip or Seth must have realized that Lucy was about to be hurt because tears started to stream down his cheeks. *"No!"*

Lucy shook her head. "Let him go. I'll do whatever it is you want, just let him go."

"I don't think so," the stranger said, tightening his grip on Lucy. "I think ye behave much better while he's here." He reached forward to grab her breast and she smacked his hand away, making him laugh. "Yes, I do believe I like this better now. The boy will get to see what you really are and I'll get to have a far more amusing time demonstrating it."

"Leave her alone," Seth shouted, kicking backwards at Mr. Bronson's legs.

The men just laughed at his efforts.

Lucy ached for him all over again. Was what they were doing to her in front of him not bad enough, must they mock him, too? She fisted her hand and swung at the man standing nearest her, hoping to catch him off guard, but he was farther away than she thought and instead of hitting him where she'd intended, she hit just off to the side of his groin.

He instantly sobered and tightened his hold on her hair. "You'll pay for that," he growled as he flung her against the stone wall where she hit her head then crumpled to the floor.

Seth shouted something and might have struggled, but Lucy wasn't sure since she couldn't see him through the sudden burst of stars and shapes that filled her vision when her head hit the wall.

A second later two firm hands were on her breasts trying to pull her to a standing position. She tried to fight, but felt powerless against him and her screams and cries mingled with the men's laughter.

Hysteria filled her at the painful chaos that surrounded her. She wanted to be free of this man and make sure her son was safe.

But she couldn't get free and the more she struggled, the more powerless she became against his strong grip. She was only vaguely aware that he'd ripped the bodice of her gown as she tried to catch a glimpse of Seth as he still fought to get free of his captor's hold.

Suddenly, a shadow crossed the front door and without warning another large, imposing form came into the room. *Lord Norcourt.* Without a second's delay, Lord Norcourt gripped the back of Mr. Bronson, and swung him around with such vigor that he released his hold on Seth, which sent the poor boy to the floor. Before Mr. Bronson could have a chance to put together what was going on, Lord Norcourt's large fist collided with his face.

The stranger who'd been accosting Lucy snarled and abruptly let her go. Spitting, he stalked over to their new guest and threw a punch that connected with Lord Norcourt's stomach.

A loud "Oooof" was all Lord Norcourt said before lifting his foot and kicking Lucy's attacker between his legs.

"Mama." Seth's weak voice grabbed her attention and her heart all over again as he inched his way toward her.

She reached for him and pulled him to her, wrapping him in her arms. "It's all right," she soothed in his ear, watching as Lord Norcourt lifted her attacker back to a standing position by his hair then proceeded to punch his face and midsection until he fell to a boneless heap on the floor.

In her arms, Seth's body shook with sobs and she tried her best to console him, but doubted she could when she was just as upset. She couldn't show it though. She needed to be strong. He needed her.

In the shadows she saw Mr. Bronson stagger to his feet, but with one swift punch to the face that sent him flying backwards into the jagged edge of the window ledge, he was sent back to the ground and silence engulfed the room broken only by Lucy's heavy breathing and Seth's silent tears that seemed louder than gunfire to her.

"You all right?" Lord Norcourt's soft voice startled her more than her attacker's aggression had.

"I'm fine," she lied.

He bent down near her and her heart picked up pace. Now that the danger was over, she was able to think straight and the first thing she needed to make sense of was why he was here.

"Why did you come back?"

"To apologize."

She closed her tired eyes. She couldn't begin to know what he was apologizing for. "I don't think I can refuse to accept your apology now," she teased.

"Yes, you can," he said quietly.

If she wasn't in such a state, she'd argue with him and demand to know what he was even talking about, but for as brave of a woman as she'd like to be, she could hardly muster up an ounce of courage right now, let alone any defiance.

He reached for Seth. "Let me help you."

"Leave her alone," Seth spat, clinging to Lucy.

"Seth—"

"It's all right, boy," Giles interjected in a gentle tone. "I'm not going to hurt you or your mama. Can you stand up so your mama can get up?"

It took some coaxing, but a moment later, Lord Norcourt had Seth on his feet. It was nearly dark in the house now, with only the low glow of the nearly set sun as their source of light. Even still, she could see her son's tear-stained cheeks and it was all she could do to hold back her own tears.

Lord Norcourt's strong hands slipped awkwardly under her arms as he helped her to her feet. As soon as she was standing, he removed his hands. "I didn't mean to look," he blurted.

Lucy sensed the nervousness in his tone and placed a hand on his forearm. "I know." With her other hand, she did her best to pull her torn bodice together to cover herself as much as she could. "Thank you for saving us," she whispered.

"You're welcome," he returned. "Will you both come with me to London?"

"I can't."

"Can't?" The disbelief in his voice almost made her laugh. Almost.

"Can't," she confirmed, casting a glance over to her unusually quiet son. With how desperate he'd been as of late for her to find another husband, she was rather surprised he wasn't arguing with her. Then again, he was probably now terrified of men after what he'd witnessed tonight.

"I didn't mean it," Lord Norcourt blustered.

Her eyes snapped back to him. "Pardon?"

"Last time. When I said I could get you a post. It wasn't as my mistress."

A new sense of understanding came over her, sobering her. "I know that. I didn't think you had meant that."

"But when Simon said—"

"Shhh." She put a finger to his lips. "I know that wasn't what you'd meant."

"How?"

Her entire body stilled. "I don't know," she admitted. "I just did."

He encircled her wrist with his warm fingers. "Then come to London with me."

She shouldn't. Going with him would only lead to trouble. The least of which was what others might think if they spotted them together. No, the fear of that wasn't nearly as large as the fear of the feelings he evoked in her. "I shouldn't."

"But you will?" he asked in a tone that broke down the last of her waning resolve.

She nodded. "Yes."

Chapter Eleven

Relief ran through Giles' being, taking with it all the hard tension that had held him captive for longer than he could remember. He turned to Seth. "Do you think you can help me load the carriage while your mama gets dressed?"

The boy didn't move.

"They won't be getting up for a while," Giles explained softly. If ever. He'd never hurt anyone before, but when he'd happened upon that horrific scene he hadn't known what else to do.

Seth gave a fleeting glance to the unconscious men lying on the parlor floor, then led Giles down the hall to a moonlit room that resembled a bedroom. Just without the bed. Strange. "Already packed?" Giles asked when his eyes collided with a large, scuffed trunk in the middle of the floor.

"Mama said we were leaving for York in the morning."

"You'll go to London tonight."

"Yes, my lord," Seth muttered as he flipped the latch on the side of the trunk. He sank to his knees and started emptying the contents without really looking at them.

Giles knelt down beside him. "Seth?"

"I should have done something," the boy said fiercely before letting out a deep exhale and falling backwards on his bottom.

Giles moved to sit beside him and pulled his knees up to his chest, then rested his elbows on his raised knees. For a moment the two sat that way. Giles wished he had something of any value to say to Seth to make him feel better about everything. But what could he say? Perhaps he should offer to hire the boy a tutor to teach him to fight. He shook his head. No. Lucy might throttle him if he taught her boy to fight. Better not do that.

"Seth, if I'd have been you, I'd have done the same thing."

"You would have?"

Giles wasn't sure, but he almost thought the boy sounded

surprised. "Yes. When I was a boy at the orphanage and I'd get in trouble, the nuns were instructed to hold me that way. It doesn't hurt so much, but if you try to move forward even a little, it'll break your arm."

"It will?"

Giles nodded and idly rubbed his arm. A sharp, humorous laugh escaped his lips. "It only took one time for my brain to remember that."

"A nun broke your arm?"

Giles bristled, then made himself relax. Seth didn't seem the sort to mock him intentionally. Likely he was just curious. "Yes," he said quietly.

"Was she as big as Berta?"

"Who's Berta?"

"She works in the butchery. She's gargantuan. Her arms are wider than trees and I swear she'd kill a man if she sat on him."

"Unfortunately, no. Sister Mary was about an inch or two shorter than your mother and as thin as a reed." He was thankful the room was dark enough that Seth couldn't see him blush at his confession. "That position—it uses a boy's strength against himself and can break just about anyone's arm—no matter how big they are, or the person holding them that way."

"Oh." Silence filled the air between them again. "So you don't think my mama thinks I'm weak because I couldn't help?"

"No," Giles said automatically. Then for a reason, he couldn't explain, he added, "And neither do I."

***

The tears that Lucy had fought so hard to keep at bay slipped from the sides of her eyes and coursed down her face at Lord Norcourt's final whispered words to her son as they sat on the floor in what had been Seth's bedroom. She'd known for a long time now that Seth wished for a father, but she hadn't truly realized how much.

She peeked around the doorjamb just in time to see Lord Norcourt push to his feet and gesture for Seth to join him.

"Is this what you were looking for?" Lord Norcourt asked,

picking up what appeared to be her lavender dress.

"Yes, my lord," Seth said.

"Here." Lord Norcourt extended the dress toward Seth. "You take this to her and I'll carry out the trunk."

Seth pushed Giles' hand back then bent to toss their belongings back into the trunk. "No, I'll carry the trunk."

Lucy shook her head at Seth's sudden deep tone and tiptoed down the hall so she'd be out of sight when Seth came through the door.

A moment later, Seth exited the room and walked in the opposite direction of where Lucy was standing.

Lucy peeked back inside the room where Lord Norcourt stood holding her gown in one hand and his other hand gripping his hair.

"Thank you," she said, walking into the room.

He jumped. "Sorry." He held her gown out toward her.

She took the dress, her fingers brushing his. Once again, his skin was warm. Perhaps he was always warm, she reasoned as she pulled the gown toward her chest. She remembered when she'd first bought this gown. It was a cast off from Lord Kresson's eldest daughter. Put on sale in a consignment shop no less than ten years ago in Bath. It had been her favorite; one of the only three gowns she hadn't sold.

"Do you need help?"

Lord Norcourt's voice startled her. "N-no. I'll just need a minute to change then I'll be out."

Without another word, he brushed past her, walked to the doorway and stopped.

"Do you plan to just stand there while I change?" she asked his back.

"Yes."

A shiver ran over her, but then something she didn't recognize came over her, too. Not wishing to examine it too closely, she quickly shed her ripped gown, praying all the memories attached to it would flee from her the moment it was off.

"Ready now?" he asked just as she finished putting on her gown.

"Almost."

"Do you need help?"

"No," she said in a broken whisper.

He turned to face her. "What's wrong?"

Lucy looked down at the discarded gown. "I don't know what to do."

"Leave it."

"But I need it," she argued. She'd never had many gowns anyway, but now that she only had so few, she couldn't afford to easily abandon one just because it was in need of repairs. "I think I can fix it. I'll just need to sew—"

"No." He took her cold, clammy hand in his large, warm one. "Leave it."

The logical side of her wanted to argue with him. She genuinely *did* need that dratted gown. Unlike him, she couldn't afford to buy another one just because this one now had a foul memory attached.

As if he could hear the war raging in her head, he said, "It's not just you who has bad memories of that dress."

And with that, her will dissolved.

They were nearing the carriage when she realized she was still holding his hand and felt a little bereft when he helped her into the carriage then let go of her to speak to the coachman.

She gazed over to where Seth sat on the opposite side of the carriage. He was looking at the moon through the window. She racked her brain for something to say to him, but couldn't think of anything that might break the palpable tension that thickened the air between them.

A moment later Lord Norcourt climbed inside the carriage. Lucy watched him in disbelief as he closed the door, lit the sconce, then made himself comfortable beside her as the carriage started to roll down the lane. How was it that being in such close proximity to him, a lord and a peer of the realm, didn't make her stomach lurch or her skin prickle with discomfort the way just the mention of the titled normally did?

She shook off the thought and looked to her son who seemed

to fight his sleep harder with each passing second.

Lucy reached over to the sconce. "Do you mind if I turn this down?"

Lord Norcourt shrugged. "No. I lit it for you."

"For me?"

He nodded, but didn't say anything.

"Well, I suppose I shall confess this to you now, I didn't bring any books or embroidery, so I don't think I'll need it."

Lord Norcourt's eyes went wide. "I—I didn't mean for..." He trailed off and let out a deep sigh. Lucy opened her mouth to explain that she was only jesting, when he spoke again. "It's so you wouldn't be afraid in the dark."

"I'm not afraid of you," she said without thinking. Not that she needed to. She could never explain it, but she knew she was safe with him. "I know you won't hurt me."

"You do?"

"Yes."

* * *

Giles hadn't experienced so many gut-wrenching emotions in the course of one evening since the time he was caught drawing in a book in the library by Sister Catherine. He'd been content while drawing, then pleased when he was done, followed by frightened and ashamed when caught, then horrified and confused when she insisted he strip off his clothes and be plunged into an ice bath to banish whatever evil spirit had come inside him and made him act so disrespectfully to a holy book. He shuddered at the memory and pushed away the snatches of memories of that night that hadn't yet unfolded in his mind. That had been an awful night and while not every aspect of the past few hours had been pleasant for him, his unruly emotions had been a close match. But in a good way. The night of his final ice bath at the hands of Sister Catherine had made his heart pound the same as it was now, but now it left him with a warm, excited feeling, not one of hatred and shame. He much preferred the one Lucy had created. She trusted him. A smile pulled at his lips. With the exception of Sebastian's wife, Isabelle, no lady had ever trusted him before. He almost snorted. To be honest, other than Isabelle, no other lady had ever given him the chance to earn her trust.

He shifted and tried to tamp down his excitement at his newfound knowledge. Sebastian had been right, seeking her out to talk to her and make things right had been a good idea. They just might be able to be friends. Which would be good for when she married Simon.

He frowned at the dull ache that built in his chest at the thought and tried to shift to get more comfortable again.

"Sorry," Lucy murmured.

His eyes shot to her direction. It was too dark to see her though. "Pardon?"

"I'm sorry," she said. "I don't mean to keep moving. I just can't seem to fall asleep."

"You weren't bothering me." He hadn't even noticed she'd been moving.

She sighed and moved in her seat in a way that brushed her hip along his thigh. He certainly felt *that*.

"Sorry, I can't seem to get comfortable."

Instinctively, he reached for her and pulled her against his body with her right cheek resting on his left shoulder. She didn't argue and wiggled a little against him, presumably to make herself more comfortable. Unfortunately, that did nothing for his comfort because whether she realized it or not, it drew his attention to where the soft parts of her chest were now touching his.

He closed his eyes and bit the inside of his lip. Pulling her against him might have been a mistake. He moved his right arm to settle across his lap so it'd better conceal his reaction to her nearness. Surely she couldn't see his trousers in the dark, but he couldn't be too careful.

Giles leaned his head against the squabs and tried to dredge up what notes made up the musical scale for C major. He *hated* music. Detested it. Well, listening wasn't so bad, but playing it was awful. Almost as bad as being made to dance. He couldn't dance in the carriage and moving his feet might bother Lucy. But he could think of notes and piano keys in his head. Hopefully it'd put a swift end to his current state like it had when this used to happen when he was younger and had gone to Paris for the first time. He'd never seen a woman without a habit on before then and couldn't help but stare at them all. Fortunately, he'd learned to control himself by thinking of music and hadn't embarrassed himself in years. He just hoped it'd work just as well this time.

In his mind, he went through all the scales he could remember: C, G, F, and A. There were more, but he couldn't remember them and it might not matter since his pulse was still racing and there was still a tight, hot coil in his stomach.

Just then, something damp touched his shoulder. He blinked and brought his hand to Lucy's face. "Lucy?"

She didn't say anything, but her body trembled. Surely he hadn't betrayed her trust because of his reaction to her. Panic built in his chest, but he couldn't think of the right words to make it better. Although, if one were interested in the positive of the situation, his body had cooled completely the moment he felt her tears and everything had settled back to how it should be in the presence of a lady who wasn't one's wife.

"I'm sorry," she said, her voice hitching on a small sob. "I just can't get the images of those men out of my mind and when I close my eyes—they're there."

Wordlessly, he pulled her onto his lap and wrapped her in his arms. "Cry."

"I'm sorry," she repeated with her face pressed into his chest. Less than a minute later her tears had soaked through the front of his shirt.

He glided his open palm up and down her back. "It's all right," he said against her hair. "We all have to cry sometimes."

Chapter Twelve

Lucy was pulled from her dreamless state by the low rumble in Lord Norcourt's chest.

"If you'll wait outside the carriage, I'll show you where to go."

"Yes, my lord." She recognized that as Seth's voice. Why was he awake?

She tried to move and make sense of everything, but her head and body hurt too much.

"It's all right." Lord Norcourt's soft voice was right by her ear. "We're at my house. I'll carry you inside."

Lucy knew she should argue, but she couldn't. She was too weary to move a muscle on her own.

"Go on inside, Seth." Lord Norcourt carried her up the front steps, the bottoms of his boots scraping against the stone with each step he took, but never once did it feel like she was slipping in his grip. "At the top of the staircase, go left. You can use the first room on the right."

"And my mama?"

"She'll be one room over."

What felt like seconds later, Lucy was being lowered against a feather mattress, then felt a heavy blanket come over her.

***

The sun was already high in the sky and flooding in through the break in the curtains by the time Lucy awoke. She sat up and rubbed the stiff skin of her face with her hands. She hadn't slept so soundly in years. If ever. Dropping her hands, she looked around. There wasn't a lot of furniture in the room, but what was there was beautifully carved, pristine, and decidedly expensive. She idly ran her fingers over the delicate design etched into the bedpost nearest her. It was lovely and regal.

Once I'm a viscount we'll have a house full of the finest things money can afford, Sam promised. *You deserve no less.* She could still see the way the sun glinted off Sam's light hair as he leaned against the big oak and smiled at her.

She twisted her lips. Sam had made so many broken promises to her that she couldn't recount them all. Nor did she wish to. She yanked her hand away as if the bedpost had burned her skin then stood. Spotting her chest across the room, she scurried over and changed out of the now crushed gown she'd traveled in and into her final gown. It wasn't nearly as nice as the purple one, just a plain tan and black dress. It'd be the perfect thing to wear to search for a new post. Which is exactly what she needed to do as soon as Seth returned. Lord Norcourt had been most kind to her and she'd forever be grateful for his generosity, but she needed to leave before his kindness would forever be tainted by memories of the one who'd done her so wrong.

Catching sight of herself in the mirror, she quickly repinned her hair and adjusted her bodice. Satisfied that she looked somewhat presentable, she made her way to the hall in search of her son.

There were only two other rooms upstairs. She knocked, waited a moment, then slowly let herself inside. This room was twice the size of the room she'd been in, but had the same amount of furniture, making it look even emptier. "Seth?"

"No, ma'am," said a maid who was changing the sheets on the bed. "He and his lordship went out to the bakery to get something special for breakfast."

Lucy ground her teeth. What more could she say to Seth to make him realize that he couldn't just go off with anyone? She wanted to groan. Apparently last night hadn't deterred him from trying to find himself a new father. She'd have to speak to him again. "Could his cook not have made some tarts?" She hadn't even realized she'd said that aloud until the maid responded.

"No, ma'am. Danes is so blind he can hardly tell the sugar from the salt." She grimaced. "'Tis better this way, ma'am."

"How long have they been gone?"

"About three minutes." The maid fluffed up the sheet then

smoothed it down. "You can wait for them in the drawing room, if you'd like."

If the downstairs were anything like the upstairs had been, she'd need no help finding the drawing room. Just as she'd suspected, she was correct. At the bottom of the stairs was a little room with only a mahogany desk, three chairs, a settee and two floor-to-ceiling bookcases devoid of any books. The room across the hall had a long dining table with five chairs going down each side and one on either end. No decorations were mounted on the wall nor runners on the table. Evidently, he preferred simplicity. She couldn't argue with that. The next room was locked.

"He always keeps that one locked," a female voice said behind her, startling her.

"I'm sorry. I was looking for the drawing room," she murmured, turning around to face the other woman. She immediately froze. The woman who'd spoken to her stood two inches taller than Lucy with her auburn hair piled atop her head with a few wisps of curls framing her smiling face. Her curious blue eyes held no condescension, only questions.

"The drawing room is just over here." She gestured to the open door behind her. "Won't you come join me?"

Did Lucy really have a choice? Swallowing her unease, Lucy followed the fancy woman, who could only be Lady Norcourt, across the hall and toward the drawing room.

"Have a seat anywhere you'd like," Lady Norcourt invited as she stepped into the room.

Lucy walked in behind her and came to a halt. There was only one settee. One short, squat, blue with gold edging settee in the center of the entire room. A small burble of uncontrollable laughter bubbled up inside of Lucy. She fought to hold it back, but couldn't and a small giggle escaped. He was a baron for goodness' sake, wasn't he supposed to have a house bursting with elaborate nonsense?

Lady Norcourt turned to Lucy and lifted a brow, her lips twitching. "Well, which side would you prefer, the left or the right?"

At that, Lucy could hold her mirth no longer and let out peals of giggles until her cheeks and stomach hurt and tears were streaming down her face. "I'm sorry," she said as she tried to compose herself, but it was of no use because Lady Norcourt was also laughing in the same young, carefree manner. Lucy straightened and tried to put a tight rein on her laughter before one of the servants thought they were cracked. "I'll take the left."

"Very well, and I'll squeeze in on the right."

Lucy scooted as far to the side as she dared without risking falling off to make enough room for the voluminous skirts of Lady Norcourt's morning dress.

Lady Norcourt gathered up as much of her skirts as she could hold and tried to put them in her lap. "There, that should afford you another inch or so."

Lucy didn't move closer as suddenly the comfort she'd felt in Lady Norcourt's presence but a moment ago evaporated. What must Lady Norcourt think of her? Did she think she was her son's mistress, or worse yet, just a woman he'd found only the night before? That seemed more logical since it had been Lady Norcourt who'd had to help her find the drawing room.

Uneasy tension squeezed her throat. Why did Seth have to insist on leaving? Were he here, they could have already been on their way, but now she was stuck—

"I'm venturing a guess that your name is Lucy Whitaker."

Lucy jerked her gaze to Lady Norcourt. "How did you know?"

"My son told me."

Lucy's heart picked up pace. "Which one?"

An amused smile touched Lady Norcourt's lips. "Actually, both of them." She adjusted her lacy glove. "Simon mentioned that a young, albeit stubborn, lady had cared for him, but it was Giles who gave me your name."

Giles? That must be Lord Norcourt's Christian name. "I take it he came to ask you for employment on my behalf."

"Giles?" She knit her brows. "No. He'd never do that. He doesn't ask things of me—" a shadow crossed her face and a sad look filled her eyes— "and for good reason, I suppose." She shook her head. "No, he came to the lending library yesterday to speak to you about something and I told him you weren't there."

"That's why he came to Shrewsbury," she whispered to herself, making sense of everything. Of course, he'd probably told her that last night, but she'd been so overwrought she couldn't remember everything he'd said.

"Yes, he seemed very intent to speak to you."

Lucy shook her head. "I don't know why. I know he didn't intend—" She broke off with a blush.

"Didn't intend?" Lady Norcourt prompted.

Lucy flushed again and gave Lady Norcourt an abbreviated account of how she'd lost her post because she'd helped Simon and that the two were quite adamant that they'd each find her employment and how Simon had misunderstood what Giles had meant with his vague offer. "I knew he hadn't meant to insult me that way, but it would seem it weighed heavily on his conscience," she concluded with a shrug.

"Yes, it would have," Lady Norcourt agreed. She shifted and bit her lip. "He has a hard time articulating things, but I'm sure you already realized that."

"Yes, my lady."

Lady Norcourt cringed. "Yes, ma'am, is sufficient." She tucked a curly tendril of her hair behind her ear. "I'm one of the few who gave up use of my title when I married Mr. Appleton, so there is no need to 'my lady' me."

"Yes, my—ma'am."

Lady Norcourt, or Mrs. Appleton, rather, flashed her a smile and a wink. "I'll let that pass, but be warned, if you slip again, you'll be in my debt."

Lucy grinned at her teasing tone. Mrs. Appleton seemed vastly different than either of her sons.

"Nonetheless," Mrs. Appleton started. "Both of my sons are nothing if not genuine and I'd be most appreciative if you'd consider helping me at the lending library."

"I'm sorry, but I don't think that's a good idea."

Mrs. Appleton gave her a sidelong glance and Lucy prayed the older woman wouldn't see through her. "Has one of them done something to make you feel uncomfortable?"

"Not at all," she rushed to say. "They were both perfect gentlemen. You did very well on that score."

A sad, shuttered look came over Mrs. Appleton's face. "I'm afraid I cannot claim the credit where Giles is concerned." The hurt that laced her words pierced Lucy's heart as a vague memory from last night came to mind. He'd mentioned something to Seth about an orphanage and a nun. Her curiosity was heightened, but it wasn't her place to ask anything.

"I'm sure you did the best you could, my lady," Lucy said, offering her what she hoped was a reassuring smile.

Mrs. Appleton returned Lucy's smile with a watery, wobbly one of her own. "Thank you, but I do believe you are now in my debt."

Lucy's eyes widened. Surely Mrs. Appleton hadn't been sincere in demanding Lucy pay her recompense.

"I should mention that while both of my sons are very genuine and sincere, so am I," Mrs. Appleton said as if she could read Lucy's mind. "As it would be, I truly do need some help over at the lending library and think it'd help you remember my name better to spend some time with me there."

"Thank you, but I—"

"Am in my debt," Mrs. Appleton reminded her, a sparkle in her blue eyes. She winked. "I can be just as stubborn."

Lucy released a breath and mindlessly twisted her skirt between her fingers. "I don't know if either of your sons told you this, but I have a son of my own, ma'am, and I can't stay in London. He's eleven and prone to trouble."

Mrs. Appleton chuckled. "I remember those days." She waved her hand through the air. "Just bring him with you. We have plenty of books he might enjoy."

Lucy stared at the woman, dumbfounded. Clearly she didn't understand Lucy's situation. "I don't want to drive your patronage away." There, that was tactful, wasn't it?

"Madam, I shan't drive you to tedium by recounting for you

all of the ways I've scandalized the *ton* over the years." She gave Lucy a pointed look. "I'll only say, the patronage I have left are the ones who care far less about who they're borrowing the book from just as long as the book itself is more exciting than their own story. Your presence won't hinder them any more than we could get a third person on this settee."

Despite herself, Lucy laughed. "All right. I relent. I shall start working off my debt post haste."

Mrs. Appleton opened her mouth to say something, but whatever it was, died on her lips when the deep, gravelly voice of Lord Norcourt filled the room, "What debt?"

Chapter Thirteen

Giles didn't think it'd be possible to be more surprised and dare he admit excited than he was when he opened the door to his townhouse and heard girlish laughter. But all of his good humor fled when he reached the drawing room to see Lucy sitting next to Lady Norcourt. Not that Lucy sitting and laughing with her had ruined his good humor; it had been her mention of a debt that made bile burn the back of his throat.

Every muscle in his body tensed as he demanded to know what trap his mother had ensnared Lucy into.

"Miss Whitaker has agreed to help me at the library," Lady Norcourt explained.

Giles searched Lucy's face but didn't know what he was looking for. "Do you want to?"

She nodded once. "Yes. Unless you don't want me there."

He shrugged. Why would he not want her there? It was his mother he didn't trust, not her. "In the hall, please?"

Lucy and his mother exchanged a look.

"I'm assuming you'd like to talk to me privately?" Lady Norcourt asked, standing.

Giles nodded and handed the box of tarts and other bakery goods to Seth.

The wide-eyed boy took the food and walked over to his mama while Giles' mother excused herself from the room and followed Giles into the hall.

Giles clenched his hands into fists. He wanted to know what her game was. Why she was manipulating Lucy this way. It was one thing to manipulate him, but Lucy didn't deserve to be used. "Why?"

"I came over to see if you ever found who you were looking for," his mother said with a tone that would suggest she was innocent of any wrong doing.

"Not that," he said, with a scowl. Though he didn't like it, he'd grown accustomed to having her come by his house at varied times since he'd come back to London. He should have known she'd come today and warned Lucy.

"I'm afraid I don't understand what you're asking, then," she said.

Giles' face heated. Of course she didn't. He tried to think of a better way to word what he wanted to know, but all that came out was, "Why?" He squeezed his eyes shut and tried to push away the feeling of embarrassment that was threatening to overtake him.

"Why did I hire her?"

Giles shook his head. "Debt." The word tasted bitter on his tongue, but nonetheless, he was glad he'd been able to form it.

"It wasn't a real debt," she said slowly.

He stared at her. Not a real debt? What did that mean? "She's not—" He broke off and let out a ragged breath.

"She's not what, Giles? Your mistress?"

Giles' eyes widened and he shook his head vigorously. "No."

"I never thought she was." She pressed her lips together and a crease formed between her eyes. "Giles, I know you don't trust me. Or even know me, for that matter. But if nothing else, I want you to know that I don't think poorly of you or Miss Whitaker for anything." She reached for him, but before she touched him, she pulled her hands back. "I don't care what your relationship with Miss Whitaker is or isn't. She's in need of employment and I'm in need of help. That's all there is to it. If she truly doesn't wish to work there, she doesn't have to. I'd never force her to or threaten to bring trouble to her doorstep if she didn't."

Giles stood silently as he tried to understand everything she had said.

"If you'd prefer I don't employ her, then I won't," she said quietly a moment later.

All of his unease and discontent with her was stolen with those words. She was being genuine. He couldn't explain how he knew it just then, but something in his heart told him she was. "Where will she live?"

A smile pulled the corner of her pink lips up and a tear ran down her cheek. "There's a small apartment above the library. It's been used for storage, but it can be cleared out and she can stay there." Her smile widened. "That is if this arrangement is acceptable to Lord Norcourt seeing as he's the one who owns the library and the building."

"It's acceptable."

"Shall we go confirm that this is acceptable to Miss Whitaker?"

It took some convincing, which thankfully Lady Norcourt handled, to persuade Lucy that she didn't need to rent a room from a boardinghouse and she finally agreed to stay in the apartment, but only in exchange for lower wages. Lady Norcourt immediately agreed with the terms. Seth seemed rather pleased with the arrangement, too. Almost as pleased as he was with the lemon pastry he devoured.

***

Because it was Thursday and one of the two days each week—the other being Monday—the library was closed, Mrs. Appleton had suggested that Lucy spend the afternoon cleaning up the little apartment and settling in.

There really wasn't much to settle, but she could use some quiet time.

Unfortunately, her quiet time was cut short with the appearance of one Mr. Simon Appleton. As soon as he arrived, Seth could no longer be subdued.

"Can I go see him?" Seth begged excitedly.

"I don't know if that's such a good idea," Lucy hedged.

"Why wouldn't it be?" He cocked his head to the side. "Shouldn't we at least see how he's faring?"

Lucy playfully wagged her finger at him. "You're a sly one."

He sent her an impish grin and darted from the room.

Lucy chuckled and followed after him. After her attack she'd been terrified that it would take a while for him to be the carefree lad he'd been. She was glad to be proven wrong.

Downstairs, she made her way over to the pair slowly so not to distract from their conversation.

"What did your mother say?" Seth asked through his laughter.

"She told him he'd better find a new home for his new pet bunny before he ate anymore of it or she'd make stew of him," Mrs. Appleton supplied with a shudder, leading Simon to join Seth in his laughter.

"What's that?" Lucy asked.

Simon sobered instantly and removed his felt hat. "M-miss Whitaker," he stammered. "Just a biology lesson, that's all."

"Did you know that rabbits eat their own waste?" Seth asked loudly.

"No." She looked to a red-faced Simon. "But my day has been made complete now that I've been made aware."

"I knew it would be," Seth clipped. "Do you know any other fascinating facts I can share with my mother, Mr. Appleton?"

"No." He glanced up at Lucy. "Why don't you go find a storybook while I talk to your mama for a minute?"

Disappointment shadowed Seth's face, but he didn't voice it and went to search for a novel.

"I'm glad you finally decided to come to London. I'll have to make a point to come by here more often now that I know I'll get to see you."

It was all Lucy could do to keep her face expressionless at his obvious attempt to flirt. It wasn't that he wasn't trying. He was, and *that* was the problem. She was at least eight years his senior. Much too old for him to be pursuing.

"I don't know if she told you or not, but my mother usually closes the library on Mondays. I'd be honored if I could show you somewhere in London that might be of interest."

Lucy bit her lip. "I—I don't know."

Simon drummed his fingers on the table. "Seth can join us."

***

From where Katherine Appleton stood behind a tower of books that needed to be put away, she saw Lucy bristle at Simon's words. A pang of sympathy for Lucy formed. Of course, most mothers should reserve their sympathy for their own child who was being rebuffed. But after having a child who was only welcome as an afterthought, she couldn't help but empathize with Lucy.

Likely though, Simon didn't realize how his words had sounded and this could still be salvaged. She paused. Did she want to salvage this? It was obvious that Simon was quite taken with her from the way he'd reacted the moment she'd told him that Lucy was in London and would be helping her at the library. But what of Lucy? Did she return that interest?

Katherine peered at the duo again. Lucy seemed quiet and reserved, just the way she had around Giles. Perhaps she was wary of both of them and their intentions. Even Katherine didn't yet know the extent of Giles' interest. He might be her son, but he hid his feelings well except when he was frustrated. Simon, though the dear boy tried, just couldn't hide his feelings no matter what they were.

She shook her head ruefully and looked to Lucy again for any sort of clue of her feelings. Nothing. Katherine tapped her toe quietly as she tried to make sense of it. Considering Lucy was an unmarried mother who went by Miss rather than Mrs. she likely had reason to be guarded around both of them.

"Lucy," she called in a tone louder than necessary. When Lucy looked her way, she continued. "Would you and Seth be interested in joining us at my house for dinner tonight?"

"Oh, no, Mrs. Appleton. I don't want to be any bother."

Katherine waved her hand through the air. "It's no bother. I invited Giles, but he declined so we'll have more than the three of us can eat." She watched Lucy's face to see if she detected any change at the mention of Giles, but was distracted when Simon let out an exaggerated gasp and threw his hands up to his chest as if he was horrified.

"Mother, surely you aren't implying you think this little slip of a lady could eat near as much as Lord Norcourt, are you?"

Katherine chuckled. "Of course not, but I think that growing boy of hers might."

"Yes, ma'am, I can," Seth added from beside her. "Especially if that includes three helpings of dessert."

Chapter Fourteen

Lucy scolded herself for wishing that Giles would join them for dinner. *Giles?* Since when had she started thinking of him as anything other than Lord Norcourt? *It's because that's what his mother calls him,* she reasoned with herself.

If only she believed that.

Seated on the red settee to her left, Seth asked Simon if he'd explain piquet or some other card game to him.

"How about another time?" Simon suggested as he brushed some imaginary dirt or lint from the top of his brown trousers.

Seth shrugged and asked if Simon had ever read a certain book.

Thankfully Simon had and it gave the two of them something to talk about. Lucy, however, could think of nothing to add to the conversation and tried not to notice the way Simon's eyes kept straying to her every few seconds.

"My husband isn't usually so late," Mrs. Appleton commented. "He must have had an important matter come up, but I don't think he'll be too much longer."

Lucy hoped she was right. Otherwise she might go mad.

Lucy was spared such a fate when not two minutes later the front door creaked open and heavy footfalls sounded in the hall. Trying not to appear too eager or nervous, Lucy kept her eyes trained on Seth until she was certain Mr. Appleton was in the room. Then she turned around and gasped.

She coughed quickly to recover her error, but it was too late and Mrs. Appleton watched her with an amused expression on her face. "I told you that my own scandals were more than enough to scare away certain patronage. Perhaps you believe me now?"

Lucy nodded but couldn't take her eyes off of the solemn-looking Mr. Appleton. She'd thought Giles and Simon had a striking resemblance and just assumed they had to look like their maternal grandfather, but seeing Mr. Appleton, if she didn't know better she'd say Giles looked identical—but with fewer wrinkles.

"Lucy, I'd like you to meet my husband, Walter Appleton. Walter, this is Lucy Whitaker and her son, Seth. Lucy has agreed to help me down at the library."

"It's a pleasure to meet you, Lucy," Mr. Appleton greeted. He flashed a smile in Seth's direction. "Seth."

Lucy greeted Mr. Appleton and nudged Seth to do the same.

"Well, now that we're all acquainted, shall we go down to dinner?" Mrs. Appleton chirped, killing the tension in the room.

"May I?" Simon murmured at Lucy's elbow.

Lucy placed her hand on the crook of his elbow the way she'd witnessed other ladies doing. From the corner of her eye she noticed the set of his jaw. Was he upset? Did he have some sort of hostility for either of his parents? No. It wasn't her place to ask.

The dining room was small compared to Giles'. Which was to be expected since Giles was a lord and was expected to have a bigger home. Their table had enough seating for eight rather than twelve. There was a large red runner that went down the center of the table and a large silver vase overflowing with tulips in the middle. Five place settings had been laid out. Mr. Appleton sat on the end with his wife on his right side and Lucy on his left. Mrs. Appleton had asked Seth to sit beside her leaving the chair to Lucy's left free for Simon.

Dinner was tolerable, if not awkward. Simon eventually started to relax and carried on a conversation with his father about their business, using the words investments, recoup, gain, and other such words she only vaguely understood.

Across the table, Seth sent her fleeting glances. He was disinterested in the conversation. So was she, but he didn't need to know that. She flashed him her best smile. Perhaps *this* was what it'd take for him to stop being so darn eager to spend time with every unattached gentleman.

Just then, the only male servant Lucy had seen since arriving excused himself from the room. When he came back a moment later, he set down a folded piece of paper at Mrs. Appleton's elbow, then went back to serving.

Mrs. Appleton murmured an apology to the table then read the note to herself before passing it to Mr. Appleton. The two exchanged a look, then Mrs. Appleton made her excuses and left. That was the oddest exchange she'd ever seen. Both Simon and his father must have thought so, too, for neither spoke of business again after she left.

Of course that could have been because Seth pounced on the opportunity of momentary silence to engage Simon in another conversation. This time about what it'd be like if carriages had wings and could fly. Simon was clearly stupefied by the very thought, and relied on logic to explain why this could never work.

Lucy pretended to listen and from the corner of her eye, she glimpsed a distant look on Mr. Appleton's face. She followed his line of vision to the window. Nothing seemed amiss at first glance; then she saw it. Along the far right side of the window, next to a tall wooden pole that supported the awning across the street was a carriage with the Norcourt crest emblazoned on the side. Though she hadn't been told everything about this family's history, she knew enough and while Mrs. Appleton was anything but subtle in her feelings for her eldest son, Mr. Appleton clearly felt the same way his wife did.

Her heart ached for him and without realizing it she reached forward and touched his arm comfortingly. She pulled her hand back before either Seth or Simon could see what she'd done, chastising herself for her foolishness.

Slowly, Mr. Appleton turned to look at her. Her face heated to what felt like one thousand degrees. He wouldn't say anything about her informal action, would he?

He didn't.

With glistening green eyes, he offered her a half-smile and whispered, "Thank you."

***

Giles clenched his fists and exhaled. "I'm sorry."

A small crease formed in the skin between his mother's eyes. "For?"

He released another deep exhalation. Then another. "Being cruel."

"I suppose I deserve some cruelty." She blinked her eyes rapidly. "I—I want you to know that I never—" She broke off with a sniffle, then sank into the chair nearest her.

Giles remained standing. She appeared to be in need of a hug. But not from him. He'd spent the afternoon trying to form an apology. That was the best he could give. Not that he was too sure she'd want a hug from him anyway. Most didn't. In fact, the Sisters had scolded him and told him to stop touching the others. That it was inappropriate and made others uncomfortable. He stiffened. He'd hugged Lucy. Had she minded? She didn't pull away, but neither did she hug him back.

His mother's voice pulled him from his fog. "Pardon?"

"We've already had dinner, but would you care to join us for dessert?"

Giles studied the tops of his black leather boots. Simon wouldn't like that. Simon didn't like *him*. He shook his head. "No."

"It's custard," she said, smiling.

His mouth watered. He loved custard. Always had. Some of his fondest memories with his mother were when they'd picnic together on the grassy hill by their country estate. She'd always let him eat his bowl of custard before the main meal—so it wouldn't get warm—then she'd complain of being too full after their meal and insist Giles eat her portion.

"Come," she urged. "Seth said he could eat three bowls— perhaps the two of you could have a race?"

"Seth?" Did that mean Lucy was here, too?

"I invited him and his mother over for dinner. They're here with Simon and...er—" she cleared her throat— "Mr. Appleton."

Giles pulled back. "No."

"Can you give him a chance?"

Not if it meant he had to witness the man paying attention to Lucy.

"Please? If not for me at least for the sake of Seth. The poor boy looks like he's on the verge of going mad with tedium at any moment."

Giles cracked a smile. He liked Seth. He was smart, but still needed to have fun. Not to mention, a firm hand. Giles still didn't like how those men in Shrewsbury had handled Seth, but it hadn't escaped his notice that the boy could get unruly without boundaries. "All right."

As soon as he agreed, he wished he could take it back, but couldn't when his mother clapped her hands, then reached for the blue sleeve of his coat and chirped, "Come along."

Reminding himself to breathe, Giles followed his mother to the dining room. He could do this. Left foot. Right foot. Left foot. Right foot. At the door to the dining room he halted.

"It'll be all right," his mother whispered, giving his sleeve a gentle tug. She stepped into the threshold. "I wanted to say that I appreciate Lucy and Seth for coming to be our dinner guests, and now we'll be joined by a dessert guest."

***

Even before Mrs. Appleton had finished her statement, Lucy's heart was hammering out of control. It must have been the older woman's smile that had given her away to Lucy. Giles was about to join them. Lucy fidgeted, praying that her face didn't betray her.

Beside her, Simon grew as rigid as a church steeple as he just stared at his mother while Giles lowered himself into the empty chair beside Seth.

"We're ready for our custard now, Daniel, please bring enough for both Seth and Lord Norcourt to each have three bowls."

"Whatever for, Mother?" Simon burst out.

"They're to have a race." She looked at Lucy and playfully wagged her finger. "He might be eight-and-twenty, but I still have faith my boy can out eat yours when it comes to custard."

"And what of your boy who is eight-and-forty?" Mr. Appleton asked, a hint of a smile pulling on the corner of his lips. "Does he not get a chance?"

Mrs. Appleton's sparkling blue eyes widened. "I didn't think —" She closed her mouth with an audible snap. "Of course."

Looking to Simon, she asked, "Would you like to compete, too?"

Lucy thought he might decline and was shocked when he agreed.

A moment later, the four of them each had three generous bowls of custard in front of them.

"You'll all be sick tonight," Mrs. Appleton commented.

"But it'll be worth it," Mr. Appleton remarked.

Lucy had a feeling he wasn't just talking about the sweet taste of the custard, but rather the company.

"All right, gentlemen, the rules state—"

"There are rules posted about this sort of thing?" Simon asked in a stilted tone.

Lucy immediately recognized that was his best attempt at humor for an uncomfortable situation and flashed him an encouraging smile. This was by far, the strangest family she'd ever encountered, and the more she was around them all, the more she realized how unusual it all was and the tension there must be between them all.

"The rules have never actually been penned, no," Mrs. Appleton allowed. "But they were passed down to me from my mother who heard them from her mother and so forth, so they are just as good as being etched in stone, wouldn't you say?"

"Oh, but of course, nobody would dare argue with Great Grandmama Beatrix," Mr. Appleton muttered, garnering him a little swat on the shoulder from his wife.

"All right, every bit of custard must be consumed," Mrs. Appleton said. "The first to do so will be declared the winner."

"Is there a prize?" Seth asked.

"'Course there is," Mr. Appleton said without hesitation. "But you needn't worry about it, boy, I don't plan to lose."

Seth grinned and shook his head. "We'll see about that."

Mr. Appleton laughed and winked at Seth then poked his lower lip out. "What of a boon for the winner, boys?"

Simon pursed his lips, but nodded. Giles gave a single nod, his expression impossible to interpret. Seth looked a little disappointed at first, but then just shrugged. Likely, if he were to win, he'd ask for what he would have wanted the prize to be anyway.

"All right, gentlemen, now that that's settled," Mrs. Appleton started. "Put your hands in your laps." She lifted three fingers into the air. "Ready? Three. Two. One. Go!"

Seth was the first to grab his bowl and spoon and start shoveling spoonfuls of the yellow fluff into his mouth. Simon used a similar tactic then used the edge of his spoon to scrape every last glob off the edge of his bowl. Giles had a different approach entirely and lifted the bowl to his lips and scraped its contents into his mouth. Oddly enough Mr. Appleton was doing the same thing and was the first to put his empty bowl down with a loud thud and lift the next.

Giles and Simon each finished their first bowl at the same time with Seth only a second behind.

Lucy couldn't help herself and laughed at the absurdity of it all.

"Is something funny?" Simon asked her between bites.

"Yes."

With that, Simon lowered his half-eaten bowl of custard to the table and for what must have been the first time since they'd met, grinned at her. A full, uninhibited grin that made him look exceedingly handsome. She turned her attention away before she inadvertently gave him the wrong idea. His father finished his second bowl and set it down with a much softer tap than the first. The look in his green eyes said he wanted to win in the worst way, but the way his face was turning green to match his eyes, said he was on the verge of being ill from so much sugar.

He picked up his third bowl and only ate two bites before lowering it back to the table and wiping his mouth. Defeat and perhaps disappointment, stamped on his face.

"You're not going to quit, too, are you, Lord Norcourt?" Seth asked suddenly. "Not that I mind winning, mind you." He shrugged. "It just doesn't seem right if it's only because everyone else quit."

Giles picked up his last bowl of custard—like Mr. Appleton, he didn't look like he wanted to torture himself with eating anymore. Lucy was about to suggest everyone agree to a draw when Lord Norcourt spoke again.

"No. I'm not quitting. I just wanted to give you a chance to catch up." Then, with a quick grin he lifted his bowl of custard back to his lips.

Seth wasn't far behind. In fact, they both appeared to be quite close and it was nearly impossible to tell who'd put their bowl down a split-second before the other.

"It appears as if we have a tie," Mrs. Appleton announced.

"No, he won," Giles said. "I dropped some on the floor."

Mrs. Appleton looked hesitant almost like she believed his tale about as much as Lucy did, then the look was gone. "Well then, Seth here is our winner, and as such, he may ask for a boon."

"Can I save it?" Seth asked, surprising Lucy.

"Of course you may."

"If you'll excuse me, I am off to see Cook about a tonic to cure the unease from overindulging on custard. Would anyone else like one? Simon? Gi—Norcourt? Seth?"

"Please," Giles said.

"I don't need one," Simon said.

"Neither do I," Seth agreed, stifling a yawn.

"You're welcome to go whenever you're ready, Lucy," Mrs. Appleton informed her as soon as Mr. Appleton was out of the room. "I know you both have had a tiring day."

"Thank you. I don't mean to seem impolite—"

"Nonsense. I didn't expect you to stay and play parlor games all night." She smiled. "You can if you'd like, of course, but I won't be offended if you're ready to go."

Giles leapt to his feet. "I'll take you home."

Lucy's skin tingled with something she didn't recognize— which was silly. She'd traveled all the way to London not just riding in Giles' carriage, but sitting upon his lap. She fought to keep the blush off her cheeks and didn't dare chance a glance at him. Or anyone else in the room who might have gotten the wrong impression from his offer. "That's most kind of you, but we can walk."

"It's too far."

He had a point. The library was three miles from the Appleton home and it was already dark. She really didn't want to walk that far anyway, but especially not in the dark.

"I can take you, if you'd like," Simon offered. "Nobody will suspect anything is amiss about seeing my family carriage going to the library at this hour."

She might have laughed at his logic had Giles not been in the room with them. She'd never been concerned about her own reputation. Being born the daughter of a servant who had a viscount's bastard at the age of seventeen, there really wasn't anything that could make it worse. At least not for her. Likely it wouldn't damage Giles' reputation to be seen with a woman who might be his mistress, but likely he didn't realize how much of a pariah she actually was or how it could affect him if someone made her past sins public knowledge. He didn't deserve that.

Sensing everyone was staring at her, waiting for a decision, she said, "All right, Mr. Appleton, if you insist, I'd be most appreciative if you'd see us back to the library."

***

Giles felt like a fool. No, Giles *was* a fool. He remained in his same frozen stance until Lucy, Seth and Simon were out of the room, too mortified by his earlier blurted offer to do anything other than breathe. And even that had become a struggle. Why had he offered to take her home? *Because he wanted to.* Well, he shouldn't. Never mind that he lived less than two blocks down the street from the library. She was interested in Simon and if their smiles and laughter earlier hadn't been enough to prove it, her accepting his offer over Giles' was enough to make it as good as chiseled in stone. Or on *his* heart. Both places would have the same impact.

Beside him, his mother said something about someone not meaning to upset someone else. He couldn't really hear her words over the blood pounding in his ears.

"Norcourt." Mr. Appleton's loud voice penetrated his thoughts more than his mother's had. "Here's a tonic."

"No, thank you." His stomach was the last thing he was concerned about now. His stupid brain, confounded tongue, and most of all his aching heart all took precedence. He forced his heavy feet to take a step backwards. "Thank you. Custard was good."

His mother jumped up. "You're welcome to stay, Giles. We can go to the parlor and talk."

"No." He flinched at the roughness in his own tone and the way his already hot face suddenly felt like it was being touched with lava. "I need to go."

His mother opened her mouth to say something more and thankfully was stopped by Mr. Appleton who didn't say anything, but just placed a hand on her shoulder.

With a nod of appreciation to the man who had such a striking resemblance to him it was unnerving, he made his way from the room and to his carriage that was still waiting for him on the street.

***

Lucy climbed inside the Appleton carriage just in time to glimpse Giles emerging from the Appleton's house. Simon murmured another apology for how long it took for the coachman to be located. Lucy waved him off and watched Giles as he ascended into his waiting carriage that was just in front of them. He was quite handsome with his tall, broad stature and chiseled looks. Most certainly what most would consider a fine catch. She jerked her eyes away from him and took an interest in arranging her skirts.

Paying her no heed, Seth plopped down next to her, pinning her skirt to the satin bench. She lifted her eyebrow at him. In a manner that bespoke his age, he gripped the part of her skirt he was sitting on and yanked it out from under his bottom.

"I'll just sit over here," Simon murmured, settling in on the bench across from Lucy and Seth.

"I'll join you," Seth said, bouncing off his current seat and joining Simon.

Simon's eyebrows shot up in surprise and he moved closer to the side to make room.

"Sorry, Mama doesn't like it when I sit on her skirts," Seth offered by way of explanation.

Simon nodded. "And does your mama like gardens, I wonder?"

"No," Seth answered for her though she knew the question wasn't really directed at him. "She hates to have to pull the weeds and gets fussy when a rodent gets into her vegetables."

Simon laughed. "I see…" An amused expression came over his face. "What of gardens full of vendors and marvels? Would that better suit the lady?"

"I'm not sure I know what you mean," Lucy said, trying to hide her unease at being called a lady. She was anything but.

Simon stretched his legs out in front of himself, accidentally bumping her ankle with his calf as he did so. "Pardon me," he murmured, moving his leg away. "Have either of you ever heard of Covent Gardens?"

"Yes," Lucy whispered at the same time Seth said, "No."

"It's not to be missed," Simon said excitedly. "There are entertainers of every kind—jesters, jugglers, men doing tricks with cards, horses, knives, anything you can think of, even actors perform there." He lowered his voice. "And sometimes they'll have displays of old war weapons or dinosaur bones. It's quite a sight."

Lucy wasn't so convinced. Sam had once explained Covent Gardens and all of their splendor to her. She'd been so excited at the prospect that one day he'd take her there that she hadn't been able to sleep for two entire nights. Now she didn't think it was possible to be any less interested in the fun they boasted.

Seth was interested though and only because of that did she not try to change the subject. Instead she stared out the slim window above Simon and Seth's heads and mindlessly noted that Giles' carriage took the same path home as they were taking to the library. Their carriage lurched to a sudden stop, halting Simon's descriptions and making Seth crane his neck to see what was going on out the window.

"Is that Lord Norcourt's house?" he asked, presumably when

he noticed the same thing Lucy had: Giles getting out of his carriage that was pulled to the side of the street and going inside.

Simon nodded his agreement then continued to describe the food at Covent Gardens.

Thankfully it was only a few more torturous moments until they arrived at the library.

"Seth, why don't you go on upstairs? I'd like to talk to your mama a moment."

Seth hesitated.

"It's all right," Lucy assured her son.

"Have you given any consideration to my earlier offer?" Simon asked after Seth was gone.

"To go to Covent Gardens?" Lucy ventured hesitantly. Perhaps she should have listened a little more intently in the carriage.

He smiled. "I'd be glad to take you there."

"I'd rather not go," she blurted.

"All right," he said slowly. He drummed his fingertips along the edge of the table. "You'd prefer not to go to Covent Gardens —" he cocked his head to the side— "or anywhere in London?"

Ah, that's what he'd meant. His offer to show her a few places around London. She exhaled. "Neither."

"Neither," he echoed in a tone she couldn't placc as either disappointed or bewildered. "May I ask why?"

There really wasn't an easy way to say this. "Simon, I know you mean well, but I can't."

"Mean well?"

She ran her clammy hands over her skirt. "I understand that you're appreciative that I was able to attend to you when you were hurt, but your family has already repaid me more than I deserve." She swallowed. "Far more. Truly, anyone with half a heart would have helped a man in need."

"You think that's why I asked you to see London?"

"Well, yes. There's no other reason…"

"Perhaps I enjoy your company," Simon rebutted.

Lucy would have fallen to the floor in disbelief if she'd not had one hand resting on the table. "Pardon?"

"Is it so hard to understand? You're very charming, when you wish to be."

She arched a brow at him. "When I wish to be?"

He nodded and stepped closer. "You don't speak often, but when you do it never fails to capture my attention."

Lucy stared at him, dumbfounded. Was he flirting with her again? A nervous giggle caught in her throat and she coughed to suppress it.

"Is it so hard to believe I might have a genuine interest in you?" he continued.

"Yes." She covered her mouth with her hand with an echoing *pop*.

"It shouldn't be," he said with a shrug. "I'm not nobility, Lucy. My half-brother might have a title, but I couldn't care less. Nor does anyone of any importance to me care whom I marry."

"Marry?" She took a shaky step backward. Marriage was the last thing she was concerned with.

"Perhaps one day, but there needs to be a courtship first," he said with a grin that confirmed he didn't understand her reaction. He reached for her, but she didn't give him her hand. "That didn't come out right. I didn't mean to insult you by alluding to your lower station. I just meant that who I marry doesn't matter to anyone the way it matters who Giles marries."

Lucy stared at him. He had to have the thickest skull of anyone she'd ever met. "While I'm flattered that you'd find a match with me acceptable, I'm afraid that I must decline." Then, without giving him a moment to say anything to make either of them any more uncomfortable, she spun around and went up to her apartment.

Chapter Fifteen

Giles gripped the arms of his chair, let out a deep breath, forced his eyes to the papers in front of him and commanded himself to make sense of it.

No such luck.

He'd been reading the same documents for two days now and couldn't understand hardly any of it.

"What's that?"

Giles' head snapped up and his hands reached out to push the papers away. In his haste, he knocked them to the floor.

Sebastian, his unannounced visitor, came to his desk and knelt down to help Giles gather the papers. "Is something wrong?"

Wordlessly, Giles took the papers from Sebastian and pushed them into a stack. "No."

"Giles?"

"How is your wife?"

Sebastian smiled and shook his head. "Clever tactic." He made himself comfortable in a chair. "I don't know yet. I've been invited to the Townsons' ball tonight and I'm hoping to see her there."

"See her?"

Sebastian crossed his ankles. "It's difficult to explain, but right now, I'll be content to see her and beg for an audience."

Giles lifted his eyebrows. "Beg?" He could hardly imagine Sebastian on his knees dressed in his dove trousers and blue coat begging anyone for anything. Actually, now that he thought about it, the mental image was quite humorous.

"Laugh if you must, but it might be my only way to get her back."

"Back? Aren't you still married to her?"

"I am." He frowned. "I was. I—" he twisted his lips and sighed— "I signed the annulment papers."

"You did?"

"It might be the only way to get her back." Sebastian knocked the sides of his leather boots together. "Now, enough about me, what is it that has caught your fancy and made you not come to White's for the past five days?" He wagged his eyebrows. "Lucy?"

Giles' face flushed. It wasn't that he was embarrassed so much that his friend knew he'd taken a fancy to her, but rather the reminder once again that he could never have her. "No."

"There are other ladies, Giles," Sebastian said quietly.

"I don't care." Giles picked up the stack of papers he'd earlier tried to make sense of and thrust them at Sebastian. "I can't make sense of these. Cosgrove said I had to marry and produce an heir within the next two years but I don't see anything in here that supports it. And I don't know what to look for." He scrubbed his face with his hands. "There are twenty-eight pages to that damn document and after reading them over for two days I have no idea what twenty-six of them mean."

Sebastian read one. "If it makes you feel any better, I don't know what I just read, either."

In spite of his frustration, Giles allowed a small smile. "I don't care if that says I have to marry to get my inheritance. I was fine without."

"So then why are you troubling yourself with trying to read it?"

Giles bit his lip. "The library."

"You think Lord Cosgrove might sell it?"

"Yes." *Then what would happen to Lucy? Or his mother?* As much as he didn't want to like her, he was starting to and he'd hate for her to lose something she cared so much for. His eye caught Sebastian and he quickly found something of interest in the distance.

"You need to hire a solicitor."

"I can't."

"Do you want me to ask my man to look at this for you? He can be discreet."

"So can I," a new voice said from the threshold.

Giles sprang from his chair with so little grace and such great force he sent his chair backward. "Mr. Appleton," he clipped.

Mr. Walter Appleton, his mother's husband, bowed. "I didn't mean to startle you. Your man said it was all right to come inside."

Giles gave him a single nod and righted his chair. He only employed a skeleton staff as it was and most days he gave them the afternoon off. Very few people ever came to see him. There was no reason to have dozens of servants buzzing about.

Mr. Appleton straightened the cuff on his black coat. "I know we have a very loose acquaintance, but before I began banking and investments, I trained to be a solicitor and would be willing to help you, if you'd like."

Giles wasn't sure if he could trust him or not.

As if he sensed Giles' hesitancy, Mr. Appleton said, "I'll be more than happy to entrust something of value to me in your care."

Giles didn't know what that could possibly be but was relieved all the same at the offer. "A-all right." He swallowed and nodded for Sebastian to allow Mr. Appleton to take the documents.

"It shouldn't take me long to read over everything." He flipped through the pages. "A day. Two at most."

"Thank you." He gestured toward the empty chair near Sebastian.

Mr. Appleton sat and exchanged a look with Sebastian. Odd. Did the two of them not like each other— Understanding hit. Mr. Appleton had no reason to like Sebastian. His son, Simon had wanted to marry Sebastian's wife. A very uncomfortable feeling settled over the room.

"I should probably be going," Sebastian said, standing.

Giles didn't want him to go, but understood.

"I know I didn't win the other night," Mr. Appleton said a moment after Sebastian was out of the room, "but I was hoping I might still be able to ask a favor of you."

Giles tensed. *A favor?* There wasn't any favor Giles could do for the man. That wasn't true. Though Giles had been absent from London society for the majority of his life, he did still have a title. Was that why Mr. Appleton was so willing to help him? Did he want to ask Giles to use his nonexistent influence to help him in some way? Without realizing it, he was grinding his teeth so hard they might soon turn to dust. He must have a tattoo on his forehead that said, "Simpleton". He'd have to check for it later.

"It's not that kind of a favor."

Giles penetrated the man with his eyes. "Go on."

"As you already know, your mother had to clear out the apartment above the library for Miss Whitaker and her son. What you may not know is that your mother refuses to part with any book that's ever been donated to the library and now that the space has been cleared there is a mountain of books—fortunately contained within the confines of a multitude of wooden crates—that has taken up residence in the back third of the library."

"Are you wanting my permission to throw them out?"

"Not all of them." Mr. Appleton idly scratched his neck. "Actually, I thought that only the ones in poor condition should be tossed. Instead, I asked Simon to take over my duties today in hopes that I could organize the books for her and came by to ask if you'd be willing to help."

"Help?" Giles croaked.

"Of course." He smiled. "I wouldn't ask you to do it alone, but I certainly don't think I could do it alone, either. I just need some help, if you're willing."

Giles was speechless. Mr. Appleton wanted *his* help? "Did my mother ask you—"

"No. She doesn't know I'm doing it and I wanted to ask you all on my own."

Giles' heart squeezed, but he couldn't say why. "Of course."

Mr. Appleton stood and gestured toward the door. "Shall we?"

***

Lucy walked Mrs. Crandall to the door and saw her out. Closing the door, she sighed. There had to be at least another hundred crates full of books to sort through. She'd only gotten through four crates in the past two days and at this rate, it might be autumn before she finished.

With a sigh she gripped the edge of the crate nearest her and pried open the lid.

"Anything worth keeping?"

"L-Lord Norcourt." Her face flushed and slowly she turned to face him, her eyes widening. Next to him was Mr. Appleton. What were the two of them doing here together? "I don't know what's in there yet. I just opened it."

"Well, then, let's see." Giles reached around her, his wrist grazing her abdomen and her skin tingling with excitement.

She cleared her throat, hoping it'd make her body quit responding in such a way to his nearness. It did not. "Mrs. Appleton asked me to put them away with the others…"

Giles didn't say anything as he lifted out a large stack of books in his big hands. He turned them to the side and read the titles, his brow furrowing. "Where did these come from?"

"Here and there," Mrs. Appleton explained, coming to join them. She took the books from him, presumably, so he wouldn't have a chance to declare them to be rubbish and order them thrown out. "People donate books to the library all the time."

"*These* books?"

Mrs. Appleton nodded. "Most of the books here were donations."

"Perhaps it's time you donate some of these to another library," Mr. Appleton suggested, taking the books from his wife. "'*Boats Afloat*'," he read with a chuckle. *'Land, Ho!', 'Bow and Stern—Not just for the Schoolroom'"*. The way he scrunched his nose up as he read the titles in an amused tone, nearly made Lucy giggle. *"'Sailing to the Savages',"* he added, shaking his head. He set the stack of books down before reading the other titles. "These seem worthy of donating on their titles alone."

"Oh, but someone might come in who wants to know all about ships or sailing," Mrs. Appleton argued.

Mr. Appleton picked up the book on top and flipped it open. "This was printed in 1625, I'd imagine there has to be something newer since then." He looked to Giles for support.

Giles shrugged.

Sighing, Mrs. Appleton said, "Oh, all right, that one can be donated." She picked up the others and held them against her chest. "But these are staying."

"Well, Miss Whitaker, I tried, but all I could manage was to get you one less book to dust."

Mrs. Appleton shook her head, her lips twitching. "I wondered why you were here."

"To rid this library of anything published before the pilgrims set sail and I've enlisted some help," he said, clapping Giles on the shoulder.

"I see." A smile split her face. "Well, then, I suppose I'll let you two get started. But just so you know, even by your own statutes, this book—" she plucked *Boat's Afloat* from Mr. Appleton's fingers— "still falls into the acceptable years."

"Very well," Mr. Appleton agreed with a chuckle. "We'll call for you when we're done." He dropped his voice to a stage whisper. "And we've already disposed of all the books we don't plan to keep."

Wagging her finger at him, Mrs. Appleton walked away.

"I suppose I'd better go help her," Lucy said, feeling uncomfortable all of a sudden.

"Why?" Giles asked. "Nobody's here."

"He's right," Mr. Appleton agreed. "If you promise not to tattle on us and what we throw out, we'd be glad for the help."

Lucy bit her lip. She shouldn't. "I don't think I can help you."

"Sure you can. You know where everything goes, don't you?" Giles picked up a large stack of books. "I don't." He turned the books over and separated the top two books from the pile. "Embroidery?"

Lucy took the books from him and rushed to put them away. When she came back, there were four more stacks of books for her to put away. Reptiles. Astronomy. Plants. Chess.

She hurried to put each type of book away and came back to find more piles, then repeated the process. It worked wonderfully for the most part, if not a little overwhelming sometimes. But after only five hours, they'd made their way through the majority of the crates.

"Who reads *this*?" Giles asked, staring down at a thick leather-bound book, his upper lip curling up.

"May I?"

Giles handed her the book. She read the title and giggled. *Prim and Proper, the Way to be a Lady.* "I know someone who might like to see this."

"You do?"

His surprised tone and baffled expression made her smile. "Seth."

"Seth?"

Lucy had the oddest urge to smooth the lines that had formed on his forehead when his eyebrows shot near to his hairline in astonishment. Instead, she nodded and said, "When we were living in Bath, Seth learned to read using etiquette guides." She shook her head and sat atop a nearby crate. "I have no idea where the ladies who were teaching the group found so many books on the subject, but they used them as reading primers, nonetheless."

"And he enjoyed them?"

"Perhaps not the books," Lucy allowed. "I think it was more the ladies who were teaching him."

"Have a fondness for his tutor, did he?"

Lucy moved her legs to let Mr. Appleton pass with a tall stack of books. Fondness wasn't near an accurate word to describe Seth's feelings. Affection was better, but still not quite strong enough. "It was the worst case of calf-love I've ever witnessed."

"Calf-love?"

"Infatuation. Obsession. Undying affection." Lucy shook her head ruefully. "I think he'd have asked her to marry him if she wasn't already married to—" She broke off. Suddenly this memory wasn't quite as sweet as she remembered.

"Did you not like her husband?"

"No, it's not that I disliked him necessarily." She noticed a loose thread on her purple cuff and developed an interest in fixing it.

"Lucy?"

She sighed and let go of the little string. "My father worked in the dairy on his father's estate and when I came of age, I was a dairymaid there."

"Did he treat you poorly?"

"Poorly?" She shook her head. That wasn't a fair term to assign to Paul's treatment of her. He'd always treated her well; it was his brother who hadn't. Not until they were older and she had something he wanted from her, that is. "Paul was always kind. Even then."

"Too kind?"

Lucy flushed violently. "Heavens, no!" She reached down into the open crate at her side and removed a stack of books. "Paul wasn't that way. His brother certainly was, but he wasn't." She thumbed through the stack and removed a moldy book followed by one that had no binding left. "What made it so awkward was that Paul had proposed marriage to me when we were younger and I turned him down— for his brother." She paused. That hadn't been so hard to confess.

"His brother didn't return the interest?" Giles asked, his rough voice startling her.

She pressed her lips together. "No."

"I'm sorry." His voice was so quiet she almost didn't hear it.

"It's of no account," she said, waving him off. "Not all brothers are the same and neither are their intentions." She was horrified as soon as she realized what she'd said. And even more so when Giles spoke again.

"No, they're not." He hoisted a tall stack of books out of the box and set them in his lap. "You shouldn't let his actions keep you from making another match."

Excitement shot through Lucy and she forced her now shaking fingers to pick up another set of books. Giles had a hard time articulating things. She knew this, but was it possible that he felt the same way for her that she did for him? "Are you offering, my lord?"

"No," he practically shouted, then blushed, presumably at calling attention to himself with his answer. "I meant with Simon."

Disappointment crashed over her and now her hands shook for an entirely different reason: mortification and dare she admit, devastation at being rejected so coldly. *He didn't mean to cause embarrassment or seem so cold*, she reminded herself. It was just his way. "I see…" She divided her stack of books into three little piles of like subjects and placed the unusable books back into the empty crate. "So then you'd approve such a match."

He looked up and met her eyes. "I'm in favor." Something was in those green orbs of his that she couldn't place. Likely the same thing that was in his tone. It wasn't hesitancy, though, which was a point in her favor should she accept Simon's offer to court her, she supposed. At the same time, it only served to devastate her more. He truly wasn't interested.

Chiding herself for wishing that he *was* even the slightest bit interested, she stood. It was better this way. At least he'd been honest with her about his lack of interest. That was more than she'd received from Sam. She choked on her bitter laughter and lifted two squat stacks of books that needed to be put away and started toward the shelves. Simon was the safer choice. She'd known that all along and now that Giles had all but given her his blessing, there was no reason she shouldn't encourage Simon were he to be brave enough to approach her again.

Simon was brave enough, it would seem. Determined, too. With just minutes before Mrs. Appleton was to lock up and force her husband and Giles to leave with her, Simon came into the library.

"Can I talk to you for a moment alone?" he asked Lucy, the color heightening in his cheeks.

"I don't know if it's proper for us to be alone—even for a moment," she teased.

His color darkened. "Indeed. I'd just meant—"

Lucy waved him off. "I know what you meant. How about if we go over there?"

He looked to where she was pointing and nodded. When they were to where he might consider a safe distance from the others, he said, "I wanted to apologize about last week. I think I said something that was taken out of context. It would seem that I have been—" He broke off, snorted, and shook his head as if he'd thought of something humorous and perhaps inappropriate to say.

She could almost guess what it was, but had no desire to acknowledge it.

"Nonetheless," he continued. "I'd like to apologize and ask if you'd reconsider—or consider for the first time—allowing me to take you to see part of London tomorrow."

Just over Simon's left shoulder, she caught sight of Giles. He was looking at her. Or at least he had been, until she'd looked at him and caught his eye. Then he immediately turned his attention back to the final crate he was unloading. She forced her gaze back to Mr. Appleton and she considered teasing him that it wouldn't be proper for the two of them to go anywhere without a chaperone and thought better of it. He didn't seem the sort to have a sense of humor. Clearing her throat, she said, "Yes, Mr. Appleton, I'd be honored to accompany you tomorrow."

"Splendid," he said, grinning. He reached for her hand, lifted it halfway to his mouth, and then gave it a slight squeeze. "I'll see you here tomorrow at ten o'clock?"

"We'll be ready," she said.

Simon grinned. "I'm looking forward to it."

Chapter Sixteen

Giles couldn't help but wonder what he'd said wrong. But something hadn't been right for whatever it was had caused every inch of him from the top of his throat all the way to his waist to feel as if it was being crushed in an invisible vise.

This horrid sensation had begun just after telling Lucy that she had his favor to make a match with Simon and had left him unable to eat or sleep ever since. To be truthful, he didn't care what faults she might think followed her. Nor did he care about whatever might have happened between her and the two brothers from before.

His heart squeezed yet again. He shouldn't—no, *couldn't*—tell her so, but it would seem she had an unnatural ability to snare the attention of brothers. She'd done the same with him and Simon. Only she'd made it seem that both of the ones from before had not been genuine and he knew without question his feelings—and Simon's—were genuine.

Groaning, he grabbed the nearby pillow and pulled it over his face. The sun was shining in through the open curtains of his room, telling him it was past time he should be getting up.

With a snarl, he thrust the pillow aside and threw back the red velvet coverlet. He had to get up and start his day. If he were fortunate, Mr. Appleton would have finished reading through that blasted document and could help him solve the mystery that seemed to be his life.

He rolled to a sitting position and combed his fingers through his hair, yawning. He was tired; there was no doubting that he wanted to sleep. He just couldn't. Standing, he whipped off his long, white nightshirt and pulled on the clothes Franks had laid out for him. He could just ring for the man, of course, but why bother? He was capable.

An hour later, he'd breakfasted (one bite of a biscuit), read the newspaper (what he deemed important anyway) and paced the floor for a solid forty-five minutes.

With a sigh, he left the room and went across the hall to the room he preferred to keep locked. He'd never been allowed to have many things until recently. As a boy living in the orphanage, he'd shared a room with eleven other boys and each was only allowed to keep only what could fit under his bed. When he'd traveled the continent with Sebastian, they hadn't had a lot of money nor room to keep things. Now, he had adequate room and a little more money than before. He tried to be temperate though and didn't decorate his house beyond what was necessary. He also preferred a clean, somewhat empty room rather than one that was crammed full of furniture and cluttered.

But this room, this room was the only such room he'd filled and he kept it locked so everything would stay contained.

The sweet smell of drying paint filled his nostrils when he opened the door. He did a slow sweep of the room, taking in all the canvases he had propped up against the walls, drying. Almost a month ago, he'd agreed to have his mother host a party in his home so Sebastian could carry out some nonsense that involved helping his estranged wife make a match. When his mother had come to see about the decorations, she'd declared this room needed to be cleared and used for entertaining that night. A card room, she'd called it. He had worked diligently since that dinner party to put everything back exactly how he wanted it.

Giles shrugged off his red coat and blue waistcoat, discarded his cravat and turned up his cuffs. He loved to paint. Or draw with pencils. Or even charcoal. He slid open the top drawer in the scratched bureau where he kept his art supplies and scoured over the bottles of paint hoping an idea of something to paint would come to him so he could get lost in his art and forget about the romance budding between Simon and Lucy.

A sudden, incessant knock on his front door put that hope to an abrupt end.

Grumbling, Giles slammed the drawer shut and stalked to the door. He waved the butler off and wrenched open the door.

"Seth?"

Seth grinned, which did nothing to put Giles' pounding heart at ease. "Can I come in?"

Giles stepped to the side to let the boy in. "Is everything all right?"

"Of course."

"Then why are you here?" he asked, folding his arms across his chest.

"My mama and Simon went to some museum together and I had nothing to do."

Giles shoved his hands into his pockets and fisted them tightly to take his mind off the jealousy that was bubbling up inside of him. "I see. They told you to come here so that I could entertain you?"

Seth shook his head vigorously. "No, my lord. It was my idea to come. I thought we should spend some time together."

Giles raised his eyebrows. "You did?"

"Of course."

There was no 'of course' to it. Something was afoot. "And why is that?"

"Well, don't all uncles spend time with their favorite nephews?"

Giles choked. "Pardon me?"

"My mama hasn't married Simon yet, but when she does you'll be my uncle!" A wide grin split his face. "Isn't that exciting?"

"Very."

Seth laughed at his dry tone. "So what is it you planned to do all day?"

"Paint."

"You paint?" Seth exclaimed, darting around Giles and going into his painting room.

Giles clenched his jaw. He'd never allowed anyone into that room. Not even his mother when she'd insisted on seeing it. He'd just said he'd have it cleared out for her. He stomped into the room, bent on scolding the boy and froze.

"You painted all of these?" he asked, standing in the middle of the room and slowly turning his head to take it all in. "I wish I could paint like that."

"You should try." Giles closed his mouth with an audible snap. What the devil was he doing encouraging the boy? "At home," he added.

Seth frowned. "And where would that be, on top of my bed or Mama's?"

"Yours."

Seth pressed his lips together as if he were trying to suppress a chuckle. "That's not funny."

"I thought it was."

"My mama sure won't," Seth said with a laugh that softened Giles' resolve. "Now, will you teach me?

"Teach you what?"

"How to paint?"

"No."

Seth blinked. "Why not? You said you were going to paint all day anyway. Will it matter so much if I'm here, too?"

"Yes. I don't teach."

Shrugging, Seth walked over to the bureau and picked up one of the brushes that were soaking in a cup of water. "All right, you don't have to teach me anything, but can I stay?"

Giles knit his brows. "And do what?"

"Paint."

"But you don't know how," Giles pointed out.

"That's because you won't teach me," Seth argued, the corner of his mouth tipping up into the smile he usually wore. "But that's all right. I'm sure I can paint something without any instruction."

"How about without making it necessary to revarnish the wood?"

"I don't know." Seth frowned and lifted his shoulders. "Without anyone telling me what I'm doing right or wrong, I might make a big mess."

The last of Giles' resolve and unease about having Seth in the room evaporated. "Well, just see that you do it over there where the carpet runner is."

***

"You look fetching today," Simon commented as they entered a crumbling white building that had the word "Museum" sloppily etched onto the side.

Lucy flushed at his compliment. He was just trying to be kind. She'd been alternating between the two same gowns ever since she'd come to London. They were both in desperate need of a scrubbing or at least a beating. "Thank you."

Simon guided her to the right. "I hope you like statues."

"Of course," Lucy lied. *Statues?* She'd seen a few when she'd lived in Bath and Shrewsbury, but hadn't really given them a lot of thought. Especially not going to a museum to see a large number of them. Perhaps Seth got the better end of this bargain—even if he did have to spend the day cooped up at the library with a very sudden stomach affliction.

"Good. A friend of mine owns this museum. It's more of his private collection, actually."

"He has a private collection of statues?" Lucy asked around the sudden giggle that had formed in her throat. *How unusual.*

"Yes, he's collected more than five hundred of them."

"Just to display?"

"No. He used to have a large townhouse in London where he had them in the gardens or the conservatory."

"Did he not think enough people were coming to see them so he decided they needed to be put into a museum?" When Simon didn't laugh at her attempt at a jest, she sobered. "Sorry," she murmured.

He started. "No, I'm sorry. I don't even know what it was you said, but I doubt it was anything to be sorry about."

Lucy slowly cast a glance over her left shoulder to see what it was that seemed to have caught Simon's attention, but she was too late and all she'd been able to see was the bottom of a flaring, crimson skirt just before it slipped around the corner.

Simon cleared his throat and offered her a smile. "Shall we?"

Lucy walked where he directed and stopped in front of the

first statue. It was about four feet tall of a woman standing with a bowed head and her hands pressed together in front of her as if she was praying. Lucy squinted. "Is her nose chipped off?"

"Yes," Simon said quietly. "She was one of the Virgin Mary statues that were ordered destroyed when King Henry VIII overthrew the Catholic Church and ordered Catholicism banned and the churches along with their contents destroyed."

"Someone saved her?"

"Yes. Perhaps someone who thought they could fix her. While in some places all of the statues and other decorations of the church were completely destroyed, in other places, they were merely ruthlessly taken down and damaged. To some that'd have been enough to make them worthless, but likely someone thought he had the skill to repair her." He shrugged. "Or just didn't care that she was incomplete."

Lucy nodded and murmured her understanding. She didn't intend to be cold toward something he obviously cared a great deal about, but all she saw was a statue of a noseless woman praying. She walked down to the next statue. It was another Mary. Though she appeared as if at one time she'd been identical, or very close, she had not fared nearly as well as the first Mary. This one was missing not only her nose, but her ears, too.

The next Mary was without most of her hair.

The next four Marys were missing different pieces, each one being less complete than the previous one. Lucy had to admit she was a bit unsettled that this man had collected so many broken Mary statues, but behind her, Simon took in each one as if it were the first time he'd seen it and it was some lost treasure he thought he'd never find.

Therefore, Lucy kept her lips pressed firmly together as they walked to the end of the first hall, which was made up entirely of statues of Mary. Twenty-three Marys if one wanted to be precise.

At the end of the hall they turned to the right and Lucy was slightly disappointed that she hadn't been able to catch another glimpse of the lady who'd caught Simon's attention earlier.

"These statues you might not find quite so interesting—"

Lucy wanted to groan. If he thought these were less interesting than the ones before, they must be terrible indeed.

"—I'm not sure where he found them, but I can certainly form a theory or two of why someone would be anxious to part with them."

Lucy walked up to the first one and laughed. "Is that a unicorn?"

Simon scowled. "Yes. Isn't it hideous?"

Compared to all of the praying Marys they'd seen, she didn't think it was so bad. "I don't know if I'd say it's hideous. I'm sure it could be worse."

"Ah, then you might enjoy the gargoyle."

"The what?"

"Gargoyle." He put his hand on the small of her back and just as quickly pulled it back. Clearing his throat, he pointed further down the hall. "It's over there."

Lucy walked to where he pointed, noting the serpents and dragons as she strolled by, then stopped when she reached this image of a half-man, half-beast standing on one hairy foot-claw with the other three raised and poised to attack with splayed fingers tipped with long, pointed nails. His mouth was open and his two dozen sharp teeth bared. His head was slightly cocked to the side with one eye opened wide and the other slightly squinting. He looked fierce. For something carved of stone, that is.

"Yes, I agree, this one is quite hideous."

"Then I shan't force you to gaze upon something so ugly for a moment longer. The next hall has more mythical creatures, but they're nymphs."

Lucy rounded the corner and cut her eyes just slightly to take in Simon's reaction to seeing the beautiful young lady in front of them swathed in red. He gave her but a glance then turned back to the statues on their right.

"See, far more fetching than the gargoyle," he said.

"Depends on who you ask." She fingered the worn lace on her sleeve. "As a lady, I think I'd much prefer to see fierce men—or beasts—with their muscles bulging than naked young ladies lounging around as if they have nothing more to do than to sun themselves and let men lust after them."

Simon developed a slight coughing fit. "I'd never thought of it that way." He ran an open hand over his chin and momentarily flickered his gaze past her shoulder. "Say, you wouldn't happen to have a fancy for ices, would you?"

"I've never had one," Lucy confessed.

"Never?" Simon asked, his eyes flaring wide. He reached for her hand. "Then we must go find a vendor right now."

Lucy did her best to keep up as Simon practically dragged her from the museum. She had the strangest feeling it had less to do with wanting to give her an experience she hadn't had before and was more of his way of escaping past the lady who'd been there. There was something unusual about that, but Lucy couldn't say what. Nor did she think it was her place to ask him.

Outside, Simon slowed down—but only a fraction and only because if he didn't they might have been trampled by a horse.

Simon helped her up onto his phaeton before climbing up next to her where he took but a moment to get situated then snapped the reins. "There used to be a vendor two streets over, but I think he was shut down so we'll have to go to Covent Gardens."

Covent Gardens? They'd already traveled over an hour together to go to the museum. How much further would it be to go to the Gardens? "We don't have to—"

"Nonsense." He flashed her a grin. "I love ices. Besides, we're only about half a mile away so be thinking of what flavor you might like."

"What are my choices?"

"Usually lemon or pineapple."

"Lemon," Lucy said automatically.

"Lemon, it is." Simon steered the horses down the street to where the ice vendor was standing with his little cart on the side of the road. "There he is." Simon quickly found somewhere to park his phaeton and secured the horses before helping her down.

Just as her feet touched the ground, Simon released her and she frantically reached her hand out to grip onto the side of the phaeton to steady herself.

"Sorry," he murmured, gripping her just above the elbows and trying to steady her. "I got distracted. I thought I saw—" He shook his head. "Never mind."

"Was it the same lady from the museum?" she asked, allowing him to lead her toward the vendor.

"Miss Hughes?" There was a note of surprise in his voice. He gave his head a shake. "No. She only caught me unawares because I didn't expect to see her there. Or anywhere to be quite blunt." He dropped his voice to a stage whisper. "She's rather an odd one. I thought I'd seen Isabelle just now, but I didn't."

"Is Isabelle a lady you should be taking for an ice today instead of me?"

He let out a sharp bark of laughter. "No. I think that might be met with some undesirable consequences." He twisted his lips into an exaggerated frown. "The most likely being her husband's fist against my jaw."

"Her husband?"

Simon nodded and ordered two lemon ices from the vendor. The man took Simon's coins and handed him their ices. "Is the bench all right or would you prefer to go back to the phaeton?"

"The bench."

Simon walked beside her to the bench and once she was seated handed her one of the ices then took a seat beside her, but he didn't start eating his own ice right away.

"At the start of the Season, I met Isabelle and after some convincing, she accepted my plea to court her." He let out another bitter bark of laughter. "She never told me she was still married."

"Still?"

Simon ate a spoonful of his ice. "She'd been involved in some sort of scandal a few years ago. Something about her trapping Lord Belgrave into a Gretna Green marriage." His light tone would suggest that he really didn't care about the scandal. Her heart warmed. Perhaps he really didn't care about her past, either. "Rumor had it that as soon as they returned, the marriage was annulled." His right shoulder went up in a stiff shrug. "I guess that fact was purely a rumor."

"So they'd never had it annulled?"

"According to Giles, no."

"And you still care for her," Lucy concluded.

"No, no, not at all," Simon rushed to say. "It's for the best that Lord Belgrave never signed the papers." He exhaled. "It's also for the best that Giles told me the truth, for if I hadn't left the house party when I did, I wouldn't have been beaten nearly to death and gotten to meet you. Instead, I'd still be trying to woo a married Isabelle."

Lucy wasn't sure how much she believed him. She couldn't argue with his travel timing, of course. But what of his calling his former love interest by her Christian name? If she were still married, she'd be Lady Belgrave, and if he wasn't so convinced that she was still married, he should continue to call her by her maiden name. Referring to her as Isabelle seemed to belie his claim that his romantic interests toward here were nonexistent. Besides, Seth had found him only a matter of days ago. That didn't seem like an adequate time for his feelings for Isabelle to have dissolved, which would mean his interest in Lucy was likely perpetuated only by his sense of loss of Isabelle. She stilled and waited for some sort of sadness or bitterness to touch her at the knowledge. But it didn't. And that only confirmed they were not the right match.

"Is that the reason you and your Lord Norcourt aren't so close?" she asked, more for a change of topic than out of her own curiosity. Or at least that's what she told herself.

"You mean because he was such a distraction that I couldn't properly woo Isabelle?"

Lucy knew by the expression on his face that as soon as he said those words, he wished he hadn't. She cast him a weak smile. "Is that what happened?"

Simon raked his free hand through his brown hair and heaved a deep sigh. "I don't know what happened." He dropped his hand to his spoon and idly poked at his melting ice. "She'd agreed to let me court her before the house party. I thought I'd be able to woo her into agreeing to marry me, but then Giles came and—" He shrugged and released his spoon.

"Did he like Isabelle, too?" She closed her mouth with an audible snap. What had possessed her to ask him that? It wasn't any of her business who Giles was interested in.

Simon shrugged again. "He might have, but I don't think so." He let out a sharp bark of humorless laughter. "Not that it would have mattered. I still think she would have chosen her own husband."

"Then how did his presence effect your relationship with her?" Again, it wasn't really her place to ask him such questions, but for some reason she was truly interested in his answer.

"I don't know what to say to him," Simon said at last.

"You mean because he doesn't always understand what's not spoken?" She prayed that'd be a delicate way to state it.

"That's only part of it." Simon kicked at the pebbles below their feet with the side of his leather boot. "We have no common ground, save our...er...mother."

Lucy took his meaning, like her, he'd noticed the striking resemblance Giles had to Mr. Appleton and though it could never be spoken, had assumed they both had the same parentage. "Have you tried to talk to him? To build a relationship with him?"

Simon snorted. "Isabelle suggested the same thing and when I tried it all came out wrong and ended with both of us uncomfortable and me bound for Shrewsbury." Though he smiled, it didn't reach his eyes.

Lucy frowned. "Surely, that's not the only time you've ever spoken to him."

"Alone, it was." At what he had to recognize as a doubtful expression on her face, he added, "I didn't even know he existed until a few weeks ago when my mother insisted I come to some dinner only to find the host not only looked exceedingly familiar, but my mother was acting very friendly toward him and referred to him as her son." He set his ice down on the bench next to him and folded his hands in his lap. "For the sake of appearances that night, my mother offered me some brief explanation of him being the child I always thought she'd lost while married to Lord Norcourt."

An overwhelming sense of painful understanding cascaded over Lucy causing her heart to crack. She knew there was more to this family than anyone might have been comfortable to tell her, but now so much made sense. Why the two seemed to be at odds every time they were in a room together. Why Simon's mood changed when Giles joined them for dessert. He'd tried to act polite, but it was just that: an act. Even why Giles seemed to dislike his mother so much seemed to fall into place. If she'd kept something like this from Simon, likely she'd kept something of equal consequence from Giles.

"Not that I want him dead," he continued, breaking into her thoughts. "I don't, so please don't misunderstand. It's just distracting. I don't even know where to start with him." He pursed his lips and twisted them. "Or with my mother. Giles wasn't in a position to tell me about his existence, but my mother was." He closed his eyes then shook his head. "I'm sorry. It really isn't fair of me to burden you with all of this."

"It's not a burden," Lucy assured him. And truly, it wasn't.

"Are you ready to go back to the library?"

"I believe so, yes."

Chapter Seventeen

Giles was almost certain he'd spent the last three days sitting on a bed of nails and with each day that passed the points grew sharper and sharper.

He'd half expected on Monday afternoon that Simon would have darkened his door and demanded he not spend any more time with Seth. Not that Giles had done anything for which to be warned away from the boy, but he actually liked Seth and enjoyed his company and that was good enough reason for Giles to suddenly lose something—if history were to repeat itself.

On Tuesday, Mr. Appleton had come by only to assure Giles he was still looking into things, but he'd had to send a formal letter to Lord Cosgrove's solicitor to request a few missing documents. He'd promised to return with more information when he received the documents and could review them. That was not comforting in the least.

Then on Wednesday, the fears from the two days prior had doubled with a simple line in the announcement section of the newspaper: Lord and Lady Belgrave were still officially married and had reconciled. Giles hated to seem selfish, but this was atrocious timing for him. This news might infuriate Simon or his father and make Mr. Appleton stop helping him, or worse, have Simon confront him and tell him to stay away from Lucy and Seth. Which was his right to do.

Giles closed his eyes while Franks set out his clothes for the day.

Thursday's grand event came in the form of an eleven-year-old boy who wished to come paint again.

"Did you not get your fill of painting on Monday?"

"No." Seth pushed his way into his house. "I was just putting the green on the trees when I had to go. I can't leave them barren, can I?"

"No, I suppose not," Giles agreed, tousling the boy's hair. "Go ahead and start. I need to dash off a note to Lord Belgrave then I'll be in to join you."

The boy scampered away, making Giles laugh as he went to his study. He sat down and penned a quick missive informing his friend that he wouldn't be able to meet him at White's again today. Sebastian wouldn't mind, of course. He was probably busy enjoying bedsport with his new wife and this only freed him up to do it more. Giles tightened his hold on his quill and counted to ten. He shouldn't be jealous of Sebastian. His wife loved him. There wasn't much more a man could ask for and Giles should be happy for him, not jealous that he himself was destined to die a virgin. He nearly snorted. He'd never even kissed a lady.

Giles tossed down his pen and made himself stand. He was not going to dwell on this. He quickly sealed the missive, then handed it to a footman and went to the painting room.

"It looks...nice."

"You think so?"

No. It looked like the boy just swished the brush around in every which direction. But that might be Seth's best and Giles wasn't in a habit of making others feel bad for their shortcomings. "Of course."

"You're lying."

Giles didn't know how to react to such an accusation and hoped Seth's smile meant he was only teasing. "Did you draw it out first?" he asked the boy.

"Draw what out?"

"What you're trying to paint."

Seth blinked. "No."

"You should. It'll help."

"I'm not very good at drawing."

Giles chuckled and picked up a pencil. "Sure, you are."

"No, I'm not."

"Have you tried?"

His face turned the color of an apple's peel. "Once."

Giles sat down on his three-legged stool. "And?"

"It was supposed to be a cactus like the one I'd seen in a book."

"A cactus?"

"It's a tall, rounded plant that has thousands of needles poking out all over."

"Ah, I've seen a picture of one of those." An image of said cactus formed in his mind. "That sounds easy to draw."

"I thought so, too," Seth agreed as the color rose in his cheeks again.

"Was it not?"

"No, it was easy to draw," he admitted. "Unfortunately, I didn't make the two arms that flanked the trunk on either side thin enough or tall enough and when I showed it to my mama she squealed and asked why I was drawing my private parts."

A rush of laughter came over Giles, wracking his entire body with mirth. "I'm sorry," he gasped between fits of laughter. Truly, he didn't mean to laugh at the boy, it was more the mental image of what the picture must have looked like and the horrified look that had to come over Lucy's face that made him react so.

"I didn't mean to," Seth said adamantly. His quiet tone extinguished all of Giles' laughter.

"I'm sorry," he repeated. "I did not mean to laugh at you."

Seth blew out a breath and studied the thinning fabric in the knees of his black trousers. "I don't know why she thought it looked like that. It had all those spines all over everything. I was only eight, I didn't have hair there like Simon does."

"Like Simon does?" Giles asked in surprise. While he didn't doubt that Simon had sprouted hair in various places of his body, he wondered how Seth would know such a thing.

"When he was injured, we had to carry him inside and mama, she—" the boy's face started to gain color at a rapid rate again— "she thought we should take his clothes off to tend his wounds. *All* of his clothes." The boy lifted chin. "I wouldn't let her. There are some things womenfolk don't need to see."

A range of emotions came over Giles, the most prominent

being sympathy. He shouldn't have laughed a moment ago. He knew better than anyone what it was like to be mocked about such matters. He'd forever remember the look on Sister Catherine's face when she'd ordered him an ice bath and made him strip off his clothes. He couldn't have been much older than Seth was and was humiliated by Sister Catherine's response when she'd seen his naked body and called all the other Sisters in to see him before prevailing upon Father Thomas to explain to Giles the things she didn't understand. He hated her for doing that to him.

"I'm sorry for laughing, Seth." The words were practically ripped from his throat. "I shouldn't have laughed. Can you forgive me?"

"Yes. I'm not upset, Lord Norcourt." He bit his lip. "I just don't understand."

"About where you went wrong with your picture or the hair?" Though his face burned, he was glad he'd been able to get the words out.

"The latter."

"You'll get it," Giles assured him. "We all do."

"When?"

"Depends on the boy. Some are ten or eleven and some are fourteen or fifteen."

"Fourteen or fifteen?" Seth shrieked as if it were an outrage.

Giles chuckled. "There was a boy at the orphanage with me who was fifteen and you'd have thought he'd have just been granted a trust with fifty thousand pounds the way he was celebrating."

"Celebrating?"

"He didn't think it'd ever happen." Giles shrugged. "He was the last one."

"Oh." He continued to bite his lip. "So I might be fourteen or fifteen before..."

"Could be. Could be sooner."

"How old were you?"

Giles idly scratched his neck and commanded himself not to become embarrassed. His conversation with the priest had been far less comfortable and he liked Seth too much to condemn him to such a fate. "Twelve."

"Lord Norcourt—"

"Giles," he corrected.

Seth's face beamed. "Giles, can I ask you something else?"

Giles clenched his teeth together. He didn't think he could take much more of this conversation. But neither did he want Seth to be forced to ask his mother or just not know. "Of course."

"Why were you in the orphanage?"

Giles relaxed slightly. That wasn't so bad. He crossed his ankles. "Well, when I—"

His words were cut off when Tarley, his butler, cleared his throat. "My lord, Mr. Appleton has come to see you. He's waiting in your study."

"Thank you," he murmured to the butler. Standing, he turned to Seth. "This should only take a few minutes. I'll answer your question when I get back." He opened the bottom drawer of the bureau and withdrew a sketchbook. "Meanwhile, why don't you practice your drawing?" He paused and playfully wagged a finger at the boy. "And no tallywags and whirligigs, you understand?"

Shaking his head ruefully at the boy's laughter, Giles steeled his nerves for what he might hear and went to his study.

Chapter Eighteen

"Which would you like to hear first, Lord Norcourt? The good news or the good news?" Mr. Appleton asked as soon as Giles entered the room.

Giles took his seat. "The good news?"

"It's all good news," Mr. Appleton assured him with a chuckle. He twisted his lips. "Well, it wasn't all good news at first, but it is now."

"What does that mean?"

Mr. Appleton put his booted ankle on top of his knee and ran his thumb along the edge of the papers in his hand. "I'm sure this won't come as any surprise to you, but Lord Cosgrove meant to take advantage of you."

A hard knot formed in his stomach and the blood drained from his head. Though why he had any reaction to something he already suspected, he didn't understand. "I assumed so. He threatened to start selling my properties if I didn't have a wife and an heir by the thirtieth anniversary of my birth."

"It appears he's already tried."

Giles involuntarily snapped the quill in his hand. "Tried?"

"He was unsuccessful."

"Unsuccessful," Giles repeated slowly.

"The other man's solicitor advised him against the transaction. Which is good or we'd have an entanglement."

Giles idly picked at the dried paint on his fingers while the man continued. He didn't want to admit as much, but he wasn't entirely sure he knew what an entanglement was or how one would respond to it.

"He won't be able to do so if you're still unwed on your thirtieth birthday, either."

"But he told me my father's will stated that he should use any means necessary, including depleting any asset and accounts not entailed to the barony to make me see reason."

"That's because he wanted to bully you into doing what he wanted." Mr. Appleton's voice held a stern edge similar to the one Father Thomas used when he was angry. He blew out a breath. "I can't know this for certain, but from what I've surmised he wanted to make a match between you and his daughter Lady Eugenia."

Giles' blood turned to ice in an instant. Were Lord and Lady Cosgrove and his mother and Mr. Appleton involved in some sort of scheme to take advantage of him? His mother had told him at that blasted house party she wanted to make amends and help him find a wife. Was her goal all along to have him marry Lady Eugenia? There seemed to be a shortage of air in the room all of a sudden.

"That'd be my reaction if being faced with marriage to her, too," Mr. Appleton commented.

Gripping the edges of his chair, Giles said, "Thank you. You may go."

Mr. Appleton froze. "I didn't realize you had an interest in her. My apologies."

"I don't." He took a deep breath. "But I won't—" *Won't what?* He racked his brain and his mouth moved. He clamped it shut before he could look any more foolish.

"Your mother didn't know."

Giles' reeling mind stilled. "Pardon?"

Mr. Appleton sighed. "Please, forgive me. I'm not always good with words."

"Neither am I."

Smiling, Mr. Appleton said, "Then we should both agree not to react until the other has had a chance to make a full explanation."

"A—All right," Giles said, idly rubbing his thumbs along the wood of his armrests.

"Your mother." He pursed his lips. "She means well. She does. And while I agree with you that she shouldn't have involved herself in your affairs, particularly that of finding you a wife, she fell into Lord Cosgrove's trap. Nothing more. She just wants to see you happy and treated fairly. She has no reason to see you marry

Lady Eugenia. That was solely for Lord Cosgrove's gain."

Giles didn't know why, but for some reason he believed him and it felt like a lead weight was suddenly lifted. "It all was a lie?"

"Yes." He thumbed through the stack of papers and handed Giles the four on the bottom. "This is the former Lord Norcourt's will. All of it. It looks more complicated than it is. I've read it over and there is nothing in it that states anything about allowing Lord Cosgrove to sell your assets or deplete your accounts."

Giles scanned the lines. "But he is still the one who manages the funds?"

"No. Yes. That part is a little complicated."

"It must be if it even makes an educated man like you confused."

Mr. Appleton chuckled. "In the event of your mother's inability to produce a suitable heir, Lord Cosgrove was granted limited control of your funds and assets. It would seem Lord Norcourt wasn't overly trusting of his friend because he was only permitted to use the funds as needed for improvements to the barony in addition to paying your mother a jointure and sending you your designated allowance. That's all. Anything earned was to be saved for your heir to inherit."

Giles hoped his disappointment didn't show. To Mr. Appleton this large sum of money might be good news, but to him, it meant very little if it was tied up in an account to be passed on to his heir. Not that he needed great wealth to be happy, but the meager allowance that the old baron had seen fit to bestow upon him could hardly cover his expenses. He might end up in debtor's prison in his attempt to get an heir. Were he ever so moved to find a wife. Which he wouldn't be. At eight-and-twenty only two ladies had ever caught the slightest bit of his interest. The first was already married, and the other... Well, she'd be married soon. And to his brother at that.

"Rather confident I'd have an heir, wasn't he?" Giles forced.

"Nearly all gentlemen have an heir," Mr. Appleton said. "It's just not always a son. But yes, he was confident you'd have a son —" he paused a beat— "and I am, too. That, and your mother are the only two things the old codger and I ever agreed upon."

Giles frowned and idly played with the plume on the broken quill. Apparently his father had thought with all of the money that would be in Giles' coffers by the time he was of an age to marry it'd be enough to buy the affections of a lady who wanted to be baroness badly enough. He dropped the now flattened and matted feather. "Thank you for looking into this. I appreciate it." Though clearly what he and Mr. Appleton considered good news varied.

"Have you an appointment?"

Seth was still here which meant he wouldn't be going to White's to meet Sebastian like he normally did. "No."

"Good, then I'll finish explaining." He flashed Giles a smile. "I did promise good news, didn't I?"

"I thought you already told me."

Mr. Appleton's top lip curled up, then transformed into a wide smile. "If that's what you consider good news, this next part you might consider to be great." He lifted his stack of papers up to his face and idly tapped the ends against his chin. "Hmmm. Can we make a bargain?"

"For what?" he asked between clenched teeth. Anytime anyone had ever wanted to make a bargain with him before, he'd come out with the rotten end. He tried to remind himself that Mr. Appleton didn't seem that sort and unclamped his jaw.

"My information for your presence."

"My presence?" Giles narrowed his eyes on Mr. Appleton, but damned if he knew what he should be looking for in the man's face to give away that he had bad intentions. "I thought my money was being exchanged for your information."

Mr. Appleton waved him off. "I'll accept no coins for this. And—" he met Giles' gaze— "I'll still give you the information without your agreement to come to dinner at my house tonight. But if you'd like to, the invitation is there."

Giles' body relaxed. Mr. Appleton was sincere. "I'll consider it."

"That's all I'd ask." He lowered the stack of papers to his lap. "Simon will be there again, but don't let that deter you. His mother

—*your* mother—she meant well and given the circumstances, I can't blame her too much for not having told him about you sooner."

"Too many things to explain, I suppose" Giles said.

"No, too much hurt to relive," Mr. Appleton said. "She just, well—" He sliced a hand through the air. "It's probably best we not talk about this now. I'd hate to put a damper on your good news."

"I thought it was *great* news," Giles teased, relieved for the change of topic.

"Right, you are," Mr. Appleton agreed with a chuckle. "Well, it's not all great, mind you. Some of it can only be termed as infuriating, but I think everything considered, you'll be satisfied."

Giles just stared at him, anxious.

"Norcourt granted Cosgrove the right to act as your guardian and overseer of all of the funds until your twentieth birthday at which time you'd inherit or if a physician deemed you were of unsound mind you'd cease to be heir and the barony and everything Lord Norcourt owned would be transferred to his nephew."

"He can have it," Giles muttered.

"No, it's yours. Well, most of it any way," he amended. "Unfortunately, the majority of the earnings from anything unentailed over the last eight years have gone to Cosgrove's coffers, but the rest is in a trust."

"For my heir?"

"Yes," Mr. Appleton said quietly. "Everything that has already been earned and deposited in that account is reserved for your heir. In addition anything else your barony continues to earn will be deposited into the trust, minus whatever funds are needed for the upkeep as determined by Mr. Forrester and Mr. Robins who have been appointed to act as the trustees until you are succeeded." He pursed his lips for a moment. "However, the good—nay, *great*—news is that any future earnings on anything unentailed are legally yours and will be deposited in your accounts starting next month."

The air left Giles' lungs in a *whoosh*. "Is it more than thirty pounds?"

Mr. Appleton chuckled. "Yes. You'll be very comfortable."

"Th-thank you," Giles said.

"You don't need to thank me. I was glad to help." He stood and handed Giles some papers from his satchel. "Keep these locked up for your records. I need to keep these for a few days longer if you don't mind. I'll bring them back next week?"

"Is there something unsettled?"

"Not unsettled, just undiscovered." Mr. Appleton picked up his satchel and started for the door.

Giles followed him into the hall. "Can I ask what?"

"You can ask, but you already know my price." He grinned and put on his coat. "I'll be back next week with more details. Until then, if you're available for dinner, we'd enjoy the company."

"Thank you," Giles murmured. He'd go have dinner over there at some point, he was sure of it. Just not anytime soon.

Mr. Appleton's fingertips fell on Giles' shoulder, staying him from opening the door. "If you'd rather not dine with all of us, but wish to come by for a game of cards or a drink, I'll take that, too."

Giles stared blankly at the man. He honestly couldn't fathom why Mr. Appleton would want to have a drink or play cards with him. Even Sebastian didn't invite him over for cither of those pursuits. And yet, there was nothing about Mr. Appleton that made him think he was being baited with the invitation. Odd.

"I'll think about it," he lied, opening the front door.

Wordlessly, Mr. Appleton took his leave.

A whirlwind of emotions swirled inside Giles as he closed the door then stepped into his painting room.

"Sorry. That took longer than I thought."

"That's all right," Seth said, his pencil moving back and forth across the paper.

Giles walked over behind Seth's chair to see what he was drawing. "Is that a horse?"

"It's supposed to be, but I can't get his front legs right. The first time, they were too short—" he flipped a few pages back in the book— "then they were too long—" he flipped the page again

— "and now they look too wide apart."

"They look fine to me. Extend the lines of the body a little longer before you draw in the back legs."

Seth made a few quick marks on the paper. "Like that?"

"Exactly."

A slow smile spread across the boy's face. "I thought you said you don't teach."

"I don't. It was merely a suggestion," he said, picking up another of his sketchbooks.

The clock behind him chimed the hour just then.

"I need to go!" Seth frantically tossed down the pad and pencil and scampered toward the door.

Giles reached for him to stay him. "You can take the paper with you if you'd like."

"I can?"

"Just don't bring it back filled with naughty drawings."

"I can come back?"

Giles stilled. "If you want to."

"I want to. I just thought…"

Giles knew exactly what he'd thought. He'd been left alone many times in a room by an adult who didn't want to be around him. "Seth, as I said before, that meeting lasted longer than I expected. Next time you come see me I'll spend the entire day with you."

"Monday?"

"Monday will be fine. Are you sure you don't want to spend time with your mama and Simon?"

"They need their privacy," Seth declared.

"Privacy?" They weren't even married yet!

"They're courting. They need time to talk and such."

"And such?" Giles choked out, heat rising in his face.

Seth twisted his lips. "Ride horses on some Row, sit on benches together, picnic at the park. I don't want to do any of that."

"You don't?"

"No. I'd rather come here, if you don't mind."

"No, I don't mind. I actually like you coming by, but don't

want to get in the way of your friendship with Simon since he's to be your papa and all." He hated the way his throat hurt as he said those words.

"Just because you're not going to be my papa doesn't mean we can't be friends, too," Seth said. "It's the same as what Mr. Appleton said to you before leaving—he just wants to be your friend even if you don't want to be friends with Mrs. Appleton or Simon." He picked up the pad of paper. "I need to be going now. I'll see you Monday."

Giles numbly watched the boy walk out the door. Either that boy was extremely perceptive or Giles really should be locked away in an asylum. He hadn't thought about Mr. Appleton's attempts to befriend him as anything other than a means to get him to reconcile with his mother—something he was more inclined to do with each passing day anyway—he might be after a friendship.

He idly scratched the side of his pencil with his thumbnail. Would it be so bad to form a friendship with the man? He seemed to be genuine with his efforts to help Giles. Perhaps the next time he offered, Giles would accept his invitation.

Chapter Nineteen

Lucy fingered the white lace that she'd just sewn onto the cuff of the blue dress that Mrs. Appleton had brought her yesterday. Mrs. Appleton had acted nonchalant about bringing her three gowns and even claimed them to be unneeded. Lucy hadn't wanted to accept such charity, mind you, but her need for suitable gowns had far outweighed her pride and she'd graciously accepted the older woman's generosity. They'd needed minor adjustments, of course. Some were done with just a needle and thread and others, like this cuff, had required new lace. Which she'd been able to buy and still managed to have a few coins left over that she planned to use to treat Seth.

The poor lad had been on his best behavior for her in the two weeks since they'd come to London and she thought it was time to reward him. It wouldn't be much, of course, because she couldn't be wasteful. Not that she had a lot to waste, but he did deserve something.

"How about if we go get an ice," Lucy said, sitting down in the chair beside him in the corner of the library.

His head snapped up from behind the pad of paper he'd been drawing on constantly for the past two days. "What's an ice?"

"It's a treat." She tugged the pad from his fingers and blinked at the picture he'd drawn. She wasn't quite sure what it was, but it looked far more appropriate than the last thing she'd seen him draw. "That looks lovely."

"Really?" he exclaimed, beaming.

"Of course." She almost wished she hadn't commented, for if he asked what she liked best about it, she wasn't sure what she'd say. "Now, go put this upstairs so we can go and get back before dark."

Thirty seconds later, Seth had deposited the sketchpad he'd found only heaven knew where upstairs and was ready to go. "Are we going to Covent Gardens to get the ice?" he asked as she locked up the library.

"No. There's a vendor not too far from here." She took an extra second to test the lock. "It's just down the street."

"Really?" The excitement in his voice was contagious and Lucy found herself grinning just the same.

"Really," she confirmed, wrapping an arm around him. She'd never tell him, or anyone this, but she'd been looking forward to getting another ice since Simon had gotten her one the day of the statue museum. Something about that one had been tainted and made it hard to enjoy. She had every intention to enjoy this one.

"This is the way to Lord Norcourt's house," Seth commented.

Lucy nearly tripped. "Is it?" she said as airily as she could manage, though she knew very well that it was.

"Yes. It's that one." He pointed to a tall, tan brick house about four houses down.

"And how would you know?" She bit her lip. She shouldn't have asked that, she should have just changed the subject while she still could.

Seth gave her a sideways glance. "We stayed there."

Lucy blushed. Indeed, they had, but she hadn't taken notice of his address then. She'd had too many other things on her mind that day.

"Besides, Simon pointed it out that night he brought us home."

"Did he now? I don't remember that." It was the truth, too. She didn't remember Simon saying anything about it being Giles' house. Probably because she was too distracted watching his carriage stop there for him to get out.

"Should we stop and see if he wants to get an ice, too?"

Seth's words brought her up short. "I'm sure he already has plans for the evening." He was a lord, a peer of the realm, she could almost guarantee he had more important things to do than go have an ice with her and Seth.

"Oh, there he is—" Seth pulled away from her— "I'll go ask him."

Before she could reach out and stop him, he'd gotten away.

Tamping down her mortification, she joined them where they stood at the bottom of the steps that led to his house.

"Mama and me are about to go get ices, would you like to come?"

"Ice?" he clipped; a shadow crossed his face.

"Flavored ice," Lucy supplied. "From a vendor."

Giles' puckered brow didn't relax, nor did his set jaw. "Flavored ice?"

"To eat," Seth said helpfully.

"I don't like ice," Giles said flatly.

Lucy had no idea how to respond to that.

Seth, however, had no reservation. "That's all right. You can still come with us. Can't he, Mama?"

"Seth, Lord Norcourt might have other plans already," she said softly.

"He doesn't," Seth rebutted. "He said he was just on his way out to the park to look at a bird. There'll be birds there tomorrow, so he can come with us tonight."

It was on her lips to suggest that just because he didn't have any pressing matter to attend to that he might not wish to join them, but was cut off when Giles said, "I'll come."

"Perhaps there'll be something else you might enjoy," Lucy offered.

Giles shrugged as if to say he didn't care either way and offered her his arm.

***

Giles didn't care what the vendor was selling, he'd enjoy the company and that was good enough.

"I think the vendor is just two more blocks up here, by the fabric shop."

Giles knew where she was talking about. He'd seen the man peddling his goods. The man was dratted annoying, he was. Yelling and hollering to get people's attention so they'd buy his goods. Had Giles had more coins in his pocket, there had been a time or two when he'd have bought something from the man just to close his mouth. Giles didn't realize he'd sold ices, however, and might

139

have hesitated before spending his coins on such a thing. He shivered. He hated ice. No, hated was too weak of a word. He *detested* ice.

"He's right there," Lucy said, giving his arm a gentle squeeze that sent fire through his veins.

As if he'd seen them coming from down the block, the vendor started running toward them. "Care to buy yer purdy la'y an ice?"

"Yes," Giles clipped. "And the boy."

The man nodded excitedly. "Yes, yes." He waved them over to his cart. "Lemon or wine flavor?"

"Lemon," Lucy said automatically.

"Eh, come now, ye'd like the wine flavor," the vendor urged.

"No, thank you. We'll take lemon."

"At least try it," the vendor encouraged, thrusting a cup full of a red substance into Lucy's face, missing her nose by a mere half-inch.

"She said lemon," Giles said, pushing the man's beefy arm away.

"T'ree lemon ices, den," the vendor said.

"Two," Giles corrected with a shiver.

"Two?" The blond-haired vendor stared at them through his grey eyes, then suddenly a smile spread his lips. "Eh, yer gwine share it, aren't ye?" he asked with a wink at Giles. "Ye'll wish she'd asked for the wine, fer sure."

Giles felt his face flush, but didn't know what to say to assure Lucy he had no such interest in sharing her ice. Not that he thought for an instant she'd want to share her ice with him. That would be...odd.

"Here ye are," the vendor said, pushing two ices in Giles' direction.

He took them and handed one to Lucy and the other to Seth before fishing the coins out of his pocket to pay the man his price.

"Shall we go eat these in the park?" Lucy asked.

"You don't have to come with me to the park," Giles said.

Lucy swallowed a bite of her ice. "Nonsense. You escorted us to the vendor to get an ice and saved us from having to suffer that obnoxious man alone. We'd like to go with you to the park." She lowered her spoon. "Unless you'd rather be alone."

"No." He cleared his throat. "Absolutely not. It's just three blocks that way."

By the time they arrived, Seth had no more than four bites left to his ice. Lucy, who must either not like the food or loved it and wanted to savor it, had eaten hers at a snail's pace and still had most of hers left.

"Where is best to sit?" she asked, lifting her right hand to her brow and scanning the park.

"This bench."

Lucy blinked down at the bench in front of her. "But won't the leaves of this tree be in our way to see the birds?"

"Yes."

"Then why would we sit there? Wouldn't it be better if we sat over there under that large tree that's by the water?"

"Yes."

"Then why don't we?"

"Your dress."

Lucy looked down at her dress. "Pardon?"

"It'll get dirty."

"That's all right," she said. "Besides, if you were really worried about it, you could always be a true gentleman and remove your coat so I can sit on it." She must not have meant to say that for as soon as the words were out, her face turned almost as red as that wine flavored ice the vendor had tried to accost her with.

"As you wish, my lady." He offered her his arm, then led her to the spot she'd indicated and shed his coat. "Here," he murmured, laying his dark blue coat out on the grass like a blanket.

"I was only teasing," she said, laughingly.

Giles shrugged and patted the fabric until she relented and sat.

"Can I put my feet in the water?" Seth asked.

"I don't know if you're allowed," his mother said.

"He's allowed. People do it all the time."

"Oh, all right, but roll up your trousers and do not go in past your knees, Seth." She pointed a finger at him. "I mean it."

"Yes, ma'am," he said, plopping down next to them and untying the laces on his boots. A moment later, his worn leather boots were off and so were his stockings. Then he was on his feet and racing away from them.

"Thank you for the ice," Lucy said.

Giles nodded uncomfortably. "You're welcome." He stretched his legs out in front of himself and watched Seth roll up the bottom of his trousers and test the water with his toes. "Is it good?"

"Yes. Would you like to try some?"

Giles turned his head to face her. "No. I don't like ice."

"They're a little tart, aren't they?" she commented, licking her lips.

"You don't have to finish eating it if you don't like it."

"No, I do." She ate another spoonful as if to prove her point. "I was just saying that for someone who doesn't like lemons—or wine—an ice might not be very enjoyable."

"I like lemons," he commented. "It's ice I don't like."

"You mean actual ice?"

He nodded.

"I don't like that, either," she murmured, watching Seth wade into the water. "Though it's cold, I always think it burns when it touches my skin."

"When did you have an ice bath?" he demanded a little more angrily than he'd intended. He couldn't say why, but the thought that anyone had made Lucy take an ice bath made him murderous.

"An ice bath?" she queried, giving him her full attention. "I've never heard of such a thing. I just meant when I don't have suitable gloves or I'm asked to run outside to retrieve something and I bump an icicle with my bare skin. It burns." She lowered her ice to her lap. "What exactly is an ice bath?"

Tension gripped his entire body. He'd let his incomplete thoughts get ahead of him and he'd spoken too much. "Nothing."

"Did someone put you into a tub of ice, Giles?"

Whether it was her soft tone or the easy use of his Christian name, he might never know but something about her innocent question broke through the wall he'd tried so hard to erect to protect himself. "Yes." He let out a deep breath. "But it was a long time ago. It doesn't matter anymore."

"I'd say that it does if it makes you not be able to enjoy a most delicious treat," she said. "Is it fair to assume this was done by the nuns at the orphanage?"

How did she know he'd lived at an orphanage? *Seth.* He'd probably told her. Giles mentally shrugged. "Yes. The Sisters thought it'd help drive out the evil spirits that had inhabited my mind and made me act a fool." He frowned. "I guess it didn't work. I still say foolish things."

"No, you don't," she said.

"I assure you, I do."

She shrugged. "Well, if you do then I must be going deaf because I don't notice them."

He knew she was just trying to make him feel better and he'd be lying if he didn't admit it had worked. Slightly. "Thank you. But spend more time with me and I'm bound to say something you'll think is foolish." He clenched his fists. Why had he just suggested she spend more time with him? That was the last thing he needed. Was it not enough he was already attracted to her? Must he make his torment worse by suggesting they spend more time together?

"We all do that."

He started. "Do what?"

"Say foolish things."

She laughed, but not in the way she normally did. It sounded like it was forced and not really full of humor. "When I was a girl, I had these two playmates I mentioned before—both boys. One day I was outside looking up at the birds, like I imagine you'd rather do than be chatting with me." She flashed him a smile. "Anyway, while I was on my back, staring up at the sky, the brothers came over and one asked what I was doing. I told him to be quiet that I was trying to watch for birds and I didn't want them to know I was there.

"He scoffed and said that if I keep laying there the birds might think I'm dead and make me their next meal. I remember being horrified at the thought and before I could give much thought to my words, I asked if they thought birds made 'humaning' a pursuit. I then only made it worse by explaining that while birding is when we humans watch birds, humaning was the bird equivalent and suggested that birds flew around trying to see different varieties humans: tall, short, light hair, dark..." She buried her red face in her hands. "I have never been so mortified in my entire life. Even now, retelling it, I am just as mortified."

"Don't be," he said, his heart on the verge of bursting. Nobody had ever shared such a humbling experience with him—excluding Seth's confession to having been wrongly accused of drawing his private parts. "I'm sure they forgot soon enough."

"They didn't," she said with a shaky laugh. "About two years later, the younger of the pair invited me to go with them to a menagerie. While there, the older brother asked if I'd come to look at the animals...or if I'd come so they could look at me."

Giles winced on her behalf. "Boys are cruel."

"They can be," she agreed. "They can also be sweet when they want to be."

He wasn't so sure of that but didn't want to argue. "You'd better finish off your ice before it melts."

Lucy looked down and stirred her spoon around the cup. "There's only a little left." She lifted the spoon half-filled with the cold, creamy substance and pointed it in his direction. "Are you sure you don't want to try a taste?"

Emboldened by her confession and statement about how he seemed to allow the nuns to keep him from enjoying ices, he leaned toward her. "Actually, I think I do." Then before he—or she —could change his mind, he sucked the offered refreshment off her spoon.

Chapter Twenty

"My lord, you have a visitor."

Giles opened the drawer under the front of his desk and swept all the papers on top of his desk inside, then shut it. "Send him in."

A second later Seth strolled through the door of Giles' study, made his way straight to the pair of empty chairs that faced Giles' desk and plopped down in the one on the left. "Ouch!"

Giles couldn't help but grin. "I don't think they're meant to be comfortable."

"Well, they're not." He moved his upper lip in a way that exposed the entire front of his teeth and wrinkled his nose.

"Would you like to do something other than paint today?" While he enjoyed painting and drawing, many of the other boys he'd grown up with hadn't and he thought perhaps Seth might wish to do something else.

"What else do gentlemen do all day?"

Giles shrugged and poked out his lower lip. "Read the newspaper. Answer correspondence. Meet their friends at White's —"

"What's White's?"

"It's a club for gentlemen."

"Can we go?" Seth asked, nearly bouncing off his chair.

"No."

"Please?"

"It's not for gentlemen your age."

"Why not?"

"Because they talk about—" he waved his hand in a circle through the air— "things."

"Things?"

"Things," Giles confirmed.

"What kinds of things?"

"Gentlemen things."

Seth's green eyes nearly quadrupled in size and his jaw dropped. "They talk about their *pizzles*?"

Giles choked on his own tongue. "No," he said banging his hand against his chest with so much force he knew he'd have a bruise there later.

"Then what do they talk about?"

Giles regained his breath. "Horse racing, cards, politics. Nothing of interest to a young lad." He scoffed. "Or me."

Seth crossed his arms. "You've never heard anything there that held your interest?"

"No." Of course he hadn't been completely honest when he'd told the boy what was spoken about. Even the pizzle comment was accurate in a way. There were some men, none who Giles wished to make further acquaintances with, who discussed their private parts and those of certain ladies they'd bedded. He'd found their talk and the images it put into his head uncomfortable at first. Now, it was just their talk that made him uneasy. He had no problem with imagining himself and Lucy doing any of the things he'd heard about.

"Giles?"

Giles snapped to present, blinking. "I'm sorry, lad. What did you say?"

"I asked what we're going to do today."

"Hmm." Giles put his feet on the desk and crossed his ankles. "I take it you've little desire to read again today?"

Seth's lips twisted. "No, my lord. I've read more in the past fortnight than I have in my entire life." He looked around the room. "Do you have any games?"

"Yes. I have about a dozen decks of cards around here somewhere and a chess set. Which would you prefer?"

"Chess."

"Very well." At least he knew where the chess set was. He didn't know how to play it, mind you, but he knew where it was. He stood and went to the far corner of the massive bookshelves. He'd stored the blasted chess set on the very top so he wouldn't have to see the thing and as he came up on his toes, he almost wished he hadn't. He stretched his fingers until they collided with the hard wood of the edge, then slid it down. "Can you pull that end table over here?"

Seth did as he was bade while Giles moved his wing-backed chairs so one was on either side of the makeshift game table.

Seth took his seat first and started unpacking the pieces. "What are the rules?"

"I don't know. I thought you did."

"No. I've never played."

"Neither have I."

Seth laughed, then froze. "You're serious?"

Giles nodded, then in unison they both started laughing. "Sorry, lad. I don't play games."

"Ever?"

"Not unless I'm forced," he said with a grimace as a painful memory of the dinner party his mother had hosted popped into his mind.

"But you're a baron, I thought the lot of you knew how to play all games. That it was taught in the schools you attended."

"It probably was. But I didn't attend school," he reminded Seth.

"That's right. I'm sorry." Seth idly spun a chess piece that looked like a horse. "Were you not allowed to play games at the orphanage?"

A sharp bark of laughter escaped Giles' lips. "No. Father Thomas said if we needed something to occupy ourselves with, we should memorize the Bible."

Seth's eyes widened. "Did you?"

"Some." He drummed his fingers along the edge of the table. "Do you know any games?"

"Draughts."

"Do we need cards?"

"No, just a board like this one—" he gestured to the chess board— "and two different color circles."

"Circles?"

Seth shrugged. "I don't know what they're called."

Giles didn't, either. "These pieces are two different colors." He pointed to the ivory and onyx chess pieces. "Do you suppose we could use these?"

"I suppose so." He counted under his breath. "There are too many pieces. We only need twelve of each."

Giles picked up four of each color and put them back in the wooden box that held the game pieces. "There. Now there's twelve of each."

Seth wordlessly started collecting the black pieces.

Giles picked up the white ones and noticed that Seth was only putting his on the black squares so Giles put his on the white ones.

"No, they need to go on the black squares."

"But mine are white."

"I know, next time we'll use the white squares if you want, but this time they all need to be on the four black squares of the first three rows."

Shrugging, Giles did as Seth instructed, then waited while the boy explained the rules.

Move your piece over the other person's pieces. That sounded simple enough.

It wasn't.

At least not at first. Apparently, you could only "jump" your opponent's piece at a diagonal, not straight forward. Not to mention, moving backward wasn't allowed.

A half hour later and Giles' luck had turned around and he was on his way to winning when suddenly Seth caught him unawares again. But not with a new rule this time. No, it was something completely different that came out of his mouth: a question.

"Giles, do you know where babies come from?"

The piece that Giles had decided earlier was shaped like an unnaturally thin phallus slipped from his fingers and hit the board with an echoing *pop*. "Yes." He picked up his piece and for the second time wished he'd tossed that one out while ridding them of unneeded pieces. "Do you?"

"No. Not really." He ran one of his thin fingers along the edge of the chess board. "I have an idea, but I don't know."

A sickening tightness formed in the pit of Giles' stomach. Father Thomas had given him a brief explanation when he was a few years older than Seth. Not too many facts, mind you. Just the mechanics of what went where and what the results would yield. To be honest, he'd learned far more from sitting in White's waiting for Sebastian to join him than he had from Father Thomas. But he still knew the mechanics at least.

Seth was too young yet to know. Wasn't he? Perhaps he wasn't. Father Thomas was loathe to talk about it with Giles and said he was only doing so because *someone* had to since Giles was still responsible for one day securing an heir. To all the other boys, he'd explained as often as he could how the best thing to do with their lives would be to become monks. Oddly enough, only one did. He blinked to staunch his meandering thoughts. Seth had come to him for an answer. Why he hadn't gone to Simon, who would one day be his papa, with such an important matter, Giles wasn't sure, but whatever his reason, Seth had come to him and he couldn't *not* help him.

Clearing his throat, he said, "If you'll tell me what you think you know, I can tell you if you're right." It was the best he could offer. The lad was still only eleven and hadn't started changing yet. His mother might kill Giles if he told Seth everything he knew. At least this way, he was just confirming facts.

Seth hummed and tapped his fingers on the edge of the chessboard as he pondered Giles' offer. "A—all right."

"Seth, if you've changed your mind and you'd rather ask your mama or Simon, I understand."

"No." He bit his lip. "Unless you don't want to talk to me about this."

"Of course I do. I was merely surprised that you'd ask me."

"Oh, well, that's because I know you won't lie to me or laugh at my lack of knowledge."

"No, I won't." He moved his piece and took one of Seth's men. "Whenever you're ready."

Seth moved his next piece. "Well, the woman has the babies."

"Yes." Giles moved another piece and captured another of

Seth's, leaving him with only two men.

"But there needs to be a man."

"Yes," Giles agreed.

"That's the part I don't understand."

Giles shifted uncomfortably. "You mean his role?"

Seth nodded. "When we lived in Bath, one of the ladies I knew started getting bigger." He held his hands out in front of him to indicate just how she was getting bigger. "When I asked her why her stomach was growing she said she and her husband were expecting a baby." He picked up one of his pieces, then set it back down and met Giles' eyes. "My mama's never been married."

Giles was at a loss of what to say. Seth was right, of course. Lucy had made it no secret to him that she'd never married. Father Thomas's warnings of fathering children out of wedlock and awful repercussions resounded in his head. He pushed those thoughts away. That was the last thing Seth needed to hear. "You're right," Giles started quietly. "On both scores. A man does need to be present and your mother wasn't married."

"Then how—" He broke off with a sigh. "I suppose not every woman I've ever known who's had a baby was married." His voice was low and quiet as if he were trying to make sense of everything he knew.

Giles swallowed hard, praying the right words would come to him so Lucy—or even Simon—wouldn't murder him for having this conversation. "Sometimes there is more to a situation or someone's reasoning than we might know."

"I know, but—" He shook his blond head. "I still don't understand. Even if she never married, but a man had to be present. Then who is the man?"

"I don't know." Fortunately, it was the truth. For if Giles had known, he might have been tempted to tell Seth.

Seth twisted his lips, put his elbows on his knees, then leaned his chin against his palms as if he were about to get lost in deep contemplation. A moment later, he sat straight up. "Do you think it could be a lord?"

Giles wasn't sure whether he should admire or be irritated at the lad's obvious longing to be a nobleman's bastard. "I don't know."

Seth took to his feet and started walking around the room. "It makes sense now."

"What makes sense?"

"Why Mama doesn't like lords."

Giles frowned. "She doesn't?"

"No. She usually snarls when she sees or hears of one."

No wonder she'd chosen Simon. Giles never had a chance. "Did she ever say why she detests them so?"

"No. But if one is my father and he didn't marry her, then it would make sense, wouldn't it?"

Indeed it would. "I suppose," he forced carelessly. Or as carelessly as he could, considering he wished there was a way to prove to her he was different before she married his brother.

"Now, I just need to find out which one."

"Why would you want to do that?"

Seth stopped his pacing. "Because I want to know."

Giles couldn't argue with that logic, feeble and petty as it might be. "Why don't you ask your mother?"

A loud snort rent the air. "She won't tell me any more than she'll tell me how a man puts a baby in a woman."

"Perhaps when you're older..."

"I suppose," Seth muttered, falling back into his chair. "Was it my turn or yours?"

"Seth, have you ever asked her?"

"Not exactly. I tried to help her find a husband before she told me to stop because no respectable man would want her."

That wasn't true. Giles wanted her. Then again, was he really considered respectable? "Did you stop?"

"Yes." He lowered his lashes. "You don't think my father is like those men from Shrewsbury do you?'

It took Giles only a second to take his meaning. "No." Honestly, he didn't know, but it was bad enough not knowing who his father was, painting him as a rapist only made it worse.

Seth moved his piece.

"Is your curiosity satisfied, then?"

"Not completely, but well enough for today, I suppose."

Chapter Twenty-One

Three Days Later

Lucy was beside herself with worry. She'd gone out in the morning to purchase provisions and the last of the fabric for her new gown with the wages she'd been paid only to return to a vacant apartment. A quick search of the library that was closed for the day filled her chest with panic. Seth wasn't there, either.

She didn't even know where to begin to look nor did she know what danger might be out there waiting for him. In the weeks they'd been living in London, they'd either been in the library or with one of the Appletons. Never alone. No matter. She needed to find him and assure herself that he was all right. Who knows what kind of trouble a boy of his age might find for himself.

She rushed out the door of the library and locked it behind her, then dashed down the street to Giles' house. She was only going to find him because he lived the closest, she assured herself, although deep in her heart she knew that wasn't the only reason.

Heedless to the angry shouts of the carriage drivers and riders in the streets, Lucy tore down the street and straight to Giles' house where she flew up the steps and pounded on his bright red door.

A moment later, the door swung open, revealing not a stodgy, greying butler as she'd expected, but Giles himself.

"I need help," she exclaimed without preamble.

Giles' strong hands closed around her upper arms and guided her inside his house. "What's wrong?" he asked, wiping away a tear on her right cheek she didn't even know she'd shed.

"Seth," she cried. "He's gone."

Something flickered over Giles' face that she couldn't recognize and just as soon as it was gone, his hand was at the small of her back, and guiding her forward. Were she not worried about her son she might have melted at the natural feeling of his touch.

Instead, it soothed her in a way she didn't think was possible at the moment. On her back, his hand moved up and down rhythmically. He didn't say anything, but he didn't have to. His touch alone was enough to calm her.

"I'm sorry," he whispered at last, steering her into the room his mother said he kept locked. "I thought you knew."

Before she could ask what he meant her eyes fell on her son's form as he sat on a stool in front of a canvas.

She was overcome with emotion and ran to him, not sure whether she should hug him or beat him. "What are you doing here?"

"Painting."

Lucy blinked back her tears and looked to the white canvas he'd gestured to. "Is it a cloud?" she suggested with a sniffle.

"No. I'm not sure what I'll paint on this one." He jerked his thumb behind him. "I tried to do an estate with rolling hills and trees with the last one, but it doesn't look right."

Lucy squinted at the unrecognizable picture he'd indicated and pursed her lips. "Just how many times have you come here to paint?"

"Two," Seth admitted with a visible swallow. "I mean this is my second. I came the first time you went with Simon, too."

"First time," she mindlessly repeated. Now she knew what he'd done all day when he'd claimed not to feel well and said he didn't wish to go to the museum with her and Simon. "You've been coming here every Monday and Thursday, then?" So much was now making sense in her mind. He always seemed breathless when she returned from her morning errands. He was probably tired from having run back to the library to beat her. She glanced around the room at all of the paintings and drawings. Now the emergence of the sketchbook made sense, too.

"I'm sorry," Giles said from behind her, his voice so soft and quiet she almost didn't hear him. "I thought you knew he was coming here."

She whirled around. "Well, I did not." Flushing with shame at her outburst, she ran her open palms over her face. "I'm sorry, you didn't deserve that. You did no wrong."

Giles' face remained expressionless. "I'm sorry," he repeated. "I should have asked him if you knew."

"No," Lucy corrected. "*He* should have asked before coming instead of lying to me." She turned toward Seth, her anger with him firmly in place now that she knew he was safe. "Why did you come here anyway?"

"When? The first time?"

Or *any* time? "You can start with that time."

"Simon said he planned to take you to a museum and that I probably wouldn't like to go."

She could accept that. Given the choice she'd have rather spent the day with Giles, too. "And the other times?"

"Because you were gone. I just thought—" He broke off with a shrug.

"That you'd come prevail upon Lord Norcourt to entertain you?"

Seth blushed. "I wasn't bothering him."

Lucy snorted. "I'm sure you weren't."

"He wasn't," Giles said, shocking her to the toes and stealing her breath.

"Surely you're just being kind," she said once she'd recovered.

"No. He's no bother."

Lucy searched his face for some hint that he was hiding something, but if he was, he'd mastered a way to hide it. Her eyes traveled down to his white shirt and noticed the top button was undone and his coat, waistcoat, and cravat were all discarded with his cuffs rolled up around his elbows, revealing his strong forearms. He was quite dashing in a strangely disheveled sort of way. She blushed. "Thank you for allowing him to spend time here and being kind about it, but I know you have other things to do and I'll make sure he doesn't trouble you again."

"It's no trouble," Giles said, his tone even and calm like it usually was. "He's welcome to stay—and so are you."

Lucy's mouth went dry. *Stay?* She couldn't stay. "Oh, I

couldn't," she stammered. "I mean, I *shouldn't*." She squeezed her eyes shut. She'd do well to stop talking. "I can't."

"All right, then you go home and I'll stay," Seth said casually.

Frowning, Lucy said, "That won't be happening."

"Then stay," Seth said, a hint of a plea in his voice.

Lucy looked to Giles. He shrugged. Which, was tremendously unhelpful, because it told her absolutely nothing about how he really felt. "We should go home," Lucy stated firmly.

"You don't have to."

Lucy didn't know who was more surprised by his words, her or Giles whose wide eyes and raised eyebrows gave away that he hadn't meant to voice them. "It's all right," she said. "I appreciate your generosity toward Seth, but we can't trouble you any further."

His hand reached out to stop her. "It's no trouble." This time his voice was solid and sure. "Stay."

"Yes, let's stay."

She barely heard Seth's voice as he continued on about learning to paint over the loud thump of her beating heart.

"All right," she whispered.

A grin wider than she'd ever seen split Giles' face and his hand tightened a fraction. Blushing, he released her. "Do you paint?"

"No."

"That's all right." He walked over to a scuffed up oak bureau that was positioned just a few feet away from where Lucy stood. "I'll show you."

An excited shiver skated up Lucy's spine.

"You never showed me," she heard Seth say followed immediately by Giles replying, "You're not a lady."

***

Giles could no more believe he'd invited her to stay than he could believe she'd agreed. "Brushes," he barked. He cleared his throat and retrieved a small metal palate from the drawer. He gripped the material in one hand and snatched an empty cup from the top with the other. "Over here."

Lucy followed him to the easel he'd positioned in front of the window. It was his favorite. He'd always liked open windows. It had been too dark in the boys' room at the orphanage. He shuddered and set the brushes and cup down with an indelicate tap.

Grabbing the dry canvas on top of the easel with his right hand, he tapped the fingertips on his left hand on top of the stool. "Sit here."

Lucy sat and repositioned her skirts while he turned to snatch her a fresh canvas. He caught Seth's eye, but the amused boy didn't say anything, just wagged his eyebrows. Giles couldn't begin to understand why and continued about his business.

"What would you like to paint?"

"I don't know." Lucy tucked a tendril of her dark hair behind her ear and looked around the room at all the different portraits he had lining the room. He really should get rid of some of them. "I never thought about it before." She met his eyes. "Apparently subjects never seem to elude your mind."

Giles reached for the last unoccupied stool and dragged it over toward her and sat down. "Sometimes I have more ideas than I could possibly paint in a lifetime." He reached for her hand and began removing her gloves so she wouldn't soil them. "Other days my mind is as dry as the bottom of a paint jar that was left out without the cap." A giggle passed her lips, doing odd things to his insides. He released her hand and cleared his throat. "Have you a fondness for—" he scanned the room to see what he'd painted that she might like— "sunsets or horses, rivers or mountains, farms or buckets—"

"Buckets?" she asked, craning her neck.

He pointed to the far end of the room where a canvas with a watering pail sitting atop a chipped and scratched wooden table was resting against the wall.

"Why a bucket?"

Her voice held no condemnation, so he answered truthfully. "I painted that the day I came back from your house in Shrewsbury. You'd asked me to fetch some water…" He trailed off unable to voice the rest.

"I see."

Giles busied himself with opening jars of paints before she could see anything else.

"Have you ever painted a human form?" she wondered.

"No. I tried once, but I find it difficult." He reached for the tan jar and removed the top. "You might do fine though."

"I doubt it," she said with a little giggle.

"You'll only know if you try." Another lock of her dark hair had fallen across her face. He carefully pushed it behind her ear. "Who would you like to paint? Simon?" he croaked, praying she wouldn't agree to wasting his materials in such a way.

"No." She pursed her lips and cocked her head to the left. "I think I'd rather paint you."

All the air left his lungs in one swift *whoosh*. Him. She wanted to paint *him*. Unable to form the words to ask her why, he sat still and watched her go about selecting which brush she thought she might need.

"Are you going to give me instruction, or will I have to ask Seth how to paint with such splendor."

"Pencil," he croaked. Clumsily, he reached for the pencil that was near the paints. "Draw it first."

Lucy took the pencil from him and brought the point to the canvas, a small smile curving her lips as she glided her pencil around to make a perfect oval. "I think I should start with faces before attempting anything more complex."

Giles didn't care what she started with—even cacti that resembled unmentionables if that's what she wanted. He just enjoyed sitting next to her as she did it.

She tapped the end of the pencil against her lips as if she were trying to remember where facial features were located.

"I'm right here, if you need to cheat," he whispered.

Her cheeks grew a fetching pink and she turned to look at him. He stayed still while she studied his face. "May I?"

Giles bit the inside of his mouth. He had no idea what she was asking, but not wanting to make a fool of himself by asking, nodded.

A second later, she lifted her delicate fingers to his skin. With her fingertips, she traced the contours of his face. His cheekbones, chin and jaw. She turned to the canvas and drew lines inside the oval. They were a little darker than he might have made them, but he couldn't bring himself to correct her. He'd just have to mention something about using more paint to cover them when she was ready.

She turned back to him and tentatively touched him again. This time she felt his eyebrows and around his eye socket, then down his nose. Who knew being touched thus could excite him so. When she'd finished drawing in the outline of his eyes and nose, she brought her fingers to his lips, inflicting the worst torture imaginable on him as her fingers brushed over them then traced the outside edge. His groin hardened instantly and his lips ached to kiss her fingers—even just ever-so-lightly, but he didn't dare. Instead, he shifted just enough to hide the way his erection tented his trousers and he trained his eyes on the canvas.

Without touching him again, she drew two flaring swoops down from either side of his chin, which he presumed was to be his neck, then she set the pencil down and reached toward the brushes that were in the water.

"Which am I supposed to use."

"Any." He coughed. "Excuse me," he said, patting his chest. "Any of them will work. But I prefer this one—" he pulled out a brush with a medium-sized tip and handed it to her— "it's easier to use for a painting such as this."

"I thought you never painted people," she said, dipping the bristles into the orange paint.

"I don't." He reached for the palate and the white paint. "You'd better mix these or I might look like a deformed carrot."

She giggled and took the white paint from him. "Do I just pour it?"

"You could, but—" he snatched a large paintbrush from the water— "I prefer to just take a scoop from each color. He dipped his larger brush into the white paint and scooped a blob onto the palate, then did the same with the orange, putting that blob on top of the white one, then swirling them around.

"Thank you." She took the palate from him and dipped her brush into the mixed colors, then brought her brush to the canvas. "Urp," she squealed, moving her brush hurriedly down the canvas to keep up with the large drip that had slid off the end. "I told you I wasn't good at this," she said on a sigh.

"Nonsense." Giles took the brush from her and smoothed out her strokes. "Less paint." He dipped her brush into the mixture, then wiped a little off the side and handed it back to her.

Lucy brought the brush back to the top of where the coloring was on the canvas and started brushing this way and that way, right and left.

Giles covered her hand with his. "This way," he whispered against her hair, leaning forward and helping guide her hand smooth and slow along the canvas.

**

If Lucy's skin heated another degree she just might disintegrate into a pile of ashes. Thankfully, Giles seemed oblivious to her body's heated reaction to him as he repositioned himself behind her and helped guide her hand's brushstroke. He moved their hands down to the pool of paint and refilled her brush before guiding her hand back to the canvas and helping her move it.

"That's it." He abruptly let go of her hand, leaving Lucy to feel bereft at the loss of his warmth and a fool for feeling that way. "I'll be right back. Keep doing that. It looks good."

Behind her, she heard him and Seth exchange a few words about dragons or some such creature. She shuddered. Dragons made her think of that museum she'd visited with Simon. She stilled her brush. Simon. He'd come to see her the day before at the library to ask if she'd be willing to go to Covent Gardens with him. She'd declined. Politely, of course. She truly did need to spend the day working on her sewing, she'd even intended to repair the holes that were in knees of three of Seth's five pair of trousers. She lowered her lashes and put more paint on her brush. Truly, she shouldn't enjoy being in his company this much. He was just being polite to her, she reminded herself as she finished filling in his face.

"Ready to do the eyes?" Giles asked, resuming his seat next to her.

Lucy reached for a thinner brush and twisted her lips. The jar of green resembled a lime's peel. Certainly not a hue that would do justice to his emerald eyes. "Is this the only green you have?"

"I had another, but it's covering that canvas." He gestured to Seth's rolling hillside mixed with dense forest. "Perhaps you can find a thick blob that's still drying from last week to use," he suggested, grinning.

"Traitor," Seth called in mock indignation. "First you help her, then you let her steal from my masterpiece."

"Cool your heels," Giles soothed. "That paint is so thick there'd be no way she'd get any off now." He handed her both the white and the brown. "Mix that green with either of these until you get the color you'd like."

"Hmm." Lucy's bold fingers reached up toward his face and brushed back the hair that had fallen into his eyes. Of course she already knew he had eyes the most beautiful shade of green she'd ever seen a gentleman have, but she couldn't very well pass up this opportunity to study them, could she? They were an unusual shade of green, almost both light and dark at the same time. Overall, they appeared dark, but a light shade of dark. She frowned. That really wasn't an adequate way to describe them. She'd seen light green eyes before, so light they almost looked hazel in some light or blue in others. Seth had eyes that color. So had his father. She swallowed. Giles' were different. They were darker. But not so dark that it'd be easy to confuse them for brown at a distance. They were very distinctively green. Like an emerald.

She pursed her lips together, debating how she'd manage to mix such a color. First, brown and green, then she'd add white, she thought. She should turn back to the colors, but she couldn't. Not yet. She started. *Why not?* Unease came over her. She was attracted to him.

Pulling her hands away, she turned back to the paint. Of course she already knew she was attracted to him. But now there was no way she could deny it. Taking a deep breath, she mixed the colors in a fruitless effort to make the color of the eyes that held her captive today and likely always would, then began painting. Though she knew she shouldn't, she'd allow herself this one day to enjoy his presence and nearness and hoped it'd be enough to last a lifetime.

***

Giles idly picked at the hangnail on his thumb with his index finger. He could sit and watch Lucy paint all day. He practically already had and he enjoyed every blissful moment of seeing her delicate profile, complete with a slight smile that pulled at the corner of her lips. That smile, as small as it might be, was enough to make a man fall to his knees, try to move mountains, or do anything else she might ask of him.

Including wave off his butler no less than three times before he could announce that the midday meal had been served. Which is exactly what Giles had done.

As three o'clock neared, Lucy's painting was almost complete. Well, almost as complete as it could be. She'd mastered his image perfectly. Perfectly, that is, to him. He didn't think it was possible to care less that the image she'd painted teetered on the edge of being frightening—especially to those of a young age. He was far too distracted by the bright smile that filled her face and the tingling and burning sensation it set off inside him.

From the corner of his eye, he saw Tarley enter the room, presumably to inform him again that the midday meal was ready. If the grumbles of Seth's stomach were any indication, he'd better not turn the man away again.

"Give us but a moment," Giles said before taking a look at the portrait on the canvas. "You did well."

"Yes, he looks like he belongs in a fable, Mama," Seth commented, coming up behind them.

A crease formed between Lucy's bright blue eyes. "You think so?"

"Yes, ma'am. He makes the perfect villain with the long crooked nose, snarling lips and bulging eyes."

Giles opened his mouth to chastise the boy for mocking his mother's efforts when suddenly a peal of infectious laughter filled the room as Lucy clutched her stomach with one hand and covered her mouth with the other.

"I'm sorry," she choked out between giggles. "I—I—I—" She broke off in another wave of laughter. This time Giles was unable to hold back and joined her and Seth in their merriment.

"The only thing he's missing is a hairy wart on the end of his nose," a masculine voice said from the door.

Lucy's laughter halted instantly. She bounced off her seat, her knees hitting the bottom edge of the canvas as she did so. Paying no mind to the wet paint she'd just gotten on her dress, she faced the man who'd just spoken, the delicate column of her throat working convulsively.

"Sebastian." Giles took to his feet and impulsively reached for Lucy's hand. He gave her a reassuring squeeze. "I didn't expect to see you today."

"No, I guess not," Sebastian said, his lips twitching. "I received your note earlier and thought I'd come by to invite you to join us for dinner tonight."

"We haven't even had lunch yet," Seth informed him.

Sebastian chuckled. "You haven't? Then perhaps all three of you ought to come over to my house for dinner. Belle would enjoy some female companionship, I'd wager," he added with a pointed look at Lucy.

Lucy's delicate hand grew stiff in Giles' grasp. "I—I—We—" She licked her lips.

"Only need to arrive at six o'clock with nothing more than an appetite." He winked. "But if you insist I allow you to paint my portrait before dining with us, I shall order all the necessary materials brought to the drawing room so you and Belle can poke fun at me together." Then, without letting Lucy accept or reject his invitation, he slipped from the room.

"We must go," Lucy breathed as soon as the front door closed behind Sebastian.

"There's no argument from me on that score," Giles said. He

lifted an eyebrow toward Seth. "You?"

"No. I'd love to have dinner with whoever that was."

"Absolutely not," Lucy said, pulling her hand from Giles'. "You know what I meant. Seth, gather your things so we can go home. I think we've imposed upon Lord Norcourt long enough for one day."

Giles' throat constricted. What had he done wrong? "Lucy," he rasped, reaching for her.

She moved away.

"Don't go." He raked his hand through his thick hair and pulled. It did nothing to help him find the right words to stay. "We don't have to go to dinner with Sebastian and Isabelle, but you don't have to leave."

"Isabelle?" He wasn't entirely certain but it seemed that her voice faltered.

"Sebastian's wife. He calls her Belle, but her name is Isabelle." He closed his mouth with a snap. There was no need for him to prattle. Surely she had already made the connection.

"If your friend married Isabelle, then I certainly don't think it's wise we go."

He jammed his fisted hands into his pockets. "Why not?"

Chapter Twenty-Two

Why not? There were dozens of reasons she and Seth shouldn't go with Giles to his friends' house for dinner. The least of which being that it would be highly improper considering she and Giles were not wed. Her heart squeezed painfully, but it didn't make it any less true. She hadn't had any business spending the day with him even and less enjoying herself so much. Joining him at his friends' house for dinner made the impropriety of it all scores worse than it already was.

"Do be serious," Lucy said, forcing a laugh and unable to meet his eyes. "I'm the daughter of a servant who used to work for nobility, I have no place at a lord's dining table." *Unless seated there in the role of his mistress.* The sting of Sam's cruel words to her the day she'd informed him that she'd conceived sounded in her head, and she winced.

"Lucy?" Giles' warm hands framed her face, an amused expression on his own and a hint of laughter in his eyes. "I'm the only one around here allowed to woolgather."

A nervous burble of laughter lodged in her throat and she pulled back. "My apologies, but we need to be going."

He dropped his hands, his face falling simultaneously. "What have I done wrong?" His ragged tone tore at her heart.

"Nothing."

"Remember, Mama doesn't like the titled," Seth whispered, then added, "Not to worry, I do."

"Seth," Lucy practically hissed. If the floor were to suddenly open and swallow her at this exact moment, she wouldn't voice a word of protest.

"Thank you, Seth," Giles said, his tone impossible to decipher. "As for your mama—" his green eyes sought hers— "perhaps she might grow a fondness for one if she spent enough time in his presence."

Lucy's breath hitched at the implication of his words. He'd said something similar to that the other day when they were at the park. She'd done her best to ignore it then, but she couldn't ignore it now. Did Giles have a romantic interest in her or was he being inarticulate again? She moistened her lips, unsure what to say.

"Sebastian is my closest friend," he continued. "He's always been most kind to me—even before he knew I had a title. His wife, Isabelle or Lady Belgrave now, is just as genuine. They won't judge either of you for anything. They have no reason to."

Lucy nodded her head numbly. Here she thought he'd been expressing an interest for her to spend more time with him and he'd just been trying to persuade her to join him for dinner with his friends. She pushed away the sadness and disappointment that threatened to creep over her. "I really shouldn't," she protested. She gestured to her gown. It was still the best one she owned. "I'm really not dressed for such an occasion."

"Neither am I." He threw a glance over his shoulder. "Neither is Seth."

Despite herself, she smiled at his logic. "But you have something you can change into that would be appropriate, I do not." It wasn't a lie. She'd worn her favorite purple gown today, the cast off from Lord Kresson's daughter, and though the gowns his mother had given to her were nice, they weren't what most would consider dinner attire.

"I don't think they invited us so they could scrutinize your clothes," Giles said, his tone not giving anything away.

"All the same, they are your friends and they'd like to visit with you, not us."

"Not at all. I'm tedious." He traced one of his long, blunt-tipped fingers down the length of her nose at the pace of a feather floating from the sky. "You're not."

A hard, inexplicable knot formed in Lucy's throat, either from his words or gesture, she didn't know. "You're not tedious," she whispered. "You're anything but."

Something unnameable flashed across his face and Lucy wished she could take back the words. But it was too late, she'd just let on to how much she already thought of him "So will you join us tonight?"

"I can—"

He pressed his fingers to her lips, halting the rest of her protest. "I just heard an agreement. Didn't you, Seth?"

"Yes, I did, my lord."

Reluctantly, Lucy pushed Giles' fingers away from her lips. "That doesn't count. Besides, I'm serious, I cannot attend any dinner dressed like this."

"Are you saying that if you were wearing a different gown, you'd go?"

She narrowed her eyes on him. He had something in mind. But what, she didn't know. "I didn't say that."

"You didn't deny it, either," he murmured. He swallowed in a way that made his Adam's apple bob. He was nervous. And yet, seemed to be pressing forward.

Lucy's resolve crumbled to dust. For a reason she couldn't begin to comprehend, he genuinely wanted her to go with him to his friends' house. "No, I didn't," she agreed. "But I can't wear…"

"Dinner is not for—" he withdrew his timepiece and bit down on his bottom lip with his white teeth— "three-and-a-half hours. Surely we can find you a suitable gown in that amount of time."

Lucy would have argued at the impossibility, but couldn't bring herself to dash his hopes so cruelly. Instead, she flashed him her best smile and said, "If you can find a suitable gown in time, then I'd be delighted to go."

A sparkle lit in his green eyes that bespoke of all sorts of mischief. Mischief she didn't understand, but made her giddy nonetheless. "Seth, ring for Tarley."

A moment later the butler arrived.

"Tarley, have all of the chests retrieved from the attics and brought into the drawing room post haste."

"Yes, my lord." The butler bowed and left the room.

A sinking feeling settled in the pit of Lucy's stomach. "I don't mean to be rude—"

"Then don't be," Giles broke in. He wagged a playful finger at her. "You said you'd go if I found you suitable attire."

"Yes, I did." She idly picked at the cuff of her gown and twisted her lips. How did she tell him this without demeaning or belittling him? She took a deep breath. "None of those will fit right."

"With alterations they might."

A snort rent the air. Followed by a loud, echoing *pop* as Lucy's hand covered her mouth and nose when she realized it'd been her who'd made such a rude noise. "Forgive me," she murmured, removing her hand. Flames licked her face. "I appreciate your efforts, but there won't be enough time to make the alterations those gowns might need to fit me."

"I know."

"Then why are you having all the chests brought down?"

"To find something suitable."

She wanted to groan in frustration. He wasn't making any sense. She clutched her hands into her skirts and stepped aside so he could brush past her, Seth right behind him.

She followed.

Across the hall in the drawing room, a footman set a large chest on the floor, and turned to go back after another.

Giles lifted the lid of the chest and untied the ribbon that held the large cloth in place that wrapped the clothes to keep them fresh. He peeled back the blanket and frowned. The gown on top looked as if it had been made for royalty. It was a dark, shimmery purple with a vibrant gold trim around the bodice and cuffs with intricate needlework covering the bodice. "Not in here," he muttered, dropping the lid with a bang.

No, Lucy agreed in her mind, there was likely nothing in that box that would be fitting for her to wear. Ever.

The footman brought in another box and paused a moment to wipe his sweaty brow.

Giles scowled as he made quick work of picking through the next chest. He slammed the lid on that one and stood, just in time to make way for the footman. When the man put down his chest, he gripped him above the elbow and walked with him into the hall where they spoke in whispered tones.

"I suppose this means we're going back to the library," Seth stated flatly.

Lucy did her best to ignore the sadness in his voice. "Is it so bad to dine with me, then?" she teased.

"Not at all," Giles said from the door. He flashed her a smile. "Can you come here a moment."

Hesitantly, she crossed the threshold and came to an abrupt stop when she nearly collided with a maid. "Yes?"

"Millie here will help with your hair and anything else you require."

Lucy blinked at him. "Pardon?"

"I know I'm a chambermaid, but I used to do my sister's hair when we were girls," Millie said, her round, red face beaming with pride.

"It's not that," Lucy assured the greying woman. "I don't have a gown."

Giles seemed to have developed a sudden deafness because he stepped past her as if he hadn't heard her and went back to the trunks. He knelt down and fiddled with the lock of the next one and made a flicking gesture with his free hand.

"This way, ma'am," Millie clucked.

Lucy should protest. This had gone far enough. It wasn't possible for him to find her a suitable dress in the under three hours they had left before the dinner was to start. Instead, she found herself being led up the stairs to the sparse bedroom she'd occupied only a few weeks before.

A sense of warmth came over her when she walked inside. She couldn't say why she liked being in the room, but she did and the thought unsettled her.

"It looks like you only got a little paint on the front of your gown," Millie commented, pointing at the front of her purple skirts.

Lucy looked down and gasped. How had that gotten there? She lifted her skirt and tried to wipe it off. But it was dry. Changing tactics, she used her thumbnail to try to pick it off.

"Don't fuss with it," Millie said, pulling at her skirt. "Lord Norcourt stains his clothes with paint all the time. I'll just take this down to the kitchens to scrub the stain while you bathe."

"Bathe?"

"It won't be a full bath, I'm afraid," she confessed, blushing. "It'd take too long to heat up enough buckets, so you'll just have to use a basin. I hope that's all right."

No. It wasn't all right. It wasn't all right at all. It was nonsense. This whole dinner invitation and expectation that she could attend with him was nonsense. "Thank you, but I really don't see—"

"I know." Millie's soft voice brought her up short. "Sometimes Lord Norcourt doesn't make sense, and sometimes he does," she allowed. "I've only been in his employ a short time—about a month or so, to be honest—but it's been long enough to learn two things about him. First, he's odd. I'm sorry to say it, and I know I'd get sacked if anyone else heard me say it, but it doesn't make it any less true. He's odd and his brain..." She shrugged. "Well, it works differently than others, I've noticed."

Lucy had noticed that, too. Not that it was a bad thing, it wasn't. Not at all. It just made it hard to know what to say or do sometimes. "The second thing?"

Millie chuckled. "That fella always has a plan. No matter how strange, obvious, or unimaginable by anyone else it might be, he always has a plan. Always. I believe this trait is actually part of the first, but you can't fight him, you just have to trust him."

Lucy blinked at the older woman. If she didn't know any better she might think this lady had formed an affection for Giles. Not a romantic one, mind you. It was more a motherly type of affection. "All right. I'll trust him."

***

Giles had a suspicion that she didn't think it would be possible for him to find her adequate attire. But perhaps that was only because she didn't know how badly he wanted to spend more time with her—selfish ingrate that he was. He stiffened and lowered his lashes to stare down at the chest that had just been placed at his feet. She was Simon's lady. He had no right to coerce her into going to dinner with him. Her spending the day with him was far more than he could have ever asked for. But oh how he wanted just a little more time with her and Seth.

Falling to his knees, he flipped open the top on the fifth chest that had been brought down. Who knew his mother had packed away so many of her gowns and those of her mother and the Lady Norcourt before her. One thing was certain, if he ever married, his wife wouldn't lack for gowns if any of these ever came back into fashion. Even if they didn't, surely they could be altered to fit if she desired it.

He released a breath. *His wife?* Likely he'd never have one of those. He tightened his grip on the lid of the chest and mindlessly untied the chord. Even if his father's will demanded he marry or be disinherited, he wouldn't. He couldn't possibly imagine marrying anyone but Lucy. An iron weight lowered onto his chest. It wasn't fair to her or him or even Simon for him to think of her that way. He freed the knot in the string and then pulled the blankets apart.

"I don't think these will work, either, my lord," Seth said on a sigh. "They're not even gowns."

Giles grinned with excitement. "I know." He released his hold on the lid of the chest and used both hands to sort the clothing. Memories of when he'd last seen them filled his mind. He might have been the simple son of a baron, but he was still of nobility and on the occasion that the Sisters would take the boys to a village, he was always to be dressed in finery. He hated it. Rather than making him feel important, it made him more uncomfortable. As if everyone was staring at him and laughing at his plight. He despised the clothes and refused to wear them when not forced to. As he outgrew them, they'd been returned to London. He hadn't cared one way or the other what had happened to them at the time, but they'd be perfect for Seth.

Giles withdrew a white shirt, green coat, yellow waistcoat, dove trousers and even a pair of black shoes with a hideous silver buckle across the top and tossed them into a pile at his feet. "This is it. You can take these chests back up, now," he said to the footman who'd just come back into the room. "Take these clothes to the kitchen and see if Franks can work some of the wrinkles out, then have him bring them up to my room."

"Yes, my lord."

"Seth?"

"My lord?"

"I thought I heard you call me Giles earlier."

"I did."

"Good, then I shouldn't have to ask you to do it again." He crossed his arms over his chest and cocked his head to the side. "How old did you say you were again?"

"Eleven."

"Hmm." Giles leaned forward and made a show of squinting as he assessed Seth's face.

"What are you doing?"

"Counting the hairs."

Seth's hand flew to his face. "What hair?"

"Those hairs." Giles tapped Seth's hairless jaw an inch away from his ear then straightened. "Well, boy, it looks like you might be in need of a shave."

Chapter Twenty-Three

Lucy dunked the cloth to the basin, lifted it and stilled. Was that *laughter* she heard from next door. Setting the cloth back into the bowl, she padded over to the connecting door and pressed her ear against it. A smile pulled at her lips. She'd been correct. It had been laughter, loud, rich masculine laughter. Both Seth *and* Giles seemed to be laughing. Her heart warmed. What could possibly be so humorous?

She pressed her ear harder against the door, but it did no good. She wondered if it'd be possible to open the door a crack and peek in. She bit her lip. She was in her chemise and most definitely didn't wish for them to see her thus; likely they were in a similar state of undress and wouldn't want her to see them, either.

What if she peeked just a little? She pressed her forehead against the door. *Peek a little?* Weren't those the same thing? Shaking off the thought, she pressed her palms to the door and willed herself to push away. But when another round of laughter filled the air, she couldn't move.

With a promise to herself that she'd try to only look at their faces and if she saw anything, she oughtn't, she'd immediately close the door, she gripped the doorknob and slowly twisted it. She slowly eased the door open a crack and peered in with one eye.

Her eye landed instantly on the pair. Giles stood with his back to her, and Seth faced him. He was rubbing his face. She squinted. They both were. She couldn't make out why though. She opened the door just a fraction more to give her a better view. Her heart slammed in her chest. *Shaving lotion.* Closing her eyes, she shut the door. Seth was too young to need to be concerned with shaving for a few more years. But that mattered very little. Giles had made him feel special and important and if she wasn't already convinced of it, there was no denying it now, she was in love with Giles.

"Is something wrong, ma'am?"

She whipped around to face an inquisitive Millie, blushing. "No." She licked her lips. "I was just…er…" She broke off and plucked at her chemise. "Is my dress done?'

"Almost. I got the stain out easy 'nough. Now it needs to dry." She walked over to the vanity and removed a silver brush from her apron. "Now, about yer hair…"

A half hour later Lucy was in need of a tonic for a headache. Her hair looked nice though. All pinned up on top of her head in a tight bun with two circles of curls pinned around it. Millie wasn't the gentlest, but she was talented.

"Wait here and I'll be back with yer gown."

Lucy wouldn't argue with that. There wasn't anywhere else she could go clad in only a chemise. A few minutes later Millie returned with the same gown she'd been wearing for over a week. "I take it he didn't have any other gown?"

A strange look came over Millie's face. "No. You can wear this one."

No, she couldn't. It was too plain to wear even for a simple dinner. She wasn't overly familiar with nobility, but she did remember the lady referring to the gown as a morning gown when she'd purchased it. "I don't think—"

Millie cleared her throat. "Remember what I said earlier?"

Right. Giles always had a plan. Even if it seemed impossible to others. She sighed. Even if she had to wear this gown, she couldn't refuse to go now, both Giles and Seth were anxious to attend. "All right."

"Very good," Millie chirped.

Careful not to muss a single hair and chance Millie insisting she fix it, Lucy put on her gown while Millie went to fetch something else.

She fastened the last button and slid her feet into her slippers, taking a moment to appraise herself.

"Lovely."

Tingles ran up her spine. "Lord Norcourt." It was only by a miracle that she'd remembered to address him so formally.

Giles walked up behind her and looked at her in the mirror.

Not to be denied the same privilege, she took a moment to look him over, too. Clean shaven, dark blue jacket over a red waistcoat and white shirt, his cravat was tied into a perfect mathematical knot with an emerald stickpin that was a perfect complement to his eyes in the middle.

She caught his eye in the mirror and blushed. "Is it time to go?"

"Not yet." He trailed his fingertips down the slope of her neck, then pulled them back when he reached her collar bone, his face turning crimson. "I've something for you."

She moved to face him. "Oh, no, I cannot accept anything."

"That's good. This isn't mine to give. It's borrowed." He lifted his right hand and there resting on his open palm was a beautiful silver butterfly brooch.

Lucy's eyes widened at the sight of all those beautiful rubies and emeralds encrusted in the outlines of the wings. If she wasn't mistaken a solid piece of pale green jade was the body. "That's beautiful," she breathed. "But I cannot wear it."

"Yes, you can."

She took a step back. "No. I can't."

He blinked his eyes twice. "Why not?"

"It's too nice."

"It is nice," he agreed. He flipped it over and unfastened it. "But not too nice. Here. You'd better put it on yourself or I'll prick you."

Hesitantly, she took the brooch from him and turned to the mirror to put it on. When she was finished, she turned around to see him holding out a purple shawl.

"It's not the same hue, but it should match nicely," he murmured, carrying it toward her. He wrapped it around her and winked. "I told you that you'd have suitable attire for tonight."

"Indeed you did."

And not only had he seen to her attire, but her prince disguised as a baron had seen to Seth's as well. Swathed in sharply pressed fabrics of green, yellow and dove (and a freshly shaven face, of course), he cut a dashing figure himself. Lucy's heart squeezed as she took him in and it was all she could do not to kiss Giles for the kindness he'd shown to both her and her son.

***

Sebastian didn't live far from him and usually he walked, but he'd insisted on the carriage tonight for Lucy's privacy. Not that it'd matter so much. Nobody knew who she was and only a fool would be daring enough to call upon either Sebastian or Giles to inquire about her identity.

Giles shoved his hands into his pockets to keep from reaching for one of Lucy's as they climbed the steps to Sebastian's townhouse. He'd tried to reassure her that she'd have a good time tonight. Openly touching her might put her back on edge rather than reassure her. He didn't want that.

"Can I bang the knocker?" Seth asked.

Giles' mind went back to the incessant knocking Seth had rendered on his door the first time he'd come over. "Twice."

Seth immediately gave the brass knocker two hearty *bangs*.

Goosey, Sebastian's butler greeted them stiffly. Goosey didn't think too highly of Giles as it was, he could only imagine what the man must think now. No matter. He'd never put much stock in the opinions of others. Usually, they were unkind where he was concerned so he found no reason to care.

The butler showed them to the drawing room and paused to ask Lucy for her name.

She froze. "I can't," she whispered.

Goosey remained impassive for a moment then lifted a haughty brow. "And what is your name, young man."

Giles lifted a hand toward the butler. "Give us a moment."

Pursing his lips, the man took a step back.

"Lucy?" Giles searched her pale face. "What's wrong?"

"This." She swallowed visibly. "I shouldn't be here."

Giles knew that feeling better than she might think. He reached for her hand and led her a few feet down the hall so they could whisper in privacy. "I'm sorry," he said. "I shouldn't have forced you to come." He clenched his fists. "I just wanted—" He broke off, unable to tell her how he felt without making a fool of himself.

"What?" Her silky tone was like a balm to a fresh cut. "What is it you wanted, Giles?"

Blood pounded in his ears at hearing his name on her lips and all logic and restraint went with it. He instinctively framed her face with his hands. "You."

"Me?"

Gulping down his unease, he nodded. "You. I want you."

She lowered her lashes and lifted her trembling fingers to his wrists. "I can't."

"I know," he admitted though it broke his heart to do so. She was Simon's. Not his. He released a shaky breath and lowered his hands. "I'll take you home."

***

Lucy felt like such a fool. She should have never allowed herself to be talked into coming here. She wasn't of the same class as Giles. He might not be the kind to make a display of his money or power, but he was still a lord and she was still but a poor, fallen commoner. Their worlds were very far apart.

"Thank you. I appreciate it." She reached for him. "I—I didn't mean to make a fool of you by taking me here only to leave this way." She didn't know why she wanted to assure him of that, but she did.

He pulled away and straightened, his movements jerky and uneven. "It's all right." The hurt in his voice was unmistakable. "Let's tell Seth and—" He broke off, his green eyes widening.

Lucy whirled around to see what he was looking at and her heart plummeted. "Did he?" she choked, unable to finish her question.

Giles nodded once. "I didn't see him do it, but I don't know where else he'd be."

Just then, Lord Belgrave poked his head out of the drawing room. "Do the two of you plan to join us or will Belle and I have the privilege of dining with this fascinating young man alone?"

Lucy could have dissolved on the spot. Who knew what Seth had said to Lord and Lady Belgrave to get him styled as "fascinating"? Frankly, she wasn't sure she wanted to know.

"We're not staying," Giles said.

Lord Belgrave's face gave nothing away. "I mean no disrespect, I'm sure he's a good lad, but I don't think there is much more for the three of us to discuss. As it is, he just finished telling us all about how you showed him how to attend his *toilette*."

A giggle borne of equal parts nervousness, discomfort, and mortification escaped Lucy's lips.

"Sebastian, don't be so dismissive. You could use a lesson or two on the matter," a petite red-haired, green-eyed lady teased, joining Lord Belgrave in the threshold of the drawing room and completing Lucy's mortification. Smiling, the lady, who Lucy could only presume was Lady Belgrave or Isabelle as everyone else called her, scooted past her husband. "Are we already walking to dinner?"

"No, Giles thought to make a quick escape and might have had I not come to check on him," Lord Belgrave said playfully.

Lady Belgrave's eyes softened and she shifted her gaze between Lucy and Giles as if she was trying to puzzle out the reason. Finally, she settled on Lucy. "This is all most improper, isn't it?" She clasped her hands together. "Why, we haven't even been properly introduced. I mentioned to my husband that little fact might pose a large problem with you wishing to join us, but he didn't seem to think so." She shook her head and sighed. "He didn't think so, of course. But then again—" she brushed her gloved fingertip over her lips and dropped her voice to a loud whisper— "he also thinks it's perfectly acceptable behavior to enter rooms through the windows rather than using doors."

Another burble of laughter escaped Lucy's lips, then yet another when her husband added, "And did you expect me to use the door in the dead of night and chance being seen? We'd have been forced to marry in a trice."

"Apparently, we already were," Lady Belgrave parried, winking at Lucy. "Only I didn't know it."

Her husband placed his hand on the small of her back. "You do now and so does the rest of London."

A slight blush Lucy couldn't place stained Lady Belgrave's cheeks. She cleared her throat. "Well, now that my scandals have been aired, shall we have a proper introduction then go to dinner?"

Giles caught Lucy's eye, a silent question in his. "I'd be honored to," she said with as much bravado as she could muster.

The meal was a grand affair—at least to Lucy—with six courses, including custard for dessert. Thankfully, Seth was allowed to dine with them. If he hadn't been, it might have been a very uncomfortable dinner for all as Lucy struggled to keep her mind on anything other than the broad form next to her and the excitement he created by just being in the room.

When the meal was over, the men invited Seth to join them in Lord Belgrave's study for whatever it is that men did in there while Lucy and Lady Belgrave went to the drawing room.

"I wanted to apologize again for Sebastian's tricks this afternoon. He means well, but sometimes I think he was on the continent too long to know what proper manners are."

"It's partly my own doing," Lucy admitted. "If I hadn't been over at Lord Norcourt's house today, he wouldn't have seen me and expected that I was his mistress." Though why his friend would want to invite his friend and his mistress over to dine, she'd never understand.

"Is that what you think?" Lady Belgrave burst out laughingly. She shook her head. "Sebastian thought no such thing. As far as I know, Giles has never had a mistress."

"He hasn't?" The words were past her lips before she realized it.

"I don't think so." Lady Belgrave popped the back of her slipper off her heel and shook her foot a little to each side. "I don't know him well, mind you. We only met less than two months ago actually, but from what Sebastian has said about the more than five years they toured the continent together, I don't think he has."

"They toured the continent together for more than *five years*?"

"I suppose there was a lot to see," Lady Belgrave said with a shrug. She pushed her foot back into her slipper. "Sebastian never told me why Giles was touring for so long, likely because he doesn't know." She snorted. "He says he didn't even know that Giles had a title until the night Mrs. Appleton, the former Lady Norcourt, hosted a dinner party."

"Do you mind if I ask why your husband toured for so long?" Lucy asked just to make conversation and stave off the impending uncomfortable silence that was threatening to engulf them at any second.

"I'll be glad to tell you, but you owe me an answer in return," she said with a grin. Then, before Lucy could retract her question, Lady Belgrave continued. "Surely you've read in the scandal sheets about the young lady of common birth who trapped a lord into marriage by posing as her sister during their assignation? I am that young lady and my husband was the lord. The scandal sheets embellished the story a little, but the gist of it is accurate enough. On our return from Scotland, our carriage was in an accident that left me abed for a long while, and spurred by some bullying by both of our fathers, he fled the country."

"Your father must be quite terrifying to make a man flee so long," Lucy murmured, tamping down a pang of jealousy. Her father hadn't even tried to confront or appeal to the man who'd done Lucy wrong. He'd condemned her for her own stupidity and barely spoke to her again.

Lady Belgrave smiled ruefully. "Actually, he is. But I think there was more to it than that. Have you ever done something wrong, and you want to make it right, but so much time has passed that you just don't know where to begin to make amends? That's the real reason Sebastian took so long to return. He didn't know where to start to repair what he'd broken."

"What brought him back?"

"I came to London to find a new husband. Only I couldn't marry since he'd never signed the papers. My turn."

Lucy's palms grew damp in a second's time. Lady Belgrave might be a commoner with a few scandals attached to her name, but none were as damning as Lucy's.

"How do you know Giles?"

The question caught her unawares. She thought Lady Belgrave

might ask about Seth's parentage, not how she knew Giles. Lucy eyed her askance. Why was Lady Belgrave so interested? Did *she* think Lucy was Giles' mistress? Suddenly uncomfortable, she quickly explained about Simon's injuries and sending for Giles.

"Simon *asked* you to send for Giles?" Lady Belgrave said, her mouth slightly agape.

"He is his brother," Lucy supplied. She hoped that didn't sound nearly as unkind to Lady Belgrave's ears as it had to her own.

Lady Belgrave nodded slowly, her jaw still unhinged. "I'm just surprised that's all." She lifted her hand to her hair and idly twisted a fallen lock around her fingers. "I knew Giles had left the house party the day after Simon and Sebastian did, but nobody knew why he left." She released her hair. "I expected it to be because his mother was driving him mad, not that they'd made amends and were suddenly claiming a relation."

So much of her last statement echoed Lucy's perceptions of Giles and his family. Giles and his mother did have a stilted relationship, but it was far more loving than the one he had with Simon. The two didn't hardly utter a word between them, and looked at the other even less. She bit her lip. Should she ask Lady Belgrave what she knew about this? It was obvious she knew something of the pair. She might also know why Giles was wont to evade his mother, which presumably was the reason Lady Belgrave thought she'd drive Giles to leave the party early.

Loud footfalls coming down the hall ended her chance to ask. Which was probably for the best.

"Ladies," Lord Belgrave greeted with an overdone yawn and a wink in Lucy's direction.

"Ready to go?" Giles asked without ceremony.

Lucy and Lady Belgrave exchanged a look. "Of course," Lucy said, standing.

Lord and Lady Belgrave walked them to the door where Giles' carriage was already waiting for them. With a quick goodbye and an expression of gratitude for the meal, Lucy hurried to Giles' carriage. It was silly, she knew, for it was too dark outside for anyone to see and if someone did, they'd never recognize her. Still, deep inside, she felt like a fraud for attending such a dinner with Giles and his friends tonight. Pushing away the thought, she made herself comfortable inside the carriage.

Seth climbed in next and automatically found a seat across from her. Then Giles climbed up and sat next to her, his body touching hers from her shoulder to her knee.

The carriage lurched forward and Giles struck a match. He lit the sconce then blew out the match, a companionable silence engulfing them all.

In the low light, she saw a flash of silver in Seth's hand. She strained to see. "Seth, is that a flask?"

"Yes, ma'am."

"And why do you have it?"

"It's for drinking."

"Yes, I know that." She fought to keep her voice even. "But why do you have one?"

"To drink from."

Lucy ground her teeth, irritation swelling in her chest. Letting him shave his nonexistent beard was one thing, allowing him to drink whiskey was quite another. "Did you drink from that?"

"The whole thing," he said proudly.

On the verge of hysteria, she looked at Giles. "You let him drink that whole thing."

He nodded slowly then leaned close to her. "Don't tell him, but I filled it with lemonade."

His words took all the anger right from her being, the air from her lungs, and the resistance of him from her marrow and with nothing holding her back she did the one thing she'd never thought she'd do: she kissed him.

Chapter Twenty-Four

Giles went rigid. In every way possible. Lucy was kissing him. It wasn't one of those long, lippy kisses he'd witnessed while walking down a back alley in Paris. In fact, it wasn't even on his lips, but rather on his cheek. His cheek that now burned as if she'd touched it with a branding iron.

Her hand found his and she gave him a gentle squeeze. "Thank you."

He didn't know what she was thanking him for, but whatever it was, he'd have to do it again if it made her react this way.

The carriage bounced, jarring him from his trance. "Can I come inside?"

Lucy's hand stiffened briefly in his, then relaxed. "You wish to talk to me?"

"Yes, please." He squeezed her hand, a memory of the night he'd walked in on her being attacked flashed in his mind. "Only to talk. Don't be afraid of me."

"I'm not."

He held her hand until they reached the library then tried to help her down. He'd had no problem helping her in and out of the carriage before, but this time it was different. In his study, Sebastian had encouraged Giles to tell Lucy exactly how he felt about her. He'd even claimed that he suspected she might feel the same. If she didn't, she wouldn't have spent the day with him or agreed to go to his friends' for dinner—even if she'd tried to leave as soon as they arrived. Her kissing him could only be further proof. Now, he just needed to find some way to put his feelings for her into the right words.

Lucy handed Seth the keys and he ran inside, clutching tightly to the trinket Sebastian had allowed him to keep. Giles opened the door for Lucy and followed her inside.

"Thank you for today," she said, lighting the candles in the candelabra.

"You're welcome." He raked his hand through his hair and took a deep, calming breath. Words swirled in his head. "What about tonight?" He cringed. That wasn't what he'd wanted to say to her.

"You mean having dinner with your friends?" She slid the shawl off her shoulders and started to fold it. "It was enjoyable, too."

"Enjoyable."

Her throat worked. "They were very kind to me."

Something was off. But what could it be? He racked his brain. She'd been uncomfortable when they'd first arrived, but she'd seemed fine at dinner. In the carriage she'd seemed fine, too. More than fine, even. Otherwise she wouldn't have been so intimate with him. Had something happened when he'd been away from her? Isabelle had been nothing but kind to him. He couldn't fathom her being cold to Lucy. "Was Isabelle?"

She made the last fold on the shawl, then removed the brooch and handed them both back to him. "Of course she was. We had a lovely discussion. It's easy to see why Simon was so upset about losing her."

Her words were the equivalent of a fist to the gut. Had she been thinking of Simon the entire time they'd been there? Paralyzing embarrassment overcame him, rooting him to the floor. Around him, the room spun. Lucy said something, but he couldn't make it out. He was a fool. Fire burned in his gut ten times stronger than it had when he was mocked as a boy. He had to leave. Go home. Hide. If only his bloody legs hadn't turned to lead. He commanded his leg to move and it did. And then his knee buckled and he dropped to the floor.

Or would have if not for Lucy's arms wrapping around his midsection, holding him up.

"Easy," she whispered, easing him onto a nearby stool.

He could feel her soft chest pushing against his and almost groaned in aggravation. It wasn't fair to have such a strong attraction to her. "Thank you," he grunted, pulling back from her.

"Are you all right? Do you need some water?"

"I'm fine." He stood and was greeted by her palm meeting his chest. "I need to go home," he mumbled, encircling her wrist with his fingers and trying to push her arm away as gently as he could.

She didn't budge. "No."

"No?"

"No. You said you wanted to talk to me. Surely it wasn't to ask me what I talked to Lady Belgrave about."

"It doesn't matter."

"I think it does." She lowered her hand from his chest and sighed. "Even if it's not that significant, I think you need to tell me what I said just a moment ago to upset you and make you wish to leave so quickly."

"I'm not upset."

She quirked a brow at him. "You have the same expression on your face as you did before you left my cottage in Shrewsbury without breakfast."

He bridled. She must think him a petulant child. "I was embarrassed."

"Embarrassed? Whatever for?"

She wouldn't understand and there was no way he could explain it to her without making it worse. "I need to—"

She pressed her lips to his. "Kiss me," she murmured against his mouth.

Yes, he needed to kiss her.

And he did.

At first, he merely brushed his lips over hers. Then again. Risking her reaction and his heart, he cupped her face and moved his lips over the top of hers, parting his and surrounding hers. Her lips were soft against his. Smaller and gentle. He liked the feel of her lips against his. Perhaps a little too much. He pulled back, flushing.

If she noticed his erection, she didn't let on.

"Was there something you wanted to say?"

"I don't think Simon will like it that I kissed you."

"No," she agreed. "He probably won't, but I don't plan to tell him."

Giles stood from where he sat on the stool and took an unsure step back. "I shouldn't have."

"I kissed you first," she reminded him.

"I know, but if you're to marry Simon—"

Her brow puckered. "Who said I was going to marry Simon?"

"Seth. That's why he comes to my house. So you and Simon can go to the park or ride horses or go on picnics and such together."

"I haven't done any of that with Simon. I went with him once to a museum, that was it."

"It was?"

She nodded. "When he came to see me after the first time, I declined his offer to take me to the park and told him that we didn't suit."

"You did? You don't?" He had no idea which of those questions he wanted answered more, but was pleasantly surprised when Lucy wrapped her arms around his neck and brought his head down toward her as she came up on her toes.

"I did," she murmured, brushing her lips over his. "And no, we don't," she murmured again, kissing him once again.

Elation that she wasn't in love with his brother as he'd feared shot through him and he placed his hands on her cheeks and kissed her back. Full and thorough this time. Taking time to explore her lips with his.

"I like kissing you," he blurted when their kiss ended.

She ran the back of her finger across his cheek. "I like kissing you, too."

His heart slammed against his ribs. "You do?"

"I do."

"I'd like to do more than kiss," he admitted. He was certain she'd said something akin to, "I can tell," in response, but didn't want to ruin the moment by asking. "Now, isn't the time though." It took almost all of the strength he possessed to say that, then the last ounce to step back and separate them.

"No, it's not," she agreed, biting her lip. "Giles, I can't..." She cleared her throat. "I can't be your mistress."

"I never asked you to," he choked out.

"I know you didn't. But I just wanted to let you know. I can't. I—I made a mistake in the past and it's affected my entire life." She closed her eyes. "And Seth's."

His hand found hers and he gave her a gentle tug in the direction of the settee his mother had set out for the comfort of her patrons. He waited for her to sit down, then he joined her. "What happened?" he asked, interlacing their fingers.

"Not a lot. He talked of marriage and even promised he'd formally ask my father. I believed him and allowed him liberties, but he never asked."

"What did he say about Seth?"

"That I needed to find a new post. He had no wish to glimpse the bastard." The hitch in her voice tore at his heart.

He brushed a kiss above her brow. "I'm sorry."

"Don't be. I was the one foolish enough to trust him when I knew I shouldn't. Unfortunately, I was the only one to suffer the consequences."

"He never relented?"

"No. His brother did though. Before I'd gotten in so far with Seth's father, his younger brother had asked if I'd marry him since he was soon to be a vicar and thought a wife would be useful, and well, because he'd always loved me. And yes, those were his exact words. Anyway, I'd refused in favor of his brother who I was led to believe loved me in a different way. The real way, the *right* way, not just as a friend the way I believe Paul loved me.

"After I realized I'd been fooled and understood the extent of the damage I'd done to myself I panicked and in a moment of desperation, I begged Paul to take me back." She released his hand and buried her face in her palms. A moment later she dropped her hands to her lap and continued. "He refused—which was for the best, but for several years he showed me a greater kindness than I deserved by sending me funds and gifts for Seth."

"Did he have expectations?"

She released a laugh that held no humor. "No."

"Then why did he stop?"

"I asked him to. Remember the other day when I mentioned the lady who taught Seth to read with propriety books? She was his wife. Between Seth's growing *tendre* for her, the rumors that circulated around the town that suggested her husband was Seth's father, and Seth's own curiosity, I realized I couldn't stay there and I certainly couldn't allow Paul to keep helping me. That's how I ended up in Shrewsbury." She let out a deep exhalation. "I'm sorry, that was far more than you asked about."

"I'm glad you told me." And he was.

"Giles?"

He loved the way his name sounded on her lips. "Yes?"

"It's been a while since we arrived. You should probably go."

Giles pulled out his pocket watch. They'd been talking—and kissing—for more than an hour. "Did you mean what you said earlier?"

"About?"

He flushed. "Kissing me."

Without warning, she leaned in and kissed him yet again. "What do you think?"

That I love you. He swallowed. Hard. "Yes," he rasped.

"You're right," she said, kissing him again. "But you need to go."

"Right." He gained his feet and helped her up. "I meant what I said earlier, too."

"That you like to kiss me?"

"That, too." He clasped her hands in his. "That you trusted me enough to tell me your past." He brought their hands up to his lips and kissed her knuckles. "I will not ask you for such liberties before marriage."

"I know."

Chapter Twenty-Five

It had been three days since Lucy had spent the day with Giles and she secretly hoped he'd invite her to do the same again tomorrow, her next day off. Both Friday and Saturday, she'd allowed Seth to leave at one o'clock and spend the afternoon with Giles as long as Giles didn't have anything else he needed to accomplish.

Both days, she'd taken it upon herself to go collect her son when she finished with work and both days, Giles had invited her in and stolen a kiss from her in the entryway of his townhouse.

She loved those moments with him, even if the whole encounter only lasted a few moments. It was five moments of bliss she'd gotten to enjoy in two days and with any luck she'd have a similar moment of bliss in a mere—she glanced at the clock—eight hours. She sighed and turned her attention back to the stack of books that had been turned in and needed to be put away.

Around her, Mrs. Appleton hummed as she acted as if she were putting away books when really she was just moving them from one place to another, probably without even looking at the titles. She was clearly distracted. And excited. She'd been in this very same cheery mood for several days now. Whatever had happened to Mrs. Appleton during her last day off had to have been just as thrilling to her as spending so much time with Giles was to Lucy.

Shaking her head at whatever strange event had transpired that made Mrs. Appleton so excited, Lucy went about her business.

A loud hissing sound broke into her thoughts. She turned around and frowned. "Not yet," she whispered to Seth.

He slumped his shoulders and went back to the corner where he'd left his newspaper—a habit she could only thank Giles for instilling in her son. Never before had her son had an active interest in reading the newspaper, but ever since last Tuesday, he'd become enthralled. At first she'd assumed he was just looking for something to do—in the form of finding trouble. But now that he could freely admit to sneaking away to Giles' house when she wasn't around, he'd informed her that reading the newspaper was a gentlemanly pursuit and since neither she nor Giles would take him to White's, he'd read his paper in the corner and pretended he was at his club.

The door to the library creaked open. "I'll be with you in just a moment," she called to their guest.

"No need, I know where to look for what I came for," said a familiar voice. Simon.

He walked over and greeted Seth by pressing his finger to his lips and slipping the boy what appeared to be a handful of some sort of candy, then came to Lucy. Truly, he wasn't a bad sort. Just not *her* sort. She couldn't explain it. He was kind enough, and seemed to be genuine. But there was something missing. She didn't feel the same excitement at the thought of seeing him or kissing him that she did with Giles and if she didn't know any better, she'd assume the same was true for him. It would seem that he wasn't truly past Isabelle and perhaps that was why he didn't seem to have excitement or evoke it.

Overall, he'd taken her reasons for not wishing to continue a courtship with him well enough.

"Woolgathering again?" he teased, jarring Lucy from her thoughts.

She pushed the three books in her hands to their spot on the shelf then turned back to the stack of books she'd piled up on the table. "Just trying to place what's happened to your mother," she said, hoping to keep the subject off her.

Simon looked over at his mother and shook his head ruefully, a small smile playing across his lips. "Can I trust you with a secret?"

"Of course." She placed her elbows on the table and leaned forward to rest her chin on her hands.

He matched her stance to where he was facing her and whispered, "It's Giles."

Chills ran up Lucy's spine. What did he know? More importantly, what did Giles' mother know? "What's Giles?" she asked, straining to keep her voice level.

"It appears he's found a lady who has struck his fancy," Simon said, waggling his eyebrows at her.

A small, strangled *squeak* emerged from her lips.

"That was my response, too," Simon quipped, his green eyes dancing with what appeared to be good-natured humor. He straightened and nodded toward his mother as she passed by them. "Nobody knows who she is, though."

"Then how do you know she exists?" Not that she wanted to cast doubt on Giles' ability to find a lady who "struck his fancy", as Simon put it. But neither did she think it would be for the best for his entire family to know it was her. Perhaps she'd better stop going to his house to retrieve Seth. Which also meant she should probably stop allowing Seth to go.

"You're about as distracted as she is," Simon commented, making Lucy blush. Had he puzzled it out? "Anyway, a few nights back, Giles sent a note to Mother requesting to borrow her best shawl and brooch—" he lifted his brows and dropped his voice— "and apparently these items have yet to be returned."

"Because of this your mother thinks he gave them to a young lady he's interested in?" She'd wondered whom he'd borrowed the shawl and brooch from. She'd even considered that he'd found them in one of those chests and didn't want her to feel bad for wearing them.

"Indeed she does, but I'm not quite so convinced."

"Well, you can take yourself and all of your negativity right back out the same way you came in," Mrs. Appleton scolded playfully. "I think it's wonderful he's found someone."

"I'm sure you do—especially since this attempt only required you to send him your best brooch and shawl, not request a favor of a friend to host a house party swarming with debutantes for him to pick from," Simon muttered, not unkindly.

Mrs. Appleton frowned. "Ophelia invited someone for you, too."

"Yes, one lady. And she still had a husband."

"To be fair to her, she didn't know that," Mrs. Appleton said softly when an uncomfortable silence had overtaken them.

"It doesn't matter," Simon said with a flick of his wrist.

Lucy's gaze shot to him. A few weeks ago, it seemed he was still smarting over what had happened between him and Isabelle and now he seemed so dismissive. Why? What had changed? Actually, it was best she didn't know.

"All I was trying to say is that you shouldn't be so sure he's found a lady just because he asked to borrow your items, Mother," Simon continued.

"I'd like to think so," Mrs. Appleton said with a sniff. "And if not, then at least he's warming up to me if he asked for my help." She clucked her tongue. "But I still think he's found a young lady."

"Think so all you'd like, but I seem to remember that he could hardly get a young lady to sit with him at a meal unless she was foisted on him by you or Lady Cosgrove."

Mrs. Appleton pursed her lips and stared at her son. "You're jealous."

"Am not," he said quickly. Too quickly. He *was* jealous.

Lucy could understand that and might have offered him some sort of reassuring gesture if she weren't afraid he'd take it as encouragement to pursue her again.

"I just think that you should wait until you know all the facts," Simon said.

"All what facts? An announcement in the paper?" At Simon's grimace, Mrs. Appleton offered an apology. Lucy had heard rumor that while Giles had told Simon the truth of Sebastian's and Isabelle's marriage, the only confirmation Simon had received had come in the form of an announcement in the newspaper that Lord and Lady Belgrave had reconciled. "The fact remains," Mrs. Appleton went on. "He has to have someone special or he wouldn't have asked *me* for help in the way of *my* finest."

She had a point. Giles and his mother weren't close by anyone's standards and if he'd asked to borrow something from her, he had to have had a reason. Lucy's heart squeezed in both a good way and a terrible way at the same time. Giles truly cared for her and had for a while otherwise he wouldn't have done that. But was it too much? Were his feelings too deep for her? Was she being fair to him by kissing him and accepting his kisses in return?

No. She was only hurting him more. Shame flooded her and made her gut tighten into one hard, painful knot.

"Well, if he does have a lady he's wooing, I'm sure he'll do something soon to secure her hand in marriage and a brooch and a shawl isn't what I mean."

Lucy had no idea what to make of his statement when Seth appeared at her side and shoved the newspaper in her face with his left hand while hitting the paper mercilessly with the index finger of his right.

Carefully, Lucy took the paper from him, laid it out on the table, read the words he'd pointed out, then felt her knees give way under her as her mind—and body—fell into the black abyss in an action many fancy ladies termed a "swoon".

The burning, pungent aroma of a horrid mix of flowers and spices filled Lucy's nostrils. She groaned and waved her hand in the air in front of her in an attempt to banish the nauseating stench.

It didn't go anywhere.

In fact, it seemed to get stronger!

"I think it's working," said a man's voice.

"I've never had to use them before, but I think you're right," came a feminine reply.

"Perhaps you should put them closer to her nose and she'll come to faster."

No! Move them away.

Bullish man didn't heed the demands of her mind and pushed those dratted things closer and when Lucy inhaled again, she got a nose full of foul-smelling smelling salts.

She coughed then blinked her eyes. Her nose itched. Bad. Batting her left hand in the air to clear the space in front of her, she sat forward and gave a hearty sneeze.

"Excuse—" *achoo*— "me."

Mrs. Appleton handed Lucy her handkerchief. "Are you all

right, dear?"

Lucy took to her unsteady feet. When had she moved to a settee? Never mind. She'd rather not know. From the corner of her eye she glimpsed that dratted newspaper in Simon's hand. Had he been fanning her with that blasted thing? She closed her eyes and repressed a groan or some other sound of vexation. "I'm fine now, thank you. May I see that again?"

All eyes went to the newspaper in Simon's hand. "You read it right." He raked a hand through his dark hair. "I have no idea where he got such a notion you'd marry him, but I'll go speak to him, if you'd like."

"No!" Simon speaking to Giles would only make matters worse. She was certain of it.

"Are you sure?" He tossed the paper down onto the settee Lucy had just vacated. "He's taking advantage of you."

"Taking advantage? Of me?" she choked. Most would say it was the other way around. That she didn't deserve him. And they'd be right.

Simon nodded. "He needs a wife and for whatever reason he's set his mind on you to fill that role for him."

"That's enough, Simon," Mrs. Appleton snapped.

Lucy bit the inside of her lip. Hard. She didn't dare tell them that she might have given him reasons to assume she might be interested in making a match with him, but she needed to tell them *something*. "Mrs. Appleton, I—"

"Need to make no explanation," Mrs. Appleton cut in. She turned to her son. "You, however, need to apologize."

"Apologize?" Simon and Lucy said in disbelieving unison.

"Apologize," Mrs. Appleton confirmed, then sighed. "Lucy dear, you'll have to forgive Simon's sour mood today, he's been having some lady troubles of his own as of late."

Lucy nearly choked. *Already?* It had barely been two weeks since she'd told him she didn't return his affection. Either he had no standards or he'd already had a lady in mind... She cocked her head to the side and nearly laughed at his grimace.

"I wouldn't call them lady troubles," he muttered with a sour twist of his lips. "If that blasted woman had the good sense to listen to reason—" He broke off with a huff. "Never mind that. We're not talking about her."

"No, we're not—you are," his mother teased, winking at Lucy.

Casting his mother what had to be the most pathetic attempt at a scowl Lucy had ever borne witness to, Simon said, "Lucy, you don't have to marry Giles if you don't wish. He needs to learn he cannot manipulate people this way."

"Manipulate?" He wasn't manipulating her, exactly. She'd kissed him. A lot. If anything, he had to have taken that as encouragement. Though, she would have liked it had he even bothered to *ask* her to marry him before just assuming she would. She stilled. Would she have said yes? Before she could have a chance to think about that any deeper, Simon's words broke into her thoughts.

"...he should have gone about finding a bride the right way by attending balls and such to find a suitable match. Instead, he's decided to be highhanded about it and foisted his suit upon someone unsuspecting who cannot refuse him. But you can if you don't wish to marry him. We'll find a way to help you."

Lucy let his final words sink in and ignored Mrs. Appleton's agreement with Simon's offer of help and question of if Lucy cared for Giles that way. All she could do was wonder if it was true. Had Giles been manipulating her this entire time? Was that why he'd been so kind to her and Seth? Was it all a ploy to get his much-needed wife to produce his much-needed heir without having to court a debutante? Another dizzying sensation overtook her and she gripped the edge of the table to keep from swooning again. While it was clear Giles intended to marry her, she couldn't say that it was any different than the way Sam had treated her.

Had she chosen the wrong brother? Again?

Chapter Twenty-Six

Giles rhythmically tapped the nib of his quill against the inkpot for no other reason than it gave him something to do to occupy himself. The announcement had run in the paper today and he was certain Simon would darken his door with plenty to say about it.

He'd better hurry and come by, Giles thought. Seth had made it a habit for the past two days to come by after lunch and Giles would be damned if he'd discuss anything with Simon while Seth was in his home. It might not be good for their already unsteady relationship if Giles were to throw the man out of his house in front of his soon-to-be nephew.

But Giles would do it.

Then it happened. No sooner had he finished his thought, a series of four loud *bangs* rattled his front door.

Tension knotted his muscles as he waited for Tarley to show the man into Giles' study.

A moment later, a red-faced Lucy crossed the threshold.

Giles jumped to his feet, or tried to. Biting back a curse at hitting both of his knees on the underside of his desk, he stood.

"What's wrong?" he unintentionally barked. He wasn't too familiar with ladies, but assumed something had to be wrong or her cheeks wouldn't be so red or shimmer with tears.

"You used me," she spat.

Used her? How had he done that? "How?" he choked.

She pulled out a copy of the newspaper and tossed it down on his desk. "It was all a game to you, wasn't it?"

"A game?" he repeated. His mind raced to make sense of what she'd meant by a game. He didn't even like games.

"You...you...were kind to me and Seth and got me to trust you," she said, swiping at the tears streaming down her face. "But it was all a game."

"A game?" he repeated again, feeling even more like a fool. "I don't understand."

"An act. You were just pretending."

"I wasn't pretending. I like spending time with you and Seth." He took a step toward her. "I like kissing you."

The way she pulled back at his words as if he'd slapped her stopped him cold. That had been the wrong thing to say.

"Lucy," he rasped, his heart twisting in his chest. He clenched his jaw to keep it steady and fought the urge to take her in his arms. That might only make her angrier with him. He swallowed convulsively. "I'm sorry." For what he didn't know. It just seemed the right thing to say.

"How could you do this? I trusted you."

"What did I do?" He knew it was a stupid question. He should already know. Unfortunately, he didn't.

"Used me." She blinked her eyes rapidly as if she were trying to hold back another round of tears. The gesture only made him weaker in the knees.

"How?" It would seem they'd just had these same words, but he still couldn't understand what she'd meant. "How did I use you?" he clarified.

"You don't care about me, you just need a wife and any wife will do."

Now it was Giles' turn to pull back as if he'd been struck. "No, I don't." He crossed his arms. "I don't need any wife."

"But your heir?"

He shrugged. "I have a cousin."

"I'm sure you do, but I'm sure you'd rather it be your own seed who inherits."

"I don't care." He crossed his arms. "I'd never given much thought to actually marrying anyone until recently, and even then, I wasn't so convinced."

"Then why did you put our marriage announcement in the paper?"

"Because I'd finally found someone I wanted to marry."

An expression he couldn't interpret came over her face.

"Wanted?"

He nodded slowly. "I wanted to marry you." He took a deep breath. "I still do, too."

"Why?"

"Why what?"

"Why do you want to marry me?"

Didn't she already know? Had he not made it clear to her?

She lifted her hand to her eye and wiped away her tears, imploring him with her eyes as she waited for his answer.

He had a crippling feeling his answer meant a lot to her. The knowledge terrified him. "I like kissing you. I'd like to do more than kiss you." Though flames licked his face at his admission, it didn't make it any less true. "I want to live with you and see you every day. I want you to be the one who grows heavy with my heir —if I'm to have one. And if not, I'll be content with that because it'll be you who I wake up next to and go to sleep with at night."

There, he'd said it. He felt like a complete fool, but he'd said it.

"Me?" she squeaked.

"Yes, you." He pulled her to him. "My mother tried to help me find a match. But I didn't want any of them."

"Why not?"

"They didn't drive me to distraction with their mere presence." He framed her face and brushed his lips over hers. "They didn't make me wonder what it'd be like to kiss them. And they certainly didn't make me mad with the desire to discover every inch of them and claim them as mine forever."

A dark shadow came over her face and something flickered in her eyes. "I can't," she choked, pulling away.

"Can't what?"

"I can't marry you, Giles."

He stared at her unblinkingly. "Why?"

"I'm not good enough."

"Good enough?" What did that mean? Of course she was good enough. She was scores better than any of the ladies his mother had tried to introduce him to.

"My past is riddled with reasons why I'm not a good match for you."

"I don't see them," he said honestly. He reached for her again, but she didn't budge. "To me, you're perfect."

"No, I'm not," she said on a shaky laugh.

He moved toward her. "Neither am I."

"But it's all right for you. You have a title."

He'd never thought of that as an excuse before. "You will, too. You'll be a baroness."

"I don't even know how a baroness should behave," she burst out, her voice uneven and three pitches higher than usual.

He squeezed her hand to reassure her. "My mother and Isabelle can help you."

Lucy shook her head. "I don't think I can be your baroness."

"Then, don't," he countered, dropping a kiss on her lips. "Just be my wife."

Chapter Twenty-Seven

The wedding could not come soon enough for Giles' liking. Until it did, he'd have to settle for making up excuses to go see Lucy at the library and sneak kisses from her whenever possible. Someone—most likely his mother—had informed her that young ladies who are soon to be a baroness shouldn't go to a gentleman's lodgings. Not even with a chaperone. And not even to collect her child.

She'd also been advised to stop working in the library. Fortunately for Giles she hadn't heeded that advice completely. She only "helped", without wages so it wasn't considered work.

He drummed his fingers on the edge of his desk and mentally counted the days until the wedding. Ten. He'd survive that, wouldn't he?

"My lord, Mr. Appleton is here to see you."

Giles' skin prickled. Which Mr. Appleton had come to see him? Surely it wouldn't actually be Simon.

It wasn't.

Mr. Walter Appleton came in and removed his grey felt hat before taking a seat opposite Giles. "Forgive me for not coming by sooner to offer my felicitations. I thought you might be occupied and wanted to come back when I had news on the other matter."

Right, the other matter. "Do you?"

"Of course." He straightened the cuff on his brown coat then bent to retrieve a slim stack of documents from his satchel.

"And?" Giles burst out when it would appear Mr. Appleton wasn't on the verge of speaking.

"There's a way you can regain control of the barony and have access to the trust," Mr. Appleton said.

"The trust for my heir?" Giles asked for clarification.

Mr. Appleton nodded.

Giles wouldn't tell the man this because it was quite clear he'd spent a lot of his time and resources to pursue this, but he was a little disappointed this was all Mr. Appleton wanted to speak to him about. "I won't need it, will I?"

"No. You certainly will not be lacking in funds. But don't you want it?"

Giles blinked. "No. Why would I?"

"Because it was unjustly denied to you."

Unjustly? He didn't think so. His father could do with his money as he wished, couldn't he? Frankly, he was relieved that the man had seen fit to allow Giles to inherit his assets and their earnings after his twentieth birthday. He didn't need the trust. "That's all right, I don't need it."

"No, it's not all right," Mr. Appleton snapped. He covered his face with his hands, then exhaled and dropped his hands back to his lap. "Giles, this is yours. You deserve it."

"No, I don't. He wanted the funds and rule of the barony to go to my heir and it will."

"Yes, but will it be your legacy to pass to your heir...or his?"

"I don't know what you mean."

Mr. Appleton lifted his right hand to his forehead and idly rubbed the bridge of his nose. "As it stands now, you are just a baron in name. None of the responsibility of it is yours. You're a symbol, if you will. The same goes for the trust. Both will pass to your son as if it were left to him by your father. Not you. If the responsibility and trust is yours, you can be the one to pass it to your son."

Giles wasn't sure he understood the difference.

"Simon isn't my only son," Mr. Appleton said quietly. "I have one other, but he... Well, he doesn't bear my name and will not inherit my legacy—but the stingy leavings from another man. Don't misunderstand, I was blessed that I have Simon to carry on my name and inherit. But sometimes I feel cheated that it isn't my eldest son who will inherit my business and modest fortune. I don't want you to face the same heartbreak."

Giles could understand that. He *did* want to be the one to pass down his title and money to his son. Not just act as a formality between the two. "What do I need to do?"

"Prove to the court that you are of a sound mind," Mr. Appleton said as if he were discussing the weather.

Giles, however, didn't take his statement so lightly. "That's impossible."

Mr. Appleton lifted his right foot and rested it on his left knee. "Can I ask for an indulgence?"

"For?"

"I'm about to speak very bluntly about your mother and your father."

Giles nodded, not sure what to make of the way he'd spoken his last word.

"I think your plight had less to do with your life's cord being wrapped around your neck and more to do with a way to punish your mother."

"Because she loved you?"

"And you." Mr. Appleton lowered his voice the way Sebastian often did when he was about to say something that Giles might not like to hear. "I never knew you as a boy since you were confined to the country, but when your mother was allowed to come to town —" he coughed— "well, she'd talk about you.

"For a long time, she fretted that you'd never talk or be able to obey simple commands. She feared leaving you alone with anyone and would plead for Norcourt to take her back to Dolsey. He'd relent, but with stipulations." His expression darkened. "He didn't think she'd provided him with a suitable heir and insisted she give him another. But she couldn't." He grew quiet for a moment. "She tried for several years, and wasn't able to conceive.

"When you got a little older, about four or five, things changed. He still wanted another son, of course, but when he'd bring her to London, instead of being uneasy and forlorn, she was full of the same excitement she'd had before she'd married." A faint smile touched his lips. "She was excited about you. When we'd dance at a ball, she'd only speak of you and whatever things you'd begun doing or found of interest." He guffawed. "She even detailed the slimy coating of a slug for me. I loved seeing her like that.

"It didn't last, though. I didn't see her again for two Seasons and when I did that sparkle in her eye was gone again. I heard a rumor at my club that Norcourt was on the verge of petitioning her for a parliamentary divorce on the grounds of adultery and a list of other claims that would leave you both pariahs. I couldn't see that happen to her and I convinced her to let me help her meet his demands."

"Why?"

"Why did I try to help her give him another son?"

"Yes." It was the oddest thing he'd ever heard.

"Because I loved her." White lines formed around the edges of Mr. Appleton's mouth as if he wanted to say more, but couldn't.

Giles wasn't sure what to make of that or of Mr. Appleton for his role. What would have become of Giles had the old baron not died? Was being sent away and unable to inherit what was lawfully his the better fate?

"I didn't know my interference would result in so much harm to either of you or I might have convinced her to let him divorce her." Mr. Appleton's whispered confession hit Giles squarely in the heart. "We both agreed when he died to marry immediately. It didn't mean everything would be fair to you, but far fairer than it might have been if she'd delivered Simon as Norcourt's unmarried widow."

"Fairer," Giles repeated in disbelief. "To me?"

"Yes," Mr. Appleton said softly. "I know that it doesn't seem very fair at all. But, please understand, the alternative would have been far less favorable for you."

"Being treated as an orphan is fair?" Giles tried to reason.

"No, but living as an orphan under the protection of a title you might one day inherit is far better than being publicly branded mentally unfit and cast aside to allow your brother to inherit what was rightfully yours." Mr. Appleton rubbed the bridge of his nose. "Had Norcourt lived or had your mother delivered Simon as his widow, Lord Norcourt had everything arranged that would leave you disinherited. That's why we married so soon."

"But the orphanage," Giles persisted. Not that it mattered it was already done. Nothing could change it now.

"Perhaps she'd be the one better to explain that."

Giles shook his head adamantly. "No. You."

Mr. Appleton looked him over as if he were trying to decide if he should tell Giles what he knew or not. Giles hoped he would. He wanted to know now, not wait for his mother to decide it was time.

"Your mother only spoke to me about it once," Mr. Appleton began slowly. "Right after you were sent away, she was informed you were not to come back until you were of an age to inherit—and only then if she didn't produce a capable son. If she called you back before then, he'd petition for divorce on the grounds of adultery and have her banished."

"Just her?"

Mr. Appleton nodded. "Just her. I don't know what he planned to do with you since claiming you were a bastard might also bring questions about Simon's legitimacy, but somehow he threatened to make sure she'd never see either of you again."

"And she chose Simon," Giles said somewhat bitterly. Not that he could blame her necessarily. Simon was a son who could make any mother proud. Giles was not.

"No, she chose you both," Mr. Appleton contradicted. "It was just the only way she could have you both. She might not have been able to be there for you as a boy, but she can now." He swallowed. "That might not have been possible had she not abided by his rules."

"But after he died. Why not then?"

"She was scared. She tried once after his death, but was notified by the orphanage that only Lord Norcourt could order you released. When she tried to petition the courts, Lord Cosgrove warned her to stop and gave her the same warning Norcourt had that if she didn't heed his warning, he'd be forced to uphold Norcourt's former plan and have you disinherited." He puffed up his cheeks and blew out a deep breath. "Perhaps it was the wrong choice. I don't know. But neither do I know by which means Lord

Norcourt would have ordered for you to be disinherited. Proving bastardy or mental unsoundness might have been difficult and I don't doubt—" his voice hitched— "he might have sought other means if necessary. Nor did your mother, or I, wish to find out."

Giles sat still for a few minutes, his mind trying to make sense of everything he'd been told. He didn't know the legalities of many things. Nor did he fully understand Appleton's connection with his mother. But he understood enough. They'd married so quickly following the old baron's death so there couldn't be a way for Simon to usurp him as baron. He understood that though he wasn't sure whether that was actually a good thing or not. Simon would have made a better baron. He understood things the first time they were said and didn't get frustrated with his own inabilities to put into words what he wanted to say. But what of the rest? Did Mr. Appleton mean that Giles had been left there at the orphanage as a means of protection? He shivered at the thought.

"Giles, did you hear me?"

"Er...no."

"I said, you were done a great injustice by being sent away and having this trust and the privilege of running your barony tied up out of your grasp. I know that, and I even accept responsibility for it, but you don't have to continue to live with it. You just need to do something about it."

"Don't you understand that I can't?"

"No, I don't understand that. What is it you cannot do?"

"Think."

"Everyone thinks, Giles. Try again."

He clenched his jaw. "Speak."

"Another ability I think you have a firm grasp of. Why, you've been arguing rather well with me for about the past hour or so."

Squeezing his eyes shut, he willed the man to leave. He opened them. No such luck.

"Are you worried they'll ask you an academic question?"

No, he was worried about being asked *any* question. Alone, in his home, where everything around him was familiar and tranquil, he wasn't so distracted or overwhelmed. Everywhere else he was reduced to a bumbling fool who either couldn't speak or said the wrong thing.

"Your lack of formal schooling will not be a strike against you," Mr. Appleton said softly. "They just want to know that you're of sound mind and are not in need of being locked away at an asylum."

"An asylum?" Giles choked. He knew he was considered odd and a little simple. But he'd never thought that would make him a candidate for Bedlam.

"Giles, that's my point. You won't be denied. You just need to go answer their questions so they can determine you're of sound mind and should have access to your trust."

"No." Giles stared down at his broken quill. "There is no need. I'm not a smart man, Mr. Appleton. They'll never agree that I'm competent enough to let me run the barony."

"Who said that?"

"Nobody had to say it, I just know."

"You seem to know a lot for not being very smart," Mr. Appleton's tone was hard to place.

Giles forced a stiff shrug. "It doesn't take a smart man to know that."

"There's more than one way to be intelligent."

"Sir, I drove Sister Catherine to smuggle the communion wine. Said she needed it after spending a day trying to get me to understand sums—and not because she felt like a saint and was in need of an extra blessing."

Mr. Appleton's laughter echoed through the room. "Have trouble understanding what to do with that extra one?"

Giles felt his eyes widen in surprise. "How did you know?"

"I had the same problem as a boy. I think Simon may have, too." His face went still almost as if he were afraid of what he'd revealed. Giles didn't know why he'd be afraid of admitting that Simon wasn't perfect at anything. Mayhap Simon would be upset if Giles knew of his imperfection.

"I won't tell him," Giles offered. That wasn't a hard promise to keep since Simon's interest in talking to him rivaled his interest in speaking to Simon.

Mr. Appleton pressed his lips together. "Right. As for the matter at hand, whether you marry or not, I think you should petition the court to acknowledge you are of sound and able mind."

"No." Giles wiped his sweaty palms on his trousers. "They'll mock me."

"Who?"

"Everyone," he burst out, banging his open palm on the smooth surface of his desk.

"I won't. And neither will anyone else."

"Yes, they will. They always do." Giles released a harsh laugh. "I still don't know what to do with that extra one."

"You add it to the next column on the left," Mr. Appleton said quietly. "Or rather, your trusted estate manager does." He dropped his booted foot back to the floor with an indelicate *tap*. "You don't have to decide today what you want to do. I'm just asking that you give it some thought."

"Why is it that you care so much?"

"As I said, I know what it's like to live my life knowing that my eldest won't inherit my legacy, but rather one that was given to him by someone else."

Something about how he said those words gave Giles a chill. "How long do I have before I have to let you know?"

"Until my death, I suppose," Mr. Appleton said, tucking the papers back into his satchel. "It won't be too late then, of course, but you'll have to ask Simon to help, though."

Giles shuddered. "I'll be sure to decide something before then."

"Very well." Mr. Appleton stood and plucked his satchel from the floor. "I look forward to seeing you at the wedding, but just so you know, you're welcome to come over to have dinner any time you'd like."

That wasn't likely to happen. It had been uncomfortable before; he couldn't imagine Simon's reaction to him now. "Thank you."

"Don't thank me," Mr. Appleton said, putting his hat on his

head. "Come over and have a drink with me."

Chapter Twenty-Eight

Ten Days Later

Lucy could hardly believe she was actually walking down the aisle to her waiting bridegroom. Fortunately it was a short walk across his mother's drawing room or her knees might have buckled beneath her at the way Giles grinned at her from the moment she entered the room. Actually, that wasn't true. If her knees were to buckle, Seth was right there to help hold her up. For he'd insisted she needed an escort down the aisle and there was no one else she'd rather it be but him.

Next to Giles who was cloaked in blue and gold stood Sebastian dressed in various shades of red. In the spot where the bride's attendant was to stand stood Isabelle. When Lucy had admitted she didn't have anyone to ask to be her attendant, save perhaps Giles' mother, Giles had suggested Isabelle. Though she and Isabelle weren't close, Lucy agreed it'd make the most sense to ask her and was somewhat relieved when Giles volunteered to be the one to talk to them both about standing up with them. Lucy should have done it, she knew, but Giles was more their friend than she was. Isabelle had graciously accepted and now she was at their wedding with a slightly uneasy expression, beautiful but uneasy. Like her husband, she was dressed in red. A beautiful ruby-colored gown with a gold and silver embroidery pattern on the bodice and gold edging around the sleeves that matched the most beautiful gold flounces at the bottom of her skirts.

For her part, Lucy had worn a silver gown that Mrs. Appleton had helped her choose from a fashion plate. The fabric shone in the light and made a soft whispering rustle every time she moved. The gown itself was plain, devoid of embellished embroidering or yards of lace. Its elegance came in the cut. High on the waist, full, billowing skirts, high capped sleeves and a rounded bodice that gave an onlooker a generous view of the top of her bosoms. Of course that would not do during a wedding (only after it, when alone with the groom), and she'd elected to wear a crushed velvet shawl over top that was a near perfect match to the color of Giles' emerald eyes.

Lost in her thoughts of love for the man standing before her, the other occupants of the room, comprised of the three Appletons, Seth, and Isabelle and Sebastian, faded away as she heard the minister speak of loving and cherishing, two things she knew she'd be able to do without question. Then the vows were repeated and before she knew it, Giles' lips were upon hers, sealing their union with a kiss that seared her heart and body solely to him.

After the ceremony, the small group made their way to the dining room for a wedding breakfast. All around Lucy, conversation buzzed, but she heard none of it through the excitement that hummed through her.

Isabelle gave her a knowing look and she blushed. Was she that obvious? The sparkle in Isabelle's eye confirmed she had been.

Lucy pulled her attention away from Isabelle and looked down the table to where Simon and Seth were chatting about something. Lucy bit her lip. She'd been worried how Simon would respond to the announcement that Lucy was indeed going to marry Giles. Oddly enough, he hadn't said a single cross word about it. Then again, he'd mysteriously been absent, something about a trip to some country estate. Lucy wasn't too sure on the details, nor had she inquired.

"Are you ready to go?" Giles whispered in her ear.

Her skin tingled. "Whenever you are."

"I've been ready since the kiss," he admitted quietly.

Her blush elicited a few chuckles around them.

Giles reached for her hand and stood. "Thank you all for coming, but we're leaving."

Though she'd never actually attended a wedding before, she was fairly certain that wasn't how one announced they were leaving.

However, nobody seemed to mind. And if they did, they kept

their lips firmly closed.

Quickly all the others stood and formed a line to congratulate them and wish them well.

First was Sebastian who gave Lucy a quick hug, then shook Giles' hand while Isabelle hugged Lucy and whispered something to her about coming to call on her soon. Lucy smiled at the lady's pleasantries and her smile grew genuine when Isabelle hugged and congratulated Giles. Next was Mr. and Mrs. Appleton. Similarly to Lord and Lady Belgrave, Mr. Appleton hugged Lucy and shook Giles' hand while Mrs. Appleton hugged—and kissed—them both. Next was a very energetic Seth who seemed to have little interest in hugging either of them but wished them well and pumped Giles' hand with so much vigor Lucy wondered if he were trying to draw water from a well.

"You'll be on your best behavior and remember your manners, won't you?" Lucy said as a gentle warning to Seth. The Appletons had been kind enough to offer to let him stay there for the next two nights.

"Of course he will," Simon said for him, clapping Seth on the shoulders with both hands. "I plan to keep him so busy during the day he won't have time to get into trouble and at night he'll be too exhausted to do anything other than sleep."

Seth grin's was contagious and soon both Lucy and Giles were grinning at Simon's words. "Thank you," she said, meeting Simon's eyes. There was something in them she hadn't glimpsed before.

Simon smiled at Lucy then turned to Giles. "Congratulations to you both." He released Seth's shoulders and dug his hands into his pockets. "I think you two suit each other perfectly." Then, without another word or waiting for a response, he touched Seth's shoulder and guided him off.

Giles turned to Lucy, his eyebrows lifted and his eyes wide.

Lucy grinned. Even when he was confused, Giles was still handsome. "He doesn't know what to say to us," she said in hushed tones, reaching for his hand. "But he's certainly trying."

Giles interlaced their fingers. "I suppose he is."

"He is," Lucy assured him as Giles led her down the stairs and to the waiting carriage.

The carriage ride to her new residence seemed to go faster than she thought it would. Perhaps that was because she was going to Giles' townhouse not as the fallen Lucy Whitaker, but as Lady Norcourt—Giles' wife.

She peered up at her still grinning bridegroom as he helped her descend the carriage in front of his house and intertwined their fingers together again. The past week had been a whirlwind filled with fittings and making plans for this wedding. Mrs. Appleton had been a wonderful help to her navigating the shops and placing orders, but it had certainly interfered with any time Lucy might have gotten to spend with Giles. That was about to be rectified, now and forever, though.

"Nervous?" Giles whispered in her ear when she was safely off the bottom step.

"Just a bit," she admitted. It had been a long time since she'd been alone with a man who had the gleam in his eyes that Giles did. It had only been the once, but she did remember the activity well enough. What she didn't remember was being excited about it.

"Don't be." He unlocked the front door, then put one arm about her shoulders and hooked the other under her knees and lifted her.

Lucy looped her arms around his neck as he carried her across the threshold and kicked the front door shut before carrying her upstairs. This time, instead of taking her to the room she'd assumed was meant for the baroness, he carried her to his room. He paused just inside the threshold to kick that door closed. "Can't have anyone peeking in on the new Lady Norcourt. It wouldn't be proper."

She giggled and brought her lips to his. It had been five days since they'd last been able to sneak a kiss, which had been nothing worse than torture, but made this one that much more exciting.

Giles carried her across the room and to the bed. Then slowly, almost reverently, he lowered her to the thick feather mattress.

"You're beautiful."

She kissed him. "Thank you. You're quite handsome, yourself."

"Am I now?" He asked between kisses.

It was on the tip of Lucy's tongue to confirm, but all words and thoughts of them faded away when his lips left hers and started to kiss a slow path across her cheek and down to her jaw.

She lolled her head to the opposite side to give him better access. Which, of course, he took.

His hands released their hold on her from when he'd carried her into the room and moved to the bottom of her throat to untie the velvet emerald cape she had draped over her shoulders to match her silver gown. Freeing the knot, he pushed the thick fabric away from her skin and moved his lips down to where he'd just exposed.

Lucy's skin tingled beneath his lips. "Giles," she whispered, digging her fingers into the back of his thick, silky hair.

Giles murmured her name against her collarbone then moved his lips back up to hers, his hands sliding underneath her body. He slowly guided her up to a sitting position with her legs hanging off the end of the bed. Satisfied, he sank to his knees in front of her, bringing his face just two inches above hers.

Lucy lowered her hands from his hair to rest on his broad shoulders. He really was a handsome man. And now he was all hers.

Neither spoke, the only sound between them was their heavy breathing and pounding hearts.

Tentatively, she ran her hands down his shoulders and to the V of his coat. She slipped her hands inside and slid her fingers under the top of his waistcoat, then moved them up to his shoulders. She could feel so much more now with only his thin lawn shirt separating their skin.

"May I?" His rasped words made her skin tingle with excitement at what he might do. Where he might touch her.

She nodded and began kneading the thick muscles in his shoulders.

He skimmed his fingers from her shoulder blades halfway down her spine then across her ribs before lifting them to the silver chord that held her bodice closed. With an audible swallow, he tugged both ends of the chord until the bow was gone and the knot slipped loose.

Lucy didn't know whose body became more frozen at that moment, his or hers. She was nearly thirty and had a child. Would he be satisfied with what he saw?

With another swallow that resembled a gulp, Giles released the ends of the silver chord and began to loosen her bodice. It wouldn't reveal everything to him, but it'd be enough for him to be able to imagine the rest.

After loosening the top two crosses, he moved his hand lower and brushed her breast with his palm. His fingers stilled, his palm pressing ever-so-lightly against her breast, leading them both to swell in a way she'd never expected.

A boldness, she didn't recognize came over her and prompted her to remove her hands from his shoulders and take hold of his wrists. She guided his hands away from the center of her chest and placed them directly on her breasts. "Touch me."

As if he'd been waiting for that sort of an invitation for a decade, he did just that. His touch was slow and tentative at first as he moved his palms over the curve of her breasts, from the top to the bottom then back and forth across the sides. "They're soft," he commented before cupping them. He gave them a gentle squeeze, looking at her face as he did so.

She didn't realize her hands were still on his wrists and gave him what she hoped he'd understand to be an encouraging squeeze.

He did.

His touches and caresses became bolder and more intense as he massaged and kneaded every inch of her breasts until she was almost certain they were going to burst right out of her bodice.

"Would you like to see them?"

"Of course," he said automatically, frantically moving his hands back to the ties that ran down the front of her bodice. Jerkily, he tugged on the ties, loosening them only marginally.

Lucy touched his wrists again, staying him. Releasing his hands, she stood and turned her back to him.

It took him only a moment to start slipping the buttons that ran down the back of her gown. With every one he slipped Lucy's pulse sped up just a little more until he reached her waist. Pushing her gown open just enough in the back, he began loosening the ties on that blasted corset she was made to wear.

With a grunt, he untied the last one. He gripped the edge of the thick fabric of both her gown and her corset and between his pushing and her maneuvering, the offending garments were off her shoulders and in a heap on the floor.

Lucy spun around to face her groom wearing nothing but a thin chemise and stockings as coverings.

"Beautiful," he rasped.

"I believe you've already said that," she teased.

"Doesn't make it any less true." His eyes drifted down her body, settling on her thinly covered breasts.

Taking a deep breath, Lucy reached her trembling fingers up to the thin straps of her chemise, gripped them tightly, then dragged them across her shoulders to the ends and without giving herself time to change her course, let them drop.

***

Every last muscle in Giles' body went rigid.

He'd heard talk of women's bodies and what men did to them between their legs, but he'd never given much thought to what Lucy would look like unclothed.

She was beautiful. Nay, she was *magnificent*. He released a pent up breath he didn't know he'd been holding. She'd allowed him to touch her soft parts earlier, would she again now that she was naked?

He dropped back down to his knees in front of her and hesitantly, brought both of his hands to her bare shoulder and locking eyes with her, trailed his fingers down her soft, pale skin. Excitement built within him as his fingertips moved over the softness of her chest. He reached the peak and she sucked in a breath, making his own catch. *She must like that.* He brushed his thumbs over her nipples again then brought his hands down to the under-curve and tested their weight.

Reluctantly, he released them. With his hands at least. There was little hope of him ever removing his eyes from those two perfect globes.

He moved his hands down her abdomen until his thumb brushed the patch of curly hair just below her waist. He flushed and moved his hands back up her body with a slowness that almost drove him insane as he neared her chest.

With a sureness he didn't feel, he cupped her perfect mounds of flesh and gave them another gentle squeeze.

She arched her back, pushing them more firmly into his hands. His eyes shot to her face.

She was biting the edge of her lip, her skin flushed.

He squeezed them again, a fraction harder.

Her hands flew to his shoulders, the tips of her fingers digging in. Blood pounding in his ears, he released his hold on her and brought his fingers to the hardened tips. He closed his fingers firmly around the tips, eliciting a gasp from her. He did it again, with a little more pressure and a strangled gasp was her response, her hands gripping his shoulders tighter if such a thing were possible.

Giles released her body and covered her hands with his as he took to his feet. He was considerably taller than her and at his full height her face was somewhere in his chest. For but a moment he wished it was the other way around. Pushing away the thought, he brought his hands back to her chest and idly brushed the tips with his thumbs.

"Do you like it when I touch you here?" He couldn't say why, but her answer was important to him.

She relinquished her teeth's hold on her lip. "Yes, Giles. I like it when you touch my breasts."

Her words were almost his undoing. He gave her breasts one final squeeze before letting go and taking a step back to regather his wits or this would be over too fast and as one fellow had mentioned at White's that left the woman disappointed. He didn't want Lucy disappointed.

Just the idea of disappointing Lucy cooled his ardor. But not too much.

Closing the space between them again, he brought his lips to hers and kissed her mouth. Then her chin. Then her throat. Then he dropped to his knees again and kissed the top of her chest. Then scattered kisses down her sternum. When he reached the bottom, he turned his head just slightly to the left and scattered kisses below her left breast. He turned the other way and this time used his parted lips to press open-mouthed kisses to the skin under her right one.

She nearly melted in his hands.

Without removing his lips from her skin, he gripped her hips, stood and carried her to the bed and pulled away from her just long enough to divest himself of his clothing, then came back to join her. Settling himself between her parted thighs, he brought his mouth back to her chest and pressed open-mouthed kisses over and around her left breast while using his hand to explore the right. He'd squeezed and held, tested the firmness, then circled and rolled her budded nipple.

Beneath him, Lucy bucked and arched her back, offering him more. Greedy man he was, he took what was offered and kissed and touched every inch he could until he couldn't take it any longer. It was time. He couldn't wait a moment longer to be inside her. To join with her in a way that no other ever would.

Kissing his way back up to her mouth, he repositioned his lower body and moved the tip of his erection over her soft, warm, womanly flesh. He stilled and bit the inside of his lip. It was too soon. He released a breath and mentally recounted the scale of C Major, then resumed his pursuit of her opening.

When he found it, he was on the brink of spending and shoved inside as fast as he could, then stilled and fought to regain his breath and composure.

Lucy's once labored breathing had slowed, presumably due to his lack of attention on her breasts. He'd have to rectify that.

Keeping himself still buried inside her, he kissed and nipped and licked and tasted her until she was writhing beneath him once more.

"Ready?" he whispered.

Her only response was to clutch his shoulders.

He accepted that as a yes, and began to move inside her.

The feeling was like nothing he'd ever experienced before. It was a mixture of pleasure coupled with an intense pressure that drove him to move faster and harder in hopes of relieving it.

Then suddenly everything from the painful coil of pressure just above his waist to the images in his mind exploded as his muscles tightened and released in waves of numbing ecstasy.

Chapter Twenty-Nine

Lucy twisted her fingers into the counterpane and tried to regain control of her breathing.

She'd known that Giles would touch her breasts.

What she hadn't known was that she'd enjoy it.

She hadn't the first time she was touched there. It had felt cold and mechanical. Forced and humiliating. Sam had just tugged her bodice down until her small, pert breasts were exposed, made some glib remark about how "they'd do", then groped and pinched at them until they hurt.

Then he'd flipped up her skirt and poked around between her legs for a few seconds before he'd found what he was looking for then pushed into her like she was some tried tavern wench and moved in and out, grunting for what felt like an eternity before letting out something akin to a battle cry directly in her ear.

Giles hadn't done any of that. His touch had been far more gentle and his kiss... She already knew it had the power to make her knees buckle with the mere brush of his lips. She'd never have imagined that she'd buck and twist and writhe like a madwoman under him, though!

Surely, he must think her a wanton.

The object of her thoughts sweetly kissed her cheek then separated their bodies. She immediately felt at a loss without him there.

He stood next to the bed and lifted the counterpane just a little higher than his waist. Taking his cue, she quickly crawled under the covers and waited for him to join her.

A moment later he was at her side and she rested her cheek on his broad chest.

She hadn't been afforded the same opportunity to look at his body and under lowered lashes, she let her gaze travel over what was uncovered.

Just as she'd imagined from his stature, his shoulders and

upper arms were thick with hard, rounded muscles. As were his lower arms, his abdomen and chest. In fact, everything she could see of his that was exposed above the covers pooled at his waist looked like it had been sculpted from marble. Except perhaps the thick mat of curling hair that covered the center of his chest and made a line down his stomach.

Her fingers itched to touch it. Would it be as crisp and coarse as it looked? Or would it be soft and silky like the hair that covered his head?

"Something wrong?"

She jerked. Had he been watching her? "No. Should there be?"

"Your eyes are open." He reached down to the covers that were resting at his waist and pulled them up to cover the exposed skin of his abdomen and chest.

"Sorry," she murmured, closing her eyes.

"Don't be sorry." He lifted his right hand up to cup her cheek and idly rubbed his fingertips along the edge of her jaw. "Did you enjoy it?"

Was he talking about the view she *had* been enjoying until he covered himself or what they'd been doing *before*? She nearly laughed. He was a man. He'd meant their former activity. "Of course."

His fingers stilled. "Are you sure? You didn't call out my name and jerk my hair like the other ladies do."

She went rigid. *Other ladies?* She'd never pinned him as one who frequented other ladies' bedchambers. Perhaps she'd been wrong on that score. Somehow his hold didn't feel quite as comforting as before and she moved to free herself.

He let her go.

Lucy pulled her arms out from under the covers and moved them on the top of the counterpane, trapping her safely under its shield.

Seemingly oblivious to her rapidly fading joy, Giles rolled onto his side and ran the back of a single finger the length of her arm, starting at her wrist and ending at her shoulder. "Lucy?"

"Hmm?"

He lowered his hand to the bed. "Was it that unenjoyable?"

It hadn't been until he'd mentioned *other ladies*. Which was ridiculous for her to even be upset over. Gentlemen were expected to be experienced in such matters before marriage. She'd just thought he was different for some reason. "It was all right."

"All right?" he echoed quietly. "Can I have another chance?"

A cutting retort was on the tip of her tongue. She repressed it. "How about tomorrow, instead?"

He blanched. "Did I bungle it that badly?"

"No. You did just fine until you mentioned your other lovers." She couldn't believe she'd just said that, but since she had, she felt relieved. It was better to just say it than to hold onto it and let it fester, wasn't it?

If Giles' slack jaw was any indication, he couldn't believe she'd put voice to her feelings, either. "My other *what?*"

Lucy closed her eyes and covered her face with her hands. "Please forgive me for saying anything. Can we just go to sleep?"

He pulled her right hand away from her face. When she didn't immediately open her newly uncovered eye to look at him, he pretended to pry it open. "There aren't... I haven't..." He cleared his throat. "You're it."

"But you just said that the other ladies call your name and pull at your hair while..." she waved a hand through the air— "you know."

"Not *mine*," he burst out, his already wide eyes nearly bulging.

Lucy furrowed her brow. "Then whose?" And how did he know of such?

Giles rolled onto his back with a groan. "At White's. The men... They speak of relations with the women they bed."

"They do?" she practically squealed.

He nodded, then reached for her hand. "I won't."

She squeezed his in return, her heart slamming in her chest at his declaration that he'd never talk to others about their private moments. "I know you won't." Without relinquishing his hand, she rolled onto her side to face him. "I'm sorry that I misunderstood."

"Don't be," he mumbled. "I'm the one who said it and ruined everything."

"You didn't ruin everything," she assured him, although it had certainly tainted the moment. There was no need to mention that, though. She moved closer to him and kissed his cheek. "I enjoyed it very much," she whispered in his ear.

"Are you sure?" He let go of her hand and rolled on his side to face her. "There are other things I can try... Things you might like better."

She had no idea what those could possibly be. "Giles, I said it was enjoyable and I meant that."

"Yes, but you didn't—"

She cut him off with a kiss.

A kiss that he quickly took control of.

Framing her face with his right hand, he held her mouth to his and parted his lips. He drew her bottom lip into his mouth and gently raked his teeth over it. He ran his tongue over the place he'd just nipped and she gasped his name.

Without warning, he rolled her onto her back and settled on top of her before sliding his hands down to her swollen breasts.

She loved having his hands touch her thus and pushed her breasts into his palms, her nipples tightening to hard points against his palms.

Giles released her bottom lip and kissed down to her ear. "Trust me?"

"Yes," she breathed. "Always."

Dropping kisses along the edge of her jawline, he released her left breast and brought his hand between her legs.

Surely he didn't plan to touch her *there*. She tensed slightly at the thought.

"Relax," he murmured between openmouthed kisses.

She tried. Unsuccessfully. "Can you just..."

"No. Not yet."

She wanted to groan. She hadn't minded his earlier invasion. In fact, that part had been surprisingly more enjoyable than she remembered. But having him aimlessly touch her there was sure to be uncomfortable.

She forced herself to focus on his caress of her breast and push away the thought of what he was about to do. He was her husband after all, it was his right to do with her body whatever he wished without complaint from her.

So focused on trying to enjoy his touch to her breast she didn't realize he'd touched her most intimate area until one long, blunt-tipped finger hit something deep inside of her.

She gasped at the intrusion.

It hadn't been uncomfortable, far from it, actually.

He did it again. This time she was more prepared and noted the way a small shower of hot sparks flew through her midsection.

He thrust again and again and each time the spray of sparks was hotter and traveled further. He paused a moment and added a second finger before resuming his movements.

Lucy's hands flew to his shoulders for purchase as her body bucked and her hips moved to match his quickening thrusts. Hot, thick tension coiled in her midsection, growing tighter with each movement.

Giles murmured her name against the side of her breast and she gasped her response, moving her hands to the back of his head to hold him there as whatever this pressure was only intensified and pushed her higher and higher, closer to the edge of an unknown that seemed to linger just beyond her reach. A moment later, he stilled for a brief second and when he thrust in again it was with his erection.

He gripped her shoulders tightly and rocked his hips, finding a steady rhythm that only intensified the dizzying sensation inside her as he pushed further inside of her than he had a moment before.

Then suddenly with one swift, deep thrust a dam burst and she was pushed over that edge as her breath hitched on his name and hot euphoria rushed over her from head to toe.

Gasping for breath and clutching Giles as if he were a lifeline tossed to a drowning woman in the Thames, she had just enough wherewithal to realize he, too, was in the throes of experiencing whatever pleasure had just overtaken her and took delight that it was her body that could bring him to completion.

"I love you," he panted between gasps for air.

"I love you, too," she choked.

"You do?" he rasped, lowering himself to rest just above her with his elbows on either side of her.

"Of course I do," she said with a shaky laugh. "Wasn't it obvious earlier when I got so upset at the thought of having to share you?"

Giles pressed his forehead to hers. "You'll never have to share me, and if anyone tells you otherwise, you be sure to tell them that I'm taken."

"And so am I."

Chapter Thirty

The week that followed their wedding had to be filled with the most fun and love Lucy had ever experienced.

During the day the three of them would paint together or go on walks and talk, and at night (or whenever they could sneak away from Seth during daylight hours), their bed was alight with heated passion.

"Are you sure you and Seth don't mind spending all day here alone?" Giles asked, straightening his cravat for no less than the fifteenth time.

Lucy rose up on her knees and holding the sheet against her naked skin, walked across the bed toward him on her knees. "Yes. Mrs. Plum mentioned yesterday that as the mistress of the house I need to come up with a menu for the week. I think it might be rather fun to do." She pressed herself against him and looped her arms around his neck. "You don't have to go if you don't want to, you know."

He swallowed audibly. "Yes, I do. If I'm to be an effective nobleman I need to resume my seat in parliament. No matter how painfully dull the meetings might be."

Lucy pulled back and smoothed down his coat. For as unprepared to be a baroness as she felt she was, she felt an overwhelming amount of pride for him pushing past his fears and taking up his seat in the House of Lords. It was his right to be there and he shouldn't let anyone or anything keep him from it if he wanted to go. Even her and her past.

She sat back on her heels and nervously chewed her lower lip. "Giles, can I tell you something before you go?"

"Of course."

She'd known this moment was coming since she'd agreed to marry him. He had every right to know. She knew that and even planned to tell him. She didn't realize it'd be so soon though and was only made more urgent when he'd announced that he intended to attend session today upon waking.

"Do you not think I should go?"

Lucy started. "No, not at all." She licked her lips. "I think you should go—but only if you want to. I'm sure there are others who don't always attend."

"I know, and I might become one of those, but I think I should give it a try. I owe it to my barony, don't I?"

"Yes, you do." She offered him a slim smile. "But I need to tell you something."

"All right."

She blinked back hot tears. If this kept him from going, she'd be devastated. Still, he had a right to know from her, not from anyone else. "Giles, there's a good chance that Seth's father will be there today."

"I know," he said simply.

"You do?" she croaked.

He nodded. "I already thought about it and if he says something to me about it, I'll just inform him that he's the most unfortunate man in existence because of his overwhelming stupidity."

Lucy would be touched at his words if she weren't still in shock that he knew the identity of Seth's father. She'd always been careful not to say his name or Paul's last name. "How did you know that Lord Bonnington was Seth's father?"

"I didn't." He shrugged. "I just knew he had a title."

Her skin turned to gooseflesh. Had he hired a Runner to investigate her? "How did you know?"

"Seth."

"Seth told you that his father was a lord?" she breathed, dumbfounded.

"Not exactly. He just speculated as much."

"Speculated?" She ignored the shrillness in her voice and clutched the sheet more tightly against herself. "The two of you spent time speculating on this together?"

"No. Just him."

"And what did he say?"

"Nothing."

She leaned her head to the side. "It couldn't have been nothing if he speculated on who his father was."

"He asked if I knew how babies were made—"

"He did?" He was only eleven, surely he didn't need to know the details about *that* yet. "What did you tell him?"

"Nothing."

She narrowed her eyes on him. "Nothing?"

"Nothing." He walked over to her and put his large hands on her shoulders. "It was when I still thought you'd marry Simon. I thought he should be the one to explain it to him, so I just let Seth tell me what he thought he knew and said I'd only confirm if he were right or wrong."

Lucy's mind swam with all the information she'd just been told. "You could have told him," she whispered. Heaven knows Seth would never come to her for the answer to that.

"I didn't know that at the time. I thought you'd want to be the one to tell him or would have Simon do it."

She could understand his position. "Well, if he asks you again, or about anything else, I'd appreciate it if you'd answer his questions."

Giles nodded. "I will."

Taking a deep breath, she said, "May I ask what he already knows?"

"That there needs to be a man and a woman involved..."

Lucy wanted to bury her face in her hands to stave off the embarrassment of what her son must know she and Giles had been doing together at night.

"...Then he said he thought his father might be a lord."

Lucy snapped her head up. "And that's all he knows? Or all he *thinks* he knows, rather?"

Giles frowned. "Do you not intend to tell him?"

"No. Never."

"Why not?"

"Because I don't want that vile man around Seth."

"I didn't suggest we invite him over for dinner, but don't you think that Seth has a right to know?"

"No."

Giles moved toward the door. "Very well."

"Very well?" What did that mean? "Giles, you aren't intending to tell him, are you?"

"Right now? No. But if he asks me again—" he shrugged— "probably."

Lucy's face heated with anger. "It's not your place to tell him that."

"You just gave me leave to explain anything to him that he might have questions about. I won't bring it up with him, but if he asks me, I won't lie to him."

"You have no right," she seethed as Giles walked to the threshold. "This isn't your secret to tell."

Giles paused in the threshold of their room and without looking back at her, said. "Nor is it yours to keep."

***

Lucy wiped her sweaty hands on the front of her gown as she waited for Goosey, Lord Belgrave's aging butler, to answer the door.

"Lord Belgrave is not accepting callers," he said with a slight snarl.

Lucy's face flushed at the words that hung between them. He must think she's a doxy coming to use her charms on a married man. Well, she was not. She handed him one of Giles' calling cards. "Even to Lady Norcourt?"

The butler looked unmoved.

Fortunately, Lady Belgrave was in need of Goosey's services at that moment and was there to spare her any further embarrassment. "Lucy?"

"Lady Belgrave."

"Isabelle," she corrected. "Do come in. I was just finishing up the guest list for a dinner party we're hosting next week when I heard Goosey being beastly." She paused. "Having been on the other side of his condescending looks once myself, I try to spare as many visitors as possible the same fate until I can convince Sebastian to sack the man." She led Lucy into the drawing room and offered her a smile. "I'm glad you came by."

"You are?"

Isabelle nodded. "When you didn't come back again after your first visit here, I was afraid I'd made you uncomfortable."

"No, not at all," Lucy rushed to say. "Between the library and wedding, I just haven't had a lot of time for social calls."

Isabelle's laughter filled the room. "Mrs. Appleton has trained you well. Here, sit."

Lucy sat on the pale yellow settee Isabelle had indicated. Isabelle, was correct. Mrs. Appleton *had* trained her well with what to say to other ladies. Unfortunately, she'd neglected to mention what one should say to their husband when disagreeing.

"Now, that I know our first encounter wasn't so miserable that it has frightened you away from my home forever, may I ask what has brought you by?"

Lucy's hands grew damp again. "I'd actually hoped to speak to your husband," she admitted.

"Oh," she said quietly. "He left about an hour ago to go to Session. You can wait here for him to return, if you'd like."

If it were possible for Lucy to be any more uncomfortable, it would have happened just then. "No, I should be going home." Well, not immediately since Seth had agreed to wait for her at the library while she ran errands. She'd need to collect him first.

Isabelle heaved an exaggerated sigh just as Lucy stood to go. "It's my needlework, isn't it?"

Lucy froze. "Pardon?"

Isabelle picked up an embroidery hoop that held a large piece of white fabric half covered with red and gold thread. "My addiction to embroidery. It always seems to drive people away, my husband notwithstanding. Sebastian has warned me every day since we reconciled that I should hide it when callers come by, but I can't. Just the thought of having to put it out of view makes my skin crawl and my sore fingers itch." She shrugged. "That must be why I can't seem to make friends."

Lucy stared at her. Was the lady addled? Isabelle was beautiful and clever, besides. Surely, she had more friends than a person needed. She quickly scanned the room for more hoops, fabric and needles. "You hate embroidery, don't you?"

"How'd you guess?" Isabelle asked before carelessly tossing her hoop on the settee next to herself.

"Then why do you do it?"

"Because I have no friends," Isabelle said, her lips twitching. She sighed. "I grew up with two playmates: my sister and the boy who is now my husband. When I came to London for a Season I was pursued only by a handful of gentlemen who were interested, but didn't have any female companions—except the octogenarian who I was a paid companion to." She plucked at her green muslin skirt. "I've never had friends before, Lucy. I don't know how to make them and I fear that after our conversation that night you came for dinner that you'll only be my friend because of our husbands and be cordial to me when we see each other in Society."

Lucy was taken aback. Isabelle didn't have any friends? And more odd, she thought *she'd* put Lucy off. She couldn't be further from the truth. "Isabelle, I haven't had many friends, either." She snorted. "Actually, we're a lot alike in that respect. I only had two playmates as a girl, as well. Both were boys and I didn't marry either of them." And what a blessing *that* was. "I know you told me about your scandal the first time I came, but it's not the same as mine. The circumstances surrounding our first meeting were unusual and I thought you were just being friendly for Giles' sake. And I appreciated that. I didn't realize... That is, I never considered that we could actually be friends."

"Well, we can," Isabelle informed her, grinning. "And we should since our husbands are such good friends."

Indeed. Perhaps it was best that Lord Belgrave hadn't been home after all. It might have been because Giles and Lord Belgrave suspected Lucy and Isabelle hadn't formed an immediate friendship that they hadn't made a point to visit the other recently. She'd have to assure Giles that he could invite his friends over anytime he'd like.

"Now, that we've officially agreed to be friends, and save the other from a miserable fate of a life subjected to feeding an unnatural embroidery addiction, can I plead with you to tell me what brought you by to see my husband?" She lowered her voice to a stage whisper. "To feed the rumor mill consisting of my needles and spools of thread once you're gone, of course."

Lucy smiled weakly at her jest and said, "Giles."

"I thought it might be." She repositioned herself on the settee. "Well, him or Simon."

Lucy lifted a hand to stay Isabelle's line of thought. "Just Giles." She dropped her hand. "We had a disagreement."

"That's bound to happen," Isabelle said, her voice devoid of blame or condescension.

"I know. We've actually had a few of them now. Mainly misunderstandings. But this one—" she worried her bottom lip— "it's different."

"How so?"

Lucy quickly informed Isabelle of her conversation with Giles earlier in the morning. "I don't want him to tell Seth. I think it'll just stir up more questions and hurt and I wanted to ask your husband if he'd help me find a way to convince Giles to change his mind."

Isabelle sat quiet for a few moments. "This strikes a little close to the heart for Giles, doesn't it?" she mused.

"How so?"

"You have met Mr. Appleton, have you not?"

"Of course I have. But what does that have to do with anything?"

"Quite a lot, I'd say. Have you ever seen him in the same room as Giles?"

"Yes, they look just alike." And for good reason if Mrs. Appleton's cryptic confession was anything to rely on.

"Have you ever considered..."

Lucy flushed. "For all of a second before Mrs. Appleton hinted that my thoughts were indeed correct."

"*Hinted*," Isabelle said. "She didn't come out and say it, did she?"

"Well, no. I don't think it's something she'd want made public."

"Likely not, but if you think about it from Giles' perspective, it might make more sense why he feels that Seth has a right to know."

All arguments left Lucy's mind and her body went numb. Giles wasn't good at interpreting hints. Either he assumed they meant the wrong thing, such as taking her confession for liking to kiss him as an agreement to marry him; or he just didn't understand them at all. If he believed that Mr. Appleton was his father, he'd never said anything to her about it. Which could only mean he was completely oblivious to their resemblance, which wasn't likely or he didn't know what to believe and longed for the same information about his parentage that he claimed Seth did.

"Thank you, Isabelle," she breathed. "I was so caught up in my own feelings and protecting Seth that I didn't consider Giles."

Isabelle reached forward and patted her hand. "You're welcome. I think this is what friends are for."

"Yes, and saving each other from a life filled with embroidery."

Chapter Thirty-One

Giles couldn't go to Session and it had nothing to do with the potential of being in the same room with the man who had once been intimate with his wife.

Instead, he rode around London trying to make sense of why Lucy was being so stubborn. Didn't Seth have a right to know who his own father was? If he weren't curious, then Giles could understand not telling him. But he *was* curious.

Eight hours later he turned Thor, his stallion, down his street and sighed. He was no closer to drawing a conclusion than he had been when he'd left.

Lucy was right, though, it wasn't his place to tell Seth the truth. Only she could do that and no matter how much Seth might beg him to, Giles wouldn't betray Lucy's trust that way.

Arriving at home, he slid his tired and sore body from the saddle and tied Thor to the post for a groom to come attend him then went inside to assure his wife that he wouldn't say anything to Seth. Even though he disagreed with her decision. He should probably leave that part off if he didn't wish to get into another quarrel.

"Where's Lady Norcourt?" Giles asked Millie when he didn't see Lucy in any of the common rooms or their bedchamber.

"She left not long after you did, my lord."

Giles' stomach lurched. "Left? To where?"

Millie ran her duster in the crack between the wall sconce and the wall. "Didn't say, my lord."

"Did she say when she'd be back?"

"No, my lord."

Giles frowned. "And Seth?"

"He went with her."

His blood turned to ice. She'd left in a carriage more than nine hours ago without telling anyone where she'd gone, when she'd be back and Seth was with her. Why? Without another word to the maid, he ran up the stairs, taking them two at a time to go check Seth's room. He flung open the door and his heart sank. The sketchbook he'd given him was gone.

That could only mean one thing: Seth and Lucy were gone, too.

***

Lucy was exhausted. After spending the majority of her day chatting with Isabelle in her drawing room, she'd had to run by the library to collect Seth. Thankfully, he'd stayed there as he'd promised he would when given the choice to go spend the day there or go on errands with her.

Another point to her good fortune was going to the library had allowed Lucy a chance to have a much-needed discussion with Mrs. Appleton that yielded satisfactory results.

Then finally, it was back to the townhouse. With any luck, she'd get back before Giles. Isabelle had received a note from Sebastian mid-afternoon telling her that it could be late into the night before he'd return.

"Can I help you down?"

She looked at her son and smiled. Giles had been a good influence on him. "I'd be honored." She put her hand in his and allowed him to help her descend the carriage.

He immediately released her hand as soon as both of her feet were on the ground. Perhaps Giles still had more work yet to do, she thought as she wrapped her arm around his shoulders and walked up the stairs with him.

"I'm hungry. Can I go see if Cook has anything she'll let me eat before dinner?"

"Yes." Lucy untied her bonnet and set it down on the chair by the door. "But nothing sweet."

With a grumble, Seth walked off.

Lucy shook her head ruefully and went upstairs to change her gown for dinner. Humming, she strolled to her bedchamber door, gripped the knob and twisted.

It didn't budge.

She frowned and tried again. *Locked.*

An eerie feeling came over her. Lucy hadn't locked their room. She didn't even have a key!

Cautiously, she pressed her ear to the door.

Nothing.

Curiosity warred with unease. Someone had to be in there, or at least *had* been in there. She should go get Mrs. Plum, the housekeeper, and have her unlock it with one of the dozens of keys she had on the giant iron hoop she wore around her wrist.

Lucy turned to go find Mrs. Plum when she noticed that the door to the room Giles had put her in that first night he'd brought her to London was open. It was the baroness' suite, or so Mrs. Plum had informed her. Giles preferred to refer to it as just another bedchamber, because the baroness' bed was the same as the baron's.

A small smile tugged her lips and she let herself into the unused room. It had an adjoining door, perhaps the locked door was a mistake and she could gain entry that way.

Her smile widened, just as she'd suspected, the adjoining door was not only unlocked, it was ajar. Idly tightening one of the pins in her hair, she went to the door and pulled it open.

Then froze.

"Giles?"

Giles, who'd been sitting in a chair with his elbows on his knees, head in his hands, and shoulders slumped, jerked to a straight sitting position and blinked at her as if he didn't believe what he was seeing.

"What's happened?" she gasped taking note of his red-rimmed eyes and the tear stains on his cheeks.

"You left."

Lucy walked over toward him and he slowly took to his feet. "I left?" she repeated.

"I came home and you were gone. I thought...thought..."

"I wasn't coming back?" she ventured.

He nodded slowly.

"Why would I leave you?"

"We quarreled."

Lucy closed her eyes for an extended blink. "Giles, I love you, I wouldn't leave you."

His facial expression didn't change.

"Do you not believe me?"

"I don't know." His words, spoken in a broken whisper, took all the starch out of her knees.

"How can you not know that I'd never leave you?"

He recoiled at her words, sending a wave of remorse over her. She should have been more careful with her words.

"I'm sorry," she whispered. "That wasn't a fair question. I just don't understand why you think I'd leave you. I love you."

"So said my mother."

Another wave of understanding overcame her. It was becoming quite evident she didn't know her husband and his pain as well as she'd thought she had. "I'm not her, Giles. I won't leave you. Ever." She reached for both of his chilled hands and interlaced their fingers. "Just because we disagree, doesn't mean that I won't still be here." She released his hands and slipped free the buttons on the front of his waistcoat then pulled his shirt from his trousers. "I love you, Giles. Everything about you."

"Even the ugly parts?"

She couldn't tell if he was attempting to jest or being serious. "There are no ugly parts."

"There are. You just haven't seen them."

She didn't believe that. Well, the part about her not seeing all of him, she did. He always seemed to take extra caution in keeping as much of himself covered as he could; therefore, she really hadn't seen much of him at all. But she highly doubted there was *anything* ugly about him. She boldly cupped his groin for the first time, feeling like a new bride on her wedding night all over again as she did so. She took a measure of pride in how he hardened instantly under her fingers. "All of you." She punctuated those words with a gentle squeeze.

He groaned.

Emboldened, she walked her fingers up to the fastenings of his trousers.

He covered her hand with his, staying her.

"Am I not allowed to see my husband, then?"

"See me?"

She nodded. "You've seen me without my clothing. Am I not to have the same privilege?"

"Privilege?"

"Don't scoff. Have you forgotten that I'm a scandal-ridden baroness? It might not be acceptable in these new circles I've entered into, but I'd like very much to see my husband. *All* of my husband."

"You would?" The surprise in his voice made her smile.

"Of course." She released the fastenings of his trousers and slid both of her hands under his shirt and up to his chest where her fingers tangled in his mat of chest hair. "I've been very curious about the texture of this."

"You have?"

She'd have laughed at the surprise in his tone, if she weren't so nervous. "Of course I have. Did you think it was only your sex who liked to look and touch?"

"Yes."

This time she did laugh at his automatic answer. "Well, that's not true." She pressed her hands flat against his broad chest and used her fingers to explore all the curves and dips his muscles created. "Just because ladies don't want to admit it, doesn't dim their curiosity any." She swallowed. "At least not this lady."

"You don't think it's unsightly?"

Lucy stilled. "What, your body?" At his nod, she said, "No. Not at all." Reluctantly, she withdrew her hands from under his shirt and smoothed down his coat. "If someone told you that it was, they were wrong. I've only glimpsed pieces here and there, so it's possible that I'm the one wrong, but I refuse to believe it." She heaved a deep sigh and said a silent prayer she wasn't wrong to push him in this way. "Unfortunately, I might never be able to make an informed decision as long as you're still wearing all of these clothes."

He hesitated but a moment, then took two steps back before kicking off his boots and shrugging out of his coat and waistcoat. Without a word, he removed his cravat and pulled his shirt over his head.

She'd seen his chest before, but this time she looked her fill without the threat of him covering himself at any moment. Her eyes did a slow sweep of him, drinking everything in down to his waistband where he was working to finish where she'd left off unfastening his trousers. He slipped the last button, then gripped the sides and lowered them, revealing his long, thick erection and the large patch of curling, dark hair that surrounded it in the middle of his muscled thighs. He blocked her view momentarily to bend down and remove his trousers and stockings, exposing his muscled calves and broad bare feet to her.

He straightened and stood silent as she took in every inch of his front before circling him to see him at every angle. Tall, and both broad and lean in the right places, he was breathtaking, if a man could be termed in such a way.

She resumed her former position in front of him, meeting his green eyes.

"And?"

"You're magnificent."

He cocked his head to the side, his lips pulling up at the corner. "That's the same word I thought when you dropped your chemise on our wedding night."

She blushed. "Is that so?"

He nodded then let out a hollow bark of laughter. "Ironic we can think the same thing about the other, but cannot communicate well."

"Indeed. But those are just mere misunderstandings. I'd wager every newly married couple has had them." She closed the area between them and looped her arms around his neck. "I'd also wager we might have another, but—" she came up on her toes as far as they'd allowed, bringing her lips within an inch of his— "I want to make one thing perfectly clear to you." She kissed his lips. "I—" *kiss*— "will—" *kiss*— "never—" *kiss*— "leave—" *kiss*—

"you."

"Never?"

"Never," she confirmed. "However, just to make sure we're both in agreement, I'd be happy to communicate it to you in another way. One that involves a bed."

"And your dress on the floor?"

"We'd better be careful we're having the same thought again," she teased, pressing her midsection against his erection.

Something flashed in his eyes and his hands found her waist, and in a second he had her on the bed where she was free to touch and explore every inch of him.

Which garnered no protest from her.

Or him.

Chapter Thirty-Two

An hour later

Giles combed his fingers through Lucy's hair, relishing the way her long, silky strands felt surrounding them. It felt almost as wonderful as having her naked body draped over his. Almost. He snorted. That was a lie. There was no comparison between the two.

He peered down at her from beneath his lowered lashes and watched her slender fingers move in mindless patterns across his chest. Why had he never considered that she might like to see and touch his body? He knew the answer to that and thrust the thought from his mind immediately. He had no call to relive the coldness of his adolescence. He wasn't a boy in an orphanage any longer. He was a husband. A father.

His chest tightened. Seth wasn't his child by nature, but he was his son in every other sense of the word. He closed his eyes. Earlier he and Lucy had only spoken of their misunderstanding, not their actual disagreement.

"Giles?"

His eyes snapped open. "Yes?"

Lucy rolled over to prop herself up on her elbow. "What's the matter?"

"Matter?"

"Every muscle from your neck to your waist just went rigid," she said as if that explained anything. "What were you thinking about?"

"This morning."

"About Seth?"

He gave her a nod. "I won't tell him."

She licked her lips. "Thank—"

A loud commotion at the bottom of the stairs cut her off, followed only a moment later by a discreet scratching at the door.

"Yes?" Giles barked in the general direction of the door.

Millie said something, the only part of which Giles heard was "Lady Norcourt".

"I'll be right back," Lucy said, grabbing the sheet and running for the door. She opened the door just enough to poke her head out, treating Giles to an unobstructed view of her backside.

She closed the door with a soft *click* and held her turned position.

"Lucy?" When she didn't respond, he padded over to her. "What's going on?"

"We have guests," she said a slight waver in her voice.

"Guests?"

She lowered her sheet. "Your mother and Mr. Appleton have come to dinner."

"They have?" He didn't know why he was surprised that they'd come. They seemed the sort who had no qualms about last minute dinner invitations.

"They're waiting in the drawing room so we'd better hurry."

Giles cupped her face with his large hands. "Lucy, you're the baroness and they've come without an invitation. You don't have to see them." At least that's how he understood the term "not at home" when making social calls.

"No, I think we should see them. It's just another misunderstanding. That's all."

"Misunderstanding?"

"Between me and your mother." She turned her face and pressed a kiss on the side of his palm. "It'll be all right."

While he was relieved that this particular misunderstanding wasn't any fault of his own, he wondered what had happened between the two that had made her so uneasy.

Stubborn woman that she was, she didn't feel so inclined to explain anything to him as she donned that simple gown she'd been working on before he'd officially asked her to marry him.

Dinner was awkward. And if Giles thought so, everyone else must have been absolutely miserable.

Except Seth who seemed to have the never-ending appetite of

a growing boy and a wish to talk to everyone about anything. It was only due to his mother's agreement to allow him to eat as much custard as he could manage while the four adults talked in the drawing room that he didn't follow them in there.

"I'm sorry," Lucy whispered to him as they followed their guests to the drawing room.

"For Seth?"

She nodded. "I'll talk to him tomorrow."

Giles pulled them to a stop. "Not to banish him to his room for meals, I hope." He might have been young, but he remembered that aspect of being nobility well enough.

"I know he can be a little impolite at times."

"He's an eleven-year-old boy. I think that's his right." He smiled at her. "Don't banish him because of it."

"I won't." She kissed his cheek. "I love you."

"I love you, too."

"Good. Just don't forget that in a minute."

That would have piqued his curiosity if it wasn't already.

"Shall we?" she said with a pointed look at the open door to the drawing room.

As instructed, a footman had moved some chairs into the drawing room. Two chairs to be exact. Both of which were being occupied, leaving only the settee available for Giles and Lucy.

Letting his wife get arranged he waited to join her. When he did, his hand automatically sought hers.

If dinner had been uncomfortable, this tension-filled silence that had engulfed them was nothing short of torture.

"Have you given any further consideration to what we talked about last week?" Mr. Appleton asked abruptly.

Actually, he had. Mr. Appleton had been right. *He* wanted to be the one to pass on his legacy to his heir. And to Seth. Obviously the title would have to pass on to his oldest son with Lucy, but Seth was his son, too, and shouldn't be forgotten. "Yes."

"And?"

"I'd like to try."

A smile so wide that his eyes crinkled split the older man's face. "I'll start working on it immediately."

"Thank you."

"Have you thought any more about anything else I said that day?"

Giles wasn't sure what the man was alluding to. Mr. Appleton had told him many things that day. "Which part?"

"The part I shouldn't have told you."

"The part about Simon not knowing how to carry his sums, either?"

At that, Mr. Appleton chuckled. "Yes, it's best to keep that secret contained to this house, but there's a reason for that."

"Because nobody can properly explain it?"

"No. I don't think that's what it is." He fidgeted with his snowy white cravat. "I think I told you I had the same trouble."

"Yes."

"And that I loved your mother for quite some time and...er...helped her in a way that defies convention."

"Yes."

"Do you remember anything else?"

"Yes," he said, his throat hoarse with raw emotion. Mr. Appleton had mentioned having another son. An older one who'd received his inheritance from another. Giles couldn't have forgotten that admission with anything less than brain fever. But that's as far as it went. He didn't dare try to draw connections between any of the secrets Mr. Appleton had entrusted him with or his growing curiosity as to why the man was helping him, lest he draw the wrong conclusion and be made a fool.

"Can I trust you with another secret that cannot leave this house?"

Giles' heart pounded in his chest. "Yes."

"I convinced your mother to defy convention one other time." He reached over and took his wife's hand in his, much the same way Giles held Lucy's hand. "I knew the moment I met her that I had to marry her. Unfortunately, she'd been married by proxy to Norcourt. That did nothing to deter me and I did everything short of abducting her to spend time with her.

"When not wooing her, I studied the law to find some means for her to escape her marriage. There wasn't any. So when she told me that Norcourt was returning from abroad within the fortnight, we agreed to one night together then to go our separate ways."

"What are you saying?" Giles choked around the lump in his throat.

"I'm not saying anything is absolute," Mr. Appleton said carefully. "But you were born only eight and a half months after your mother's wedding to Lord Norcourt."

"Thank you."

"For what? Being the reason you were mistreated and separated from your mother?" Mr. Appleton burst out unevenly.

"No. For telling me the truth."

"He's always wanted to tell you, Giles," his mother said softly. "I thought it was best for everyone if it was never actually spoken of. Once again I was wrong and beg your forgiveness. I didn't want you to be hurt or to ruin any friendship that might have formed between the two of you. I've accepted that you might never forgive me. I didn't want to ruin this relationship, too."

He'd softened marginally toward his mother over the past few weeks, but her final words made every wall he'd erected around his heart toward her turn to dust. "What changed?"

"Lucy."

"Lucy?"

"She came to see me at the library today," Mother said. "She mentioned that she thought it might be important to tell you the truth." She dried her eyes and cast him a watery smile. "She asked if the two of you could come to dinner sometime later in the week, but when I mentioned it to Walter, well, as you can see he didn't want to wait."

Giles turned to his wife, unsure what to say.

"You were right this morning," she said softly.

"I was?"

She laughed. "Don't act so surprised."

"I am surprised. I'm never right."

"You were this time. I just didn't—" she frowned— "no

couldn't realize it at first."

"What changed your mind?"

She used her free hand to gesture to the room. "This." She cleared her throat. "While I'd like to accept everyone's thanks, I can't. It wasn't me who realized this needed to be said, or at least acknowledged. Lady Belgrave pointed it out to me."

"Isabelle?" everyone asked in unison.

Lucy nodded. "I hope none of you are angry with me for talking to her about it." She angled her body so she was looking only at Giles. "When I went to see her today instead of helping me find ways to convince you to agree with me, she made me realize how important the very same thing was to you."

"Does that mean?" He hoped she could share the rest of this particular thought so he wouldn't have to embarrass her by putting voice to it.

She squeezed his hands in response, and whispered, "Yes, I'll tell him when he asks."

Heedless to the fact that his mother—and father—were in the room watching them, Giles lifted Lucy's left hand to his lips and kissed her knuckles. "Thank you."

"Perhaps I'll have to go see Isabelle tomorrow and offer her my thanks, as well," Mother mused a moment later after Giles and Lucy had turned back to join their conversation. She twisted her lips and puckered her brow as if she were in deep contemplation. "She might even be able to offer me a suggestion or two on how to get Giles and Simon on friendly terms."

"She just might be willing to help if only to spare herself from having to spend the day embroidering something," Lucy murmured, then took an uncomfortable swallow. "But if you'd like my suggestion, I think it might help the most to have a candid conversation with Simon similar to this one."

Silence fell over the room for a moment or two, broken only when Giles' mother released a deep, uneven breath and said, "You're likely, no you *are* right and that's just what we'll have to do as soon as we get home."

When they were gone and Lucy and Giles were alone again,

Giles pulled her into his arms and pressed his forehead to hers. "Thank you," he whispered, cupping her face with his large hands.

"You're welcome. Hopefully, after they go home and offer some explanations to Simon things will improve for everyone's relationship."

He hoped so, too. It would actually be rather nice to have a brother, or at least another friend. In the meantime, however, he'd much rather show his wife, and closest friend, just how much she meant to him now and always would.

Epilogue

August 1818
Devon

"We don't have to go today, if you don't wish to," Lucy said to Giles when he walked up behind where she was looking at herself in the mirror of the guest bedchamber they shared at Briar Creek.

"And disappoint Simon by missing his wedding?" Giles asked. "I think not."

Lucy laughed and bent to retrieve her shawl. "All right, then we'd best be going."

"Wait."

She stilled. "Yes?"

"If you're not comfortable, we won't go."

"Me?"

Giles pushed a lock of her fallen hair behind her ear. "Did Mother tell you who was presiding?"

"Yes, Paul, Sam's brother." Lucy waited for unease to overcome her. It didn't. That's all Paul was to her: Sam's brother. Not the boy who'd been her playmate and had defended her when his brother was being beastly. Not the brother whose intentions had been genuine when they'd gotten older. Not the man who'd offered to support her and Seth out of invisible chains of morality or duty. He was just Paul, the younger son of a viscount who'd chosen the life of a vicar.

"Does Seth know?"

"That I bear a strong resemblance to the minister?" Seth asked candidly, coming into their room.

Giles choked on his surprise.

"But he's not really my uncle," Seth continued.

"Not legally, no," Lucy agreed carefully. She'd had to be careful in how she explained their connection to Paul and Liberty and that he could never refer to them publicly as anything other than Mr. and Mrs. Grimes. To the world, they were not a relation.

"I know. But not in any other way, either. Not like Uncle Simon."

Lucy smiled at her son. Seth and Simon must have had an exceptional two days together when Seth stayed with the Appletons after the wedding because there hadn't been a single week that had gone by since then when Simon hadn't come by to fulfill his role as "favorite uncle", bearing candy or other trinkets and playing cards or taking him somewhere. Presumably not to the Statue Museum, she thought wryly. Of course, when Simon came, he took a few minutes to seek out Giles. When asked, Giles always shrugged and said they didn't talk about anything of consequence, but to her, that was of the most consequence: at least they were speaking.

"Just like Lord Bonnington," Seth said suddenly, pulling Lucy from her thoughts. "He's not really my father."

A stillness fell over the room.

"Not like you are," he continued, looking at Giles. He idly rubbed his fingers together at his sides and took a hard swallow. "Giles, c-can I— That is...er..."

Lucy's heart pounded on her son's behalf. She knew what he wanted to ask. He'd confided his secret in her last night when she'd told him the identity of his father. What she didn't tell him was Giles had confided the same wish some time ago, but didn't want to ask Seth and have him agree because of obligation or for his mother's benefit. He wanted it to be genuine.

"...would it be all right with you if I—" he fidgeted and balled his hands into fists.

"Called me Papa?" Giles ventured, a question, and perhaps his heart, in his tone.

"Yes, sir. But only if—"

"I wouldn't have it any other way, son," Giles cut in with a face-splitting grin that made Lucy's heart swell with love for the two people she loved the most in this world.

For the next six months anyway—then there'd be a third...

If you enjoyed *Desires of a Baron*, I would appreciate it if you would help others enjoy this book, too.

Lend it. This e-book is lending-enabled, so please, share it with a friend.

Recommend it. Please help other readers find this book by recommending it to friends, readers' groups and discussion boards.

Review it. Please tell other readers why you liked this book by reviewing it at one of the following websites: Amazon, Barnes and Noble, or Goodreads.

Gentlemen of Honor Series
Regency set series that is coming in 2014!

Secrets of a Viscount—One summer night, Sebastian Gentry, Lord Belgrave hauled the wrong young lady to Gretna Green. When her identity is exposed, the only obvious solution is to get an annulment. Only, just like his elopement plans, things didn't go as planned and while she has reason to believe they are no longer married, he knows better. Wanting to make things right for her, he offers to help her find a husband —what neither counts on is it just might be the one she's still secretly married to.

Desires of a Baron—Giles Goddard, Lord Norcourt is odd. Odder still, he has suddenly taken a fancy to his brother's love interest, the fallen Lucy Whitaker. Lucy was once thrown over by a lord and she has little desire to let it happen again, but she's about to learn that his desires just might be enough for the both of them.

Passions of a Gentleman—Having been thrown over twice already, Simon Appleton has given up his pursuit for a wife—especially if his only choice is the elusive Miss Henrietta Hughes. But when he discovers a secret about her, he's not above helping to protect her...

If you'd like to stay current on Rose's releases, please visit her website at www.rosegordon.net to sign up for her new release newsletter.

While you wait for the next Regency, why not take a trip to Fort Gibson where three handsome Army Officers are about to find love where they least expect it!

Fort Gibson Officers Series
American-set historical romance series that takes place in Indian Territory in the mid-1840s.

The Officer and the Bostoner—While on her way to meet her intended, Allison Pearson was abandoned by her traveling party at a desolate Army fort in the middle of Indian Territory. It's a good thing there is a handsome, smooth talking officer named Captain Wes Tucker will temporarily marry her until her intended can reclaim her.

<u>The Officer and the Southerner</u>—Lieutenant Jack Walker sent off for a mail-order bride. Ella Davis answered the ad. Jack forgot to mention a few living details, and Ella's about to let him know it!

<u>The Officer and the Traveler</u>—Captain Grayson Montgomery's mouth has landed him in trouble again! And this time it's not something a cleverly worded sentence and a handsome smile can fix. Having been informed he'll either have to marry or be demoted and sentenced to hard labor for the remainder of his tour, he proposes, only to discover those years of hard labor may have been the easier choice for his heart.

Scandalous Sisters Series

Three American sisters have arrived in England for a brief visit, but they're about to all find something they never bargained for: love.

Intentions of the Earl—Faced with never-ending poverty, a gentleman is offered a handsome sum if he'll ruin a certain young lady's future—only she has other plans, and it might entail her ruining *his*.

Liberty for Paul—There's only one thing Liberty Banks hates worse than impropriety: one Mr. Paul Grimes, and unfortunately for her, it's her own impropriety that just got her married to him!

To Win His Wayward Wife—Not to be outdone by her sisters' scandalous marriages, Madison Banks is about to have her own marriage-producing scandal to a man who, unbeknownst to her has loved her all along.

Groom Series

Four decided bachelors are about to have their freedom ripped right from their clutches with nothing to show for it but love.

Her Sudden Groom—When informed he must marry within the month or be forced to marry the worst harpy ever to set foot on English shores, the overly scientific, always logical Alex Banks decides to conduct his courtship like a science experiment!

Her Reluctant Groom—Emma Green has loved Marcus, Lord Sinclair for as long as she can remember, so when he slips up and says he loves her, too, it should all be so simple. But it's never that simple when the man in question was once been engaged to and jilted by Emma's older sister.

Her Secondhand Groom—What Patrick Ramsey, Lord Drakely AKA Lord Presumptuous wanted was an ordinary village girl to be a "motherness" to his daughters and stay out of his bedroom; what he's about to get is something so much more.

Her Imperfect Groom— Sir Wallace Benedict is a thrice-jilted baronet who is about to finally have his happily-ever-after, if only the family of his one-true-love, would stop being so darn meddlesome!

Banks Brothers' Brides

The first two are prequels to the previous series and the second two are follow ups.

His Contract Bride—Since just a lad, Edward Banks, Lord Watson knew Regina Harris would one day be his bride, he'd seen the paper to prove it many times; only someone forgot to inform Regina...

His Yankee Bride—John Banks wants *nothing* to do with the scandalous, sweet talking, ever-present, American beauty named Carolina, or so that's what he keeps saying...

His Jilted Bride—Amelia Brice has a secret...and so does Elijah Banks. Hers is big...but his is bigger!

His Brother's Bride—Presented with a marriage contract his twin brother has signed but cannot fulfill, Henry Banks has to form a plan to save the Banks name, even if it means pretending he's his brother, or worse yet, marrying a lady who holds a grudge against his family.

About the Author

USA *Today* Bestselling and Award Winning Author Rose Gordon writes unusually unusual historical romances that have been known to include scarred heroes, feisty heroines, marriage-producing scandals, far too much scheming, naughty literature and always a sweet happily-ever-after. When not escaping to another world via reading or writing a book, she spends her time chasing two young boys around the house, being hunted by wild animals, or sitting on the swing in the backyard where she has to use her arms as shields to deflect projectiles AKA: balls, water balloons, sticks, pinecones, and anything else one of her boys picks up to hurl at his brother who just happens to be hiding behind her.

She can be found somewhere in cyberspace at:

http://www.rosegordon.net

or blogging about *something* inappropriate at:

http://rosesromanceramblings.wordpress.com

Rose would love to hear from her readers and you can e-mail her at rose.gordon@hotmail.com

You can also find her on Facebook, Goodreads, and Twitter.

If you never want to miss a new release, click here to subscribe to her New Release list or visit her website to subscribe and you'll be notified each time a new book becomes available.

Printed in Great Britain
by Amazon

54742135R00147